YOU WILL NEVER SEE ME

Also Available by Jake Hinkson

Find Him
Dry Country
No Tomorrow
The Big Ugly
Hell on Church Street

YOU WILL NEVER SEE ME

A NOVEL

JAKE HINKSON

CROOKED LANE

NEW YORK

Published in the United States by Crooked Lane Books, an imprint of The Quick Brown Fox & Company LLC.

Crooked Lane Books and its logo are trademarks of The Quick Brown Fox & Company LLC.

Library of Congress Catalog-in-Publication data available upon request.

ISBN (hardcover): 979-8-89242-320-5
ISBN (paperback): 979-8-89242-321-2
ISBN (ebook): 979-8-89242-322-9

Cover design by theBookDesigners

Printed in the United States.

www.crookedlanebooks.com

Crooked Lane Books
34 West 27th St., 10th Floor
New York, NY 10001

First Edition: October 2025

The authorized representative in the EU for product safety and compliance is eucomply OÜPärnu mnt 139b-14, 11317 Tallinn, Estonia, hello@eucompliancepartner.com, +33757690241

10 9 8 7 6 5 4 3 2 1

For Sophie Ann Hinkson,
the bravest person I know

The world is violent and mercurial—
it will have its way with you.

—Tennessee Williams

Part I: Thursday

Alice Hardy

CHAPTER

1

WE COLLAPSED TOGETHER in front of his full-length mirror. Me on the hardwood floor, Jason straddling me, his hairy chest rising and falling against my back. We lay tangled together until he climbed off of me and flopped onto his bed. While he stripped off the condom and tossed it in the trash, I pushed myself up from the floor, my breasts and thighs peeling away from the polyurethane like sunburnt skin, and crawled onto the mattress next to him. Leaving space between us, he laced his fingers together over his hairy belly. We both stared up at the ceiling. For a while, we just lay there catching our breaths and trying to think of something to say to each other. Finally, I turned on my side and kissed his shoulder. In return, he grinned at me like you'd nod at a stranger on the train.

"Look at that," I said, poking at the red spots on my knees. "Hope that doesn't leave a mark."

"Hey, you're the one who pulled me down on the floor."

"I like that mirror."

He grinned and returned his attention to the ceiling.

I stared at him.

"What?" he said, without looking at me.

"Just wondering what you're thinking about."

He tilted his head, as if to get a better view of his own thoughts. "Oh, nothing special."

"Well, what was the last thing? What was the last specific thought you had?"

"I thought, 'I'd sure like to get on the business end of those tits.'"

I nudged him. "Smart ass."

He shrugged. "What are *you* thinking about?"

He didn't care, I knew. He was just volleying the question back to me so he could stop talking.

I rolled over on my back and stared at his cracked ceiling. The plaster was creased and split, with chipped paint and old water stains. It looked like a topographical map.

"I don't know," I said. "Worrying a little bit, I guess."

I felt him draw further away from me. He sat up and reached for the plastic cup of water on his bedside table. "Yeah . . ." he said.

"My son. He's going to Los Angeles in the fall, you know. Studying film at USC. At least that's the way it looks."

"Uh-huh."

"I'm worried about him being so far away."

"Hm."

He lay back down, leaving a few extra inches of space between us.

"All that distance," I said. "Not just geographically, but, you know, culturally. Morally. Spiritually."

He said nothing, so I looked at him to make sure he was listening. He raised his eyebrows in a *what are you gonna do* gesture. The bare minimum to let me know he was technically still with me. I couldn't be surprised by that. I wasn't with him because he was a good listener.

But I still felt compelled to ask, "Are you listening to me?"

"Sure."

"Well?"

"Well what?"

"Do you have anything to say?"

"About the moral and spiritual distance between here and Los Angeles? No."

"I just want to know you're listening."

He turned and looked at me. "Uh-huh."

I sat up. I pressed the sheet to my chest, suddenly embarrassed to be naked. "What's your problem tonight?"

He wiped at his eyes with his thick fingers and yawned. "You weren't complaining about me having a problem five minutes ago."

"Well, now I'm trying to talk to you."

"Well, that's where you went wrong," he said.

He sat up and swung his legs off the bed and started pulling his clothes from the pile on the floor. Not as if he were mad. He did it as if he had simply decided to get up and get dressed, like I wasn't even part of the equation.

"So I went wrong trying to share something about my life?" I asked.

"About that part of your life, yeah. Jesus Christ, I don't want to hear about your kid. Especially not while we're laying here in bed. That's your idea of pillow talk? Next you'll be telling me about your husband."

Now I was pissed. I pushed myself to the end of the bed, away from him but in grabbing distance of my own clothes.

"'I don't want to hear about your life.' You don't think that's a shitty thing to say to someone? You weren't leading with that when I walked in here. You asked me how my day was."

"You say that like you caught me in a lie. I was being nice, asking how your day was. I didn't ask you to tell me about your family for Christ's sake."

I slipped into my bra and fastened it. "I get it. You don't care about my family. Or me."

"You want your family to care about me?" he asked. "You gonna go home and tell them all about what you did tonight? Of course not. It'd ruin your life if they knew about me, wouldn't it? So why try to—"

"This is bullshit," I muttered, pulling up my skirt and grabbing my blouse.

Jason was dressed now except for his bare feet. Leaning against the unpainted plaster wall in his work jeans and dirty T-shirt, he sighed.

"Look, Alice," he said, "you didn't come over here to talk about your kid. You didn't come over here to *talk* at all. You came over here to have someone pull your hair while they fucked you in front of a mirror. You came over here to *forget* you have a husband and a kid. So don't start pretending this is something it isn't, with you getting all high and mighty about the conversations we're *not* having. I gave you exactly what you wanted when you walked in my front door. And now that you got it, don't start acting like I'm the piece of shit. You're the one who's here slumming it with the hired help."

I didn't look at him as I kept dressing. When I had laced up my short black boots, I went into the living room and retrieved my coat from the middle of the floor.

Jason's old mutt Spartacus was sitting by the window, staring down at the street below. He always avoided us after we had sex, as if he felt implicated in our transgression. As I yanked on my coat and looked around for my purse, the dog glanced over his shoulder to watch me. Then he turned his attention back toward the street, as if he was worried about something going on down there.

Jason followed me to the door. His eyes were as empty as the dog's.

"You're leaving, just like that?" he said.

"What's it look like?"

"I hope you don't think I'm going to run after you."

"Oh, I know you're not," I said, turning the lock on his door.

"Look—" he said, but I was already out the door and stomping down the stairwell before he could finish.

He lived on the third floor, so he could have caught up to me if he'd tried, but he was true to his word. He didn't follow me downstairs.

I hurried down the darkened sidewalk. Swaying pools of white light from streetlamps punctuated stretches of empty darkness before me. It had been cloudy and overcast all day and now there was no moon out tonight.

I shook my head. *What was that back there? Did you really try to talk to him about Tuck? The only accessory in the man's apartment décor is a full-length mirror facing his bed, for God's sake.* But I knew who he was before I ever set foot in his bedroom. Jason might be an asshole, but he'd never hidden what he wanted from me. And, more to the point, it was the same thing I'd wanted from him. *So why are you suddenly trying to inject dignity into this totally bullshit, futureless affair?*

I was so baffled and angry it took me a moment to realize I didn't know where I was going.

I stopped.

I glanced back.

Looking around, I couldn't remember where I'd parked.

Am I going the wrong way?

I started walking again, faster this time, trying to recognize the cars lining the street, the fronts of apartment buildings. But nothing looked familiar. When I passed an alley I was sure I hadn't passed before, I stopped walking.

Shit, no, I think I am going the wrong way. I parked back up the street.

As I was turning around, I heard someone in the alley behind me.

Before I could see him, he slammed into me. I stumbled over my own feet, screaming. I tried to put out my hand to break my fall, but my thumb caught on my purse strap and the pavement flew up and smashed into me. Frantic, I scrambled to my knees.

"No," I grunted. "Don't." I don't know why I said that. It just came out. *No. Don't.*

Fingers clawed my scalp, balled my hair into a fist and jerked me up. A thick arm clamped under my neck, and the man dragged me back into the alley.

I started to scream again, but my scream died choking in the crook of his arm.

In the darkness, he pulled me to my feet, my eyes flashing starbursts. My purse, still slung around my chest, slapped my hip.

"Don't yell or I'll hurt you bad," he said.

"Please," I said, reaching for my purse. "Here, take my wallet."

"I don't want your wallet," he said.

As my eyes adjusted to the dim grayness of the alleyway, I saw my attacker for the first time. He wore jeans and a hoodie. He was clean-shaven, his hair neat and trimmed. He held a hunting knife to my throat, with a blade longer than my hand. He leaned close to me so I would have to look in his eyes. He stared at me as if he'd hated me all his life.

"Please don't do this," I said.

"Shut up," he said.

My unbuttoned coat hung open. He reached for my blouse, and I grabbed his hands. He tried to rip my blouse open, but when he did I fought against him. I was stronger than he expected, so he did it again, harder. My blouse ripped at the buttons, but he had jerked too hard this time and my flailing arm knocked the knife out of his hand.

He cursed and punched me in the stomach, and I dropped to my knees, gulping for air. He cursed me again as he felt around in the dark for the knife.

I tried to get up to run, but when I did I heard the blade scrape against the pavement under my shoes.

He heard it too, but as he threw himself into me again, trying to pin me against the wall, I felt my fingertips brush the handle of the knife. I pulled it into my hand and brought it up and swung it at his face in the dark. He yelped and backed up, and I kept swinging the knife, slashing at the darkness.

He fell back into a puddle of water in the middle of the alley. I staggered to my feet, pushing myself up the wall, waving the knife in the darkness, sure that he would lunge at me again.

But he didn't. The shadowy figure on the ground kept his hands to his throat even as he tried to get to his feet. I was too afraid to run because I was scared he'd jump at me. Instead, he fumbled about, unable to work his legs at the same time his hands were clasped to his throat. In my shock and confusion, for a moment I thought he was trying to choke himself, almost as if he were doing a parody of guilt and self-punishment.

He only managed to get to one knee, kneeling in the puddle, before he reached out a hand to steady himself on the pavement, but as soon as his hand left his throat he gurgled and panicked, falling, both hands trying to contain the blood escaping his body.

My head was swimming. I squeezed my eyes shut to regain my balance. I pressed against the wall, its rough bricks steady at my back. When I opened my eyes, the man on the ground wasn't moving anymore. His hands had not left his throat, but I could hear the wet wheeze of air still coming from his mouth.

I finally made myself move, watching him as I inched along the alley wall back toward the street. His form was a heavy black shadow on the ground, but I was afraid that the moment I turned around he would jump at me from the darkness again.

I kept inching along until the wall ended and I stumbled back out on the sidewalk. Winds buffeted me and stirred the treetops. I staggered toward Jason's apartment in the swaying light and darkness.

Behind me, a vehicle turned down the street. A big blue and white SUV, a Chicago city police cruiser. My hand shot up instinctively to flag them down. All I had to do was step into the street, but I caught myself. I froze in the dark.

I lowered my hand and jumped back so I wouldn't be seen.

The police didn't stop, didn't see me or the body lying crumpled in the alley.

I watched the police cruiser. I wanted to yell at it, call it back here. But I stood shivering in the shadows until the vehicle had slipped away, disappearing in the night.

I pushed myself out of the shadows. I began to run back to the apartment, but as I ran, I realized with horror that the knife was still in my hand. Without stopping, I dropped it like a dead rat, and I didn't stop running until I got to the front door of the building and pushed my way inside.

CHAPTER

2

"HELLLLOOOO," HIS VOICE squawked through the foyer intercom.

"Please let me up," I said quietly. My breathing was heavy in my chest, but I wasn't yelling. I spoke quickly, but I wasn't frantic. I didn't make that choice consciously. It wasn't even shock yet. Something simply told me to be quiet until I got inside the apartment with Jason and shut the door behind me.

He didn't respond. Instead, the foyer's interior door buzzed, and I pushed through and went upstairs.

He was standing in his doorway, arms crossed, a smug look on his face. He probably expected an apology, maybe even hoped for some makeup sex. Or perhaps he was bracing himself for another round of the argument from before.

But when I reached the top of the stairs, his arms dropped.

"Alice?"

He stepped toward me, taking my hand, helping me inside.

I blinked at him, walked to his couch and sat down.

"What happened?"

As I sat down, my blouse hung open because it was ripped down the middle. When I pinched it closed, I realized my hands were scratched and red.

"Alice, what happened?"

He looked toward the window, as if the answer might be hovering just outside the glass.

I closed my eyes. "A man attacked me. I went . . . I think I went the wrong way. And I was walking and he just . . . jumped on me."

"Oh, Jesus Christ, did he . . ."

He stopped himself. He didn't know how to say it, how to ask me if I'd been raped.

I shook my head.

"He had a knife, and we were struggling. The knife fell, and I picked it up. I picked it up and I swung it at him. I must have gotten him. But everything was too dark to tell."

"He ran away?"

"No, he just . . . fell down. In the middle of the alley. He stopped moving after a while, and I got up and left."

"Wait, you mean he's still . . . he's still there?"

"I think so."

"Where?"

"In the alley. Where it happened."

"Which alley?"

"How the fuck should I know which alley?" I snapped. "I didn't stop to write down the address."

I let go of my blouse and put my head in my hands.

Jason took a deep breath and ran his hands through his hair. Slowly, he asked, "You're saying you killed this guy?"

I looked down at my palms. I'd scratched them when I fell, and now they hurt as if I'd burned them on something. "I need lotion. I need to clean up." I looked at myself. My skirt was split on the side and twisted around. Through my ripped stockings, I could see that my knees were bloody.

Jason got down on his knees in front of me. He made me look at him. I felt like I was looking at him for the first time. I'd never seen him flustered before.

"Alice, I need you to tell me. I need to know. Is the man who attacked you dead?"

"I don't know," I said calmly.

"Was he still breathing when you left?"

"If he wasn't breathing, I would know he was dead."

He ignored that, stood up and rubbed his face. "Okay," he said. "The guy's alive. We think. We think the guy is alive. Okay." He nodded. "We have to call the police, an ambulance."

"An ambulance? He tried—"

"I know, but you stabbed him. If he's bleeding to death out there we can't just tell the cops that we shrugged and said, 'Well, the fucker had it coming.' Even if the fucker had it coming. We have to call 911."

I stared at my red palms.

"No, wait," I said. "Just wait. I have to get my head around this." I felt a stillness come over me. It helped me somehow that Jason was not his usual calmly confidant self. It forced me to be the calm one.

"Okay, but listen," he said, "while you're getting your head around it, that asshole could be out there bleeding to death."

"I know." I pushed my hair back out of my face. "Look, we need to stop and think about this clearly for a second. If we call the police . . . then what happens? The police come, the ambulance, then the reporters. This becomes public. People are going to ask what I'm doing in West Town at ten o'clock at night. Greg will find out about us. *Tuck* will find out about us." Thinking about my husband was bad enough, but it almost sent me into tears to think about my son at this moment. My son. My unfinished man.

An image flashed in my mind: Greg driving home from Wrigley Field, taking my call, his face turning grim as I explain where I am, what happened, Tuck watching him, whispering, "What's wrong? Is Mom okay?"

"They can't find out," I said. "Not like this. It's so sordid and awful." I thought of my friends and the people in my department seeing me on the evening news, pulling up the video online to rewatch it, asking, *Why was she alone in West Town? Where were*

Greg and Tuck? "I mean, let's at least consider the consequences of calling 911 first," I said.

Jason walked to the window and looked down at the street.

"You stabbed him?" he asked.

"I don't know. I think so. It was quick, and it was in the dark, and I was panicking the whole time. I was swinging the knife, like wildly swinging it out in front of me and that's when he fell down. I think it was his throat. His hands were on his throat."

"Then maybe he's already dead."

"Can they . . . the police, if we just left him there, could they figure out it was me?"

Jason held up his hands. "What do I know about the police? On *CSI* they can solve everything with a strand of hair and a drop of blood."

"That man attacked *me*," I said. As I said it, my scraped hands began to shake. I rubbed them together like I was cold. "*I'm* the victim here."

"Of course."

"He came at me in an alley with a knife."

"Jesus. I know."

"So if I . . . if I killed him in self-defense, that's morally defensible. Right?"

"Of course. Absolutely."

"Right. Then why would I . . . If I did nothing wrong, why should *I* be the one who has to pay for it? If I don't report it, then that's *my* business. It's between me and . . .. and that man out there. He made *his* choice. His choice was to attack some stranger in an alley. Why should *I* have to pay for *his* choice?"

Jason's mouth twisted around, as if he were actually chewing on the idea. Finally he nodded. "You shouldn't."

"If I killed him—"

Killed. The word itself was so shocking. I might have ended someone's life. That thought almost short-circuited my brain. I just stared at my red palms.

Then Jason said, "We need to know if he's alive."

"What?"

"We have to know. If he's alive, we have to get help. We can't let him die out there. Slashing some mugger in an alley, that's self-defense. Letting him bleed to death so no one finds out you're having an affair . . . that's something else. We have to go check."

He grabbed his socks balled up on the floor and went to get his work boots from a small dirty rug by the front door. Spartacus followed him, thinking they were about to go for a walk. Instead, Jason took him to the bedroom and closed the door.

"I'm not going back out there," I said.

"I don't know where he is, Alice. You have to show me. Besides," he said, "I'm doing this for you."

I didn't move. Then I thought of something else.

"The knife."

He looked up from tying his laces. "What about it?" he said. Then his mouth opened. "You left it out there."

"Yes, I dropped it on the ground."

"Fingerprints."

"Oh, Jesus. Jesus."

He nodded and grabbed his coat. "Let's go. I know you're scared. I'm scared too. But there's no danger. We'll be together. We'll figure it out." He offered me his hand. "C'mon. We'll be okay. The guy is hurt. Or maybe worse."

I didn't know which possibility scared me more.

* * *

The first thing I noticed was the absence of anything going on. As we walked back to the alley, dark clouds curtained the night sky, and the wind, scented with rain now, blew a plastic bag down the street. An occasional car whooshed by a couple of streets over. But other than that, nothing. No cop cars, no ambulances, no crowd of spectators.

And no knife.

"Where'd you drop it?"

We stopped in a swaying pool of white light.

"It was here, I think." I couldn't be sure, but I recalled the knife falling from my hand and landing on the pavement. I remembered the split in the concrete near where it fell. "I think it fell right here against this crack." I clutched my torn blouse together with my left hand and pointed with my right.

Jason turned on his cellphone's flashlight and looked out into the darkness. Nothing.

A car turned down the street. Jason cut his light. The car passed. A woman with three children. None of them paid us any mind.

"Are you sure it was here?" he asked.

I pointed ahead of us into the dark. "That's the alley."

He held my hand and turned on the light again as we walked toward the alley. The light from his phone was weak and faintly blue against the dark, but as we got closer we could both see that there was nothing in the alley. There was the puddle. Some old fast food bags balled into wet globs. Some loose gravel where the edge of the pavement had crumbled after the last bad snowstorm.

But there was no man lying there, dead or otherwise.

Jason lifted the light above his head so he could try and look further down the alley. But the light was too weak and there was nothing to see, anyway.

The man was gone.

The sky started to spit raindrops in the dark, one or two at a time. The ground was discolored, but in the dark it was hard to tell where the blood was.

"You're sure this is the alley?"

"Yes. At least . . . Yes, it is. I'm sure."

He cut his light. A raindrop hit my face.

We walked back to the apartment with more and more raindrops impatiently tapping the sidewalk around us.

"What does it mean?" I said.

He pushed open the front door to his building. "Let's get you something to put on. You can't go home like that."

We climbed the stairs to his apartment in silence. Then I went to the bathroom to clean up while he searched for something for me to wear. Once I shut the bathroom door and sat down on his toilet lid to take off my shoes and stockings, however, I just stopped and stared at the hexagon floor tiles. They alternated black and white, and I thought nothing at all as I stared at them.

Eventually, a knock on the door jarred me out of my trance. "You okay in there?"

"Yeah. Yeah, I'll be out in a second."

"Been in there a while . . . You okay?"

I realized I had no idea how long I'd just been sitting there staring at the floor, letting my mind reconstitute itself.

"I said I'll be out in a second."

"Okay, well, when you're ready I got you something to wear."

I washed my hands and knees, and when I walked out he handed me a Blackhawks jersey. It was a women's small, girlie pink and white.

"My sister left it here last time she visited," he said. "I bought it for her at a game and she forgot it when she left."

That sounded a lot like a lie, but at that point I didn't care.

I put it on, walked into his den, and sat down on the couch.

Jason followed me. "So," he said, "what do you think happened out there? He got up and left?"

I lifted my scratched palms in the universal expression of *I don't know.*

He sat down on the arm of the couch and stared at me. I realized he was calm again. As calm as I'd ever seen him. "So . . . let me ask you something," he said. "And I just have to ask this at least once, so I don't feel like a complete asshole later. You didn't by any chance . . . make up the whole 'I got jumped in an alley' thing did you?"

I blinked. I showed him my palms. "What the fuck, man? Does this look like I made it up? Why would I *make it up*?"

He shrugged. "So you could come back?"

I stood up and headed for the door. "Could you please walk me to my car? I can't do this with you right now. I have to go home."

"Look, don't be pissed at me, I had to ask."

"You had to ask if I made up almost being raped and murdered in an alley? In order so I could come back here and do what? Talk to you again?"

"No, but to get me on your side maybe . . ."

I just glared at him until he finally heaved his shoulders in surrender. "Okay, Jesus, okay," he said.

He trailed me out the door and into the night without a word. The air had turned warm with the approach of rain. We walked right to my car up the street. It was even closer than I'd remembered.

"Look," Jason said, clearly realizing he had to say *something*, "I guess the guy pulled himself together enough to get up, grab his knife, and get out of there. That's good for you. It means you're . . . you know, it means you're not culpable or whatever."

I unlocked my door and almost got in the car, but first I turned around. "If I made it up," I said, "if I'm *fucking insane* enough to do that, where'd the blood come from on my blouse? In your mind, when you concocted the scenario where I made up an attack, how'd I get the busted knee, the scratched hands, the bloody clothes?"

"Alice . . ."

"No, tell me."

He shrugged. "Well, I mean, look. And this is only because you're making me answer you, okay, not because I actually think it. But you could have, you know, you could have thrown yourself down. So it could be your blood, from your hands and your knee . . . Something like that."

I couldn't think of what to say to that. I really couldn't. Instead, without speaking another word, I gathered what was left of my scraped and battered dignity and got in my car and drove home.

CHAPTER

3

ON MY WAY home, thunder clapped once, as if to get everyone's attention, and then the sky collapsed. Rain poured out of black clouds, illuminated by white flashes of lightning, and even with my wipers going full speed my windshield looked like it was underwater as I turned onto my street. Then, as quickly as it had begun, the rain suddenly exhausted itself. By the time I pulled into my garage, the storm was over. As the garage door closed behind me, the night was quiet again.

I walked inside. Greg and Tuck weren't home yet, and the kitchen was silent and still, but the tiny pieces of our lives—notes on the refrigerator, junk mail and bills on the island, jackets hanging on pegs by the door—were all around me. It almost overwhelmed me, but I caught my breath and pushed myself forward.

I carried my bundle of ruined clothes to the bathroom and stripped naked. I got in the shower and washed myself, the hot water scalding my skin pink. I soaped up my wounded knees and hands and flushed them out, then washed my hair.

When I climbed out, I wrapped myself in a towel and looked over my clothes. My stockings were split at the knees. My skirt was torn on the side. The blouse was missing two buttons, with a third dangling loosely from the ripped fabric.

There was blood at the knees of the stockings, which I could be fairly certain was mine, and a spray of blood on the blouse, which I could be fairly certain was not. The clothes were incriminating, but for what exactly did they incriminate me? My attacker, whoever he was, apparently got up and walked away, making sure to grab his knife as he went.

In the kitchen, I dragged out the trash can from under the sink. It was half full of coffee grounds, eggshells, old food wrappers and one large plastic cup that should have been put in the recycling. I pulled the cup out. Someone in this house apparently went to Taco Bell today. I moved the cup to the recycling, and then shoved my clothes down under the garbage. I tied up the bag and left it by the door.

I bandaged my knee and walked back to my bedroom. Tossing the Blackhawks jersey on the bed, I got dressed quickly in jeans and a lime V-neck. I scooped up the jersey Jason had given me to wear home and took it to the laundry room. The fact of the matter was I could have left it lying in the middle of the floor and neither my husband nor my son would have ever noticed—first, because neither of them ever came in here of his own volition, and second, because neither ever paid attention to what I wore. I folded the jersey and slipped it in with some of my clothes. It was now about as likely to be discovered by my family as the Ark of the Covenant.

I walked out of the laundry and stopped. Why was I keeping that jersey? To give back to Jason? Did I ever want to see him again after tonight?

I ignored that question and grabbed the trash bag with my ruined clothes. I carried it outside and buried it in at the bottom of our wet garbage can at the curb.

Back inside, I finally sat down on the couch and took a long, slow, deep breath. The room slowly started to tilt and rotate, reality reconfiguring itself around me. I closed my eyes. When I opened them again, I tried to get my bearings, but it was difficult because everything in my house suddenly seemed foreign and strange. A mauve lap blanket and mismatched throw pillows piled at the end of the couch. Abandoned socks under the ottoman. Old DVDs of Ken Burns documentaries stacked beside the television. Shelves full of my books on religion and politics, Greg's books on baseball and mathematics.

My gaze finally settled on the display of family photos on the wall, the ones I'd arranged like a family tree—both sets of grandparents at the bottom, Greg and me in the middle, then through-the-years pictures of our son branching out at the top, with room above him for his family one day.

But as I stared at my house, my belongings, it all looked so strange, so artificial, to me now, like a display at IKEA. I had no memory of the books I read. Even the pictures of my own family, pictures of my own face, looked concocted, like the generic photos of models that came with the frames.

The only thing that seemed real was the mess I'd left on the coffee table hours before. The stack of quizzes I still needed to grade for my Religion and Gender course, and a glass half full of melted ice ringing the coffee table. I'd left it all here when I'd gotten Jason's text.

Well if you're alone for the night, he'd written, *why don't you come over?*

Now I sat there in the middle of my home, amidst the strange sights of my everyday life, and I trembled. I had to clasp my hands together to keep them from shaking.

I was still trying to calm myself when I saw the headlights of Greg's car flash over the windows. I steadied myself.

Be calm. Be normal.

They parked in the driveway and came in through the garage. Tuck came loping in first. He was wearing the new special edition Cooperstown Cubs cap he'd bought the week before. It was black with white stitching and he liked it because it matched his *Eraserhead* T-shirt, but Greg had teased him by saying it made him look like a White Sox fan.

He gave me a wave on his way through the den. He was headed upstairs to his room, cellphone already in hand, to FaceTime his girlfriend Julia.

"Hey," I called after him, "how'd it go?"

"Cubs lost."

"Oh. Too bad. Hey, c'mere a second and talk to your dear old mother."

He sighed, but knowing that protest was futile, he wandered over and plopped down beside me for a second, one eye still on his phone.

"So," I said, "they lost?"

"Brewers friggin' *destroyed* them, four to nothing."

"Sorry to hear that. Did you have fun, at least?"

"Sure." He looked up from his phone and smiled. "Dad spilled his beer, and the guy wouldn't give him a free refill."

We could hear Greg in the kitchen closing the garage door and resetting the house alarm.

"You tried to get a free refill?" I called out to him. "Why would you think they'd do that?"

He wandered in, wearing the same faded-blue Cubs cap he'd had since we met in grad school. "I spilled it right in front of the guy," he said. "I mean, he didn't see it happen, but I was like five feet away from the stand. He was just being an asshole."

Tuck laughed and started to get up, eager to go call Julia. Since we're not the most physically affectionate of families, he seemed surprised when I grabbed him and hugged him tight. He patted my shoulder, politely rather than sweetly. Aside from a few aspirational strands of wiry hair, his jawline was smooth and hairless. I kissed his cheek.

"What was that for?" he asked.

"Just a freebie 'cause I love you," I said, clearing my throat.

He smiled and shook his head like my strangeness was unfathomable. He squeezed my hand as he stood up. "Well, thanks for the freebie," he said, and I watched him walk across the room and start upstairs. My Tuck. My son. My unfinished man.

Greg sat down on the couch beside me and tossed his scorebook on the coffee table. He looked at me.

"Are you crying?" he asked.

I wiped a tear away. "I heard the Cubs lost."

He smiled and put his feet up, happy to be relieved of the obligation to discuss my emotions. "Yeah. I know you're heartbroken about that."

"How was the ol' father-son bonding?"

He gestured at the empty end of the couch. "Clearly, he can't bear to be away from me." He tossed his cap on top of the scorebook and scratched his head. "How about you? What'd you do tonight?"

I took a deep breath. "Goofed off mostly. Watched *The Good Place*."

He glanced down at my clothes. "You change clothes?"

"You know what I did? I was taking out the garbage, and I fell in the driveway. Really skinned my knee. Ruined my stockings. Scratched my hands." I showed him my hands.

"What suddenly compelled you to take out the trash?"

"What do you mean?"

"You haven't taken out the trash in twenty years, Alice."

That was a bit of an exaggeration but only a bit. I usually made Greg or Tuck do it.

"It stunk," I said.

He nodded and glanced at my ungraded papers and the glass of melted ice on the table. He picked up the glass and wiped away the water ring staining the oak.

Standing up, he said, "You must have really been caught up in that show."

Then he carried the glass to the kitchen.

And that was that. I guess as far as he could tell, I seemed normal. A little emotional maybe, but with Tuck leaving for college soon, I'd been a little emotional lately. No big deal.

Greg climbed the stairs to get ready for bed. I could hear Tuck, suddenly energized with a boundless desire for conversation, in his room talking on the phone to Julia. And I sat downstairs, the same woman, as far as my boys knew, that they'd left at home earlier that evening.

* * *

That night as my husband and son lay sleeping, I stared at the curtains pulled over the bedroom windows.

My palms still stung, and my knee still throbbed. I was still angry at Jason. I was still sick that I'd been at his place to begin with.

Mostly, though, I was in a state of shock. My mind was still struggling to accept what had happened. The pains lingering in my body were undeniable, but the thing itself—the fact of it—seemed *impossible.*

A stranger had attacked me on the street.

I had always considered the world a terrifying place. I'd crossed streets to avoid men, pretended to have cellphone conversations when I passed strangers on the sidewalk, carried my keys like a weapon ready to gouge at eyeballs as I walked to my car at night.

But I'd always consoled myself with facts and statistics, with the knowledge that attacks by random strangers were relatively rare. I comforted myself with the sheer improbability of a man jumping out of the dark at me.

But now that one had, I could not for the life of me understand *why* he had done it. Answers presented themselves, of course. Misogyny. Sickness. Psychosis. But those were just psychological explanations, intellectual hypotheses. They didn't really answer anything. Maybe I just wanted to know *why me.* But there was no answer for that, either. Why *not* me, after all. *He maketh his sun to rise on the evil and on the good, and sendeth rain on the just and on the unjust.* That was scripture. That was Gospel truth, but it didn't help me any more than the psychological explanations did.

I don't want your wallet, he said. And then he tried to tear my clothes off.

When it happened I didn't know what he intended to do. Jason thought the man was going to rape me, but if he had, I don't think he would have stopped there.

Will you let yourself think it? I asked myself in the dark. *He stared at you like he wanted to kill you.*

But you don't know that. Maybe he was going to—

No! Stop! Just stop and clear your mind. Stop thinking about all the things that might've happened. You're here now, safe in bed, with your family around you and the doors all locked.

But where did he go?

I thought I killed him.

What if he followed you home?

That thought drove me out of the bed to recheck the alarm and all the doors and windows again. I even peeked in on Tuck's room to make sure he was okay.

Then I went back to bed and tried to settle my mind.

I turned toward my husband. He lay on his side, his back to me, dreaming his dreams. He always traveled far in his dreams, seeing many things and many people, with one exception. He told me once he hardly ever dreamed of me. Almost never.

Maybe you get enough of me in the real world, I'd teased him.

He'd considered that for a moment and said, *Or maybe I just don't have any unresolved feelings about you.*

I rarely dreamed, but when I did I always dreamed of him. I didn't mention that maybe my feelings were less resolved than his.

Now I put an arm around his wide shoulders.

"I'm sorry, Greg," I whispered very softly, my voice hardly more than a breath itself.

My husband did not hear me though. He just lay beside me like a great toppled tower, collapsed and dead to this world, wandering his dreamworlds without me.

Part II: Thursday

Owen Pall

CHAPTER

4

THE FIRST THING I did that morning was fuck up big time. I was sticking a GPS tracker on the underside of a vintage 1967 El Camino when the car's owner, a bullnecked nightclub bouncer named Josip Vukov, suddenly walked out of his house. I was still down on one knee when I heard him grumble, "What the fuck?"

I looked up to see a big guy in a shiny bronze velour tracksuit and pristine white Gucci sneakers barreling toward me.

"Oh, hey, is—"

I was about to spin some bullshit about how I was just looking at the car. *Hey, is this a '67? My old man had one of these. Must have cost a fortune to restore.* Something like that. I didn't get the chance, though. Before I could say another word, Vukov came down on me like an avalanche.

With him pounding away on me, all I could do was cover my head and try to squirm free. I managed to get just far enough to kick up at him. When my foot caught him in the balls, he staggered backwards, and I rolled over.

Getting to my feet, I saw the tracker on the ground under the El Camino. I scrambled over to grab it, but as I reached down for it, Vukov kneed my skull into the rear fender of his car.

My vision cut out for a second like a faulty television. My ears popped and then started ringing so loudly they screamed.

I'm not sure what Vukov would have done next if the cops hadn't shown up, but I don't think he was planning on helping me to my feet. When the blue lights started flashing, he just cursed and hollered something in Serbo-Croatian toward the door of his house. The door slammed shut, and I got the impression that something inside was being hidden, flushed, or hustled down the back steps.

Vukov put his hands in the air.

I lay back against the El Camino's rear tire. Every few seconds, purple spots popped in my vision. I thought I could feel my brain moving around.

"Don't bleed on my vehicle, asshole," Vukov told me, his eyes still fixed on the blue lights.

"Sorry," I said, pushing myself off of his car. While I did, I quietly slipped the GPS back into my pocket.

* * *

I am not held in high esteem by the men and women of the Chicago Police Department, but at least I knew the cops who'd arrived to break up the fight. Officer Styrczula stuck Vukov in the back of their cruiser to question him, while Officer Karras led me to my car to take my statement.

He hitched his thumbs on his protective vest. "So, Owen," he said. "What's happening, man?"

"Working," I said, rubbing my throbbing skull.

"You call getting your ass beat 'working'?"

Karras was smaller and older than his partner, with an olive complexion, graying temples, and forearms carpeted in thick black hair. He also had a mangled upper lip that had been unevenly reassembled after some drunk hit him in the mouth with a barstool. That was long ago, but now the lip didn't really work right. Whenever he smiled, he looked like he wanted to spit.

"It's a living," I said.

"Not much of one."

"Well, we agree on that."

"So what's the story here?"

"Surveillance job."

He glanced at the neighbors hanging around on front stoops gawking at us.

"Real covert, man."

Officer Styrczula ambled over. Although he was Chicago born and raised, Styrczula looked like one of the rednecks I'd grown up around back in Arkansas. Tall, broad-shouldered, barrel-chested. His face was as white as writing paper except for places where it was so pink it looked like he'd been stung by bees. "So what's the deal, Pall? According to Mr. Vukov over here, you were trying to steal his car."

"I look like a car thief to you?"

"You look like a cheap extortionist to me," Styrczula said. "You look like the kind of guy who'd blackmail his own mother. I mean, as long as you wanna know what you look like to me."

"I ever been caught blackmailing anybody?"

"They never caught the Zodiac Killer either. Didn't make him any less of a murderer."

I turned to Karras for some kind of help.

Karras asked his partner, "Vukov want to press charges?"

"Believe it or not, Mr. Vukov don't wish to further involve the Chicago Police Department in this dispute."

Karras shrugged. "Guess he figures he got his point across with the ass-kicking."

I cleared my throat. "Well, look, although he assaulted me without any provocation, I'm ready to let it go too. No reason you guys should do any more paperwork than necessary."

Karras said, "That's real considerate of you."

Styrczula squinted at me. "He says you were fucking around with his car. GPS, right?"

I pulled out the tracker and showed it to them.

Styrczula smiled. "I knew it."

Karras jerked his thumb back at Vukov. "You know he's connected to the Glavaš crew?"

Oh, Jesus Christ.

"Uh, no," I said. "No, I did not know that. I thought he was a nightclub bouncer."

"Oh, I'm sure he's bounced some people, alright," Karras said.

"Those sneakers alone probably cost $500," Styrczula said. "No idea how much it cost to restore that El Camino. Think he paid for that tossing drunks out of a nightclub?"

I poked at my eye sockets. One of them already felt a little puffy.

"Great," I said. "Well, then, maybe *you guys* should be watching him."

But as soon as I said it, the realization hit me. I looked around. Up the street sat an old white van with a faded sign on the side that read Simpson's Quality Vacuums. I nodded. It was covered in red rust spots like acne scars and looked like a piece of crap, but I was willing to bet there were guys in the back of that van wearing earpieces and staring at monitors.

I turned to the cops. "That's how you got here so fast," I said. "The feds called you."

Neither of them replied to that, but Karras asked, "So who's got you following a Croatian legbreaker?"

"C'mon, guys," I said, "I can't tell you who I'm working for."

Karras glanced at the Vukov apartment, where Vukov's wife, a frightened-looking woman named Vesna, stared out the front window at us. At me. When the cop saw her, she jerked the curtain closed.

"Oh, God, not her," he said. "Tell me this ain't another cheating husband job."

When I didn't answer, the cops exchanged looks of shared contempt. "What a piece of shit," Styrczula grumbled.

Karras asked me, "You didn't learn your lesson from Buzz?"

I looked down at the pavement like I was being yelled at by an adult.

Styrczula shook his head and asked his partner, "What you want to do, Lou?"

"Go let that dumbass out of the car. I'll send this one off."

Styrczula left.

Karras told me, "You know, you pissed off a lot of people today, kid. And not just the batinaš over there who kicked the shit out of you. You fuck up a federal stakeout—you get their guy arrested for assault before they can follow him to wherever he's supposed to go today—and they'll cut your balls off."

"How was I supposed to know?"

"That's what you said about Buzz. 'How was I supposed to know?' Maybe don't do sleazy matrimonial work in the first place."

"I'm just hustling like everybody else, man. And can you knock off the *kid* shit? I'm thirty-six years old, for Christ's sake."

"Hey, to me you're still the pimply kid sweeping the floors at Dean's office. But, okay, I'm getting old, Dean's dead and gone, and you're thirty-six. Fine. It's your office now, and you're a big boy. Do what you want with it. We all got to eat. But you and I both know that when Dean was running that place, he stayed away from the adultery racket."

"Yeah, well, I'm not Dean."

"Finally," Karras sighed, "something we can agree on."

I dug my car keys out of my pocket.

"Any parting words?" I asked.

The cop leaned in so close to me I could see the faint white dots at the edges of his scars, where stitches had once held his gnarled upper lip together.

"Yeah," he said. "You can protest your innocence all you want, but I know how the double-dipping scam works in the divorce racket. Wife pays you to follow her husband, but when you get the dirty footage of him banging the babysitter or whatever, you offer it to him at an inflated price. He pays, and you tell her you didn't find shit. Then you pocket her original fee plus the shakedown from the husband."

"I ever been—"

"No, you ain't ever been caught in the act. Not yet anyway. It's just a matter of time, though. You're going to fuck up one of these days and get yourself charged with extortion. But here's my parting words of advice. Don't go trying to play *this* guy." He jerked his thumb over his shoulder in the direction of Vukov. "I don't want to be the one who has to scrape your brains off the sidewalk."

* * *

I discovered my shirt had been ripped in the fight, so I was driving back to my apartment to change when my phone buzzed.

Vesna Vukov, FaceTiming me.

I pulled over beside a fire hydrant to answer her call. Her thin, pointed face popped up on my screen. Her hand was pressed to her mouth, and her limp blonde hair hung over her ears like old drapes.

When she saw me, she dropped her hand from her lips. "Are you okay?" she said.

"Is he still there?"

"No, he went to the club to meet somebody."

"You didn't tell me he's a fucking gangster."

"I told you he's a bad guy."

"You didn't tell me he's a *fucking gangster.*"

"Does it matter? I need a divorce. He's a bad guy. I got to get away from him before he kills me one day over nothing."

"Yeah, well, I need to get away from him before he kills me for trying to run surveillance on him."

"You said you'd help me."

"Wrong. I said I'd do a job for you. I'm not a marriage counselor, Vesna. I'm not a cop or a knight in shining armor. You understand? You want a savior, go find Jesus. I don't do anything I don't get paid for, and I don't get paid enough to put myself in danger."

"I need to get custody for my kids."

"Well then, I suggest you hire a lawyer."

"So what are you telling me now? You no longer work for me?"

"That's right. You're starting to understand. I no longer work for you."

"You are a coward," she said. "You are a fucking c—"

I put my phone away. Why listen to the rest of that? I might be a coward, but at least I'd be a coward with two working kneecaps.

* * *

I drove home to change and open up the office, but I ended up taking four Advil PMs, crawling into bed and staying there for the rest of the day.

At six P.M. my alarm went off. I didn't want to get up, but other than the now defunct Vukov case, I only had one other paying job on my docket.

Another marital surveillance job, God help me.

My skull still felt like a cracked egg, but I pushed myself to the edge of the mattress anyway. I sat up and slapped myself awake.

"Get out of bed, boy," I said. "The only thing worse than poor is dead."

CHAPTER 5

Ronnie Dunlap left his house at seven P.M., just the way his wife told me he would. Ronnie and Heidi lived in Portage Park, in a champagne-yellow brick bungalow on a quiet residential street of similar bungalows and shaded green lawns. When Ronnie's garage door opened and he backed out and headed off down the alley behind his house, I was parked at the other end, waiting for him to leave. I waited until he turned left, and then I followed him.

As I passed the Dunlap garage, I saw that the lights were on in the house, but I didn't glimpse anyone through the windows. Ronnie was going out alone, leaving Heidi at home to watch their daughter, Tobi.

The Dunlaps owned their nice brick home in Portage Park. They didn't rent. Ronnie Dunlap was thirty-five years old. Heidi, thirty-two. Tobi, twelve. Ronnie was an EMT, Heidi was a speech pathologist. Other than that, all I knew about the Dunlaps was that they had been married for thirteen years, and Heidi thought that Ronnie might be cheating on her.

I followed Dunlap's car, a gray 2018 Ford Taurus with a dented bumper, as it left their neighborhood. When he turned onto Milwaukee Avenue, I stayed a few vehicles behind him, and we drove at a leisurely pace. In Logan Square, he slowed down and grabbed a parking space in front of El Cid, a Mexican restaurant. I drove past him for a bit, swung back after a while, and pulled over near the intersection so I could watch him.

He climbed out of his car, paid for parking, and walked into the restaurant.

I found a place to park and strolled by the restaurant. Glancing through the front window, I didn't see him among the diners, but I knew the place also had an open-air patio in the back. It wasn't really warm enough to eat outside yet, but people in Chicago have a flexible definition of "warm enough," so I knew I should check to see if he was back there.

A narrow concrete passageway painted festive green ran alongside the restaurant. At the end, a sign announced Welcome to Mexico! In the patio, beneath colorful Mexican banners streaming overhead, people sat at wrought iron tables next to six-foot tall propane heaters going full blast, eating enchiladas and drinking margaritas. Sure enough, in the back, next to a high wooden fence, Ronnie Dunlap sat at a table by himself eating chips and dip while he looked over a menu.

A waitress walked up and asked me if I wanted a seat.

"Just looking for my wife," I said. "Maybe she's up front."

I walked back out to my car to wait and see if anyone showed up to join Dunlap for dinner, but the only newcomers came in groups. After a while, Dunlap came out of the restaurant, still by himself.

He walked to his car, got inside, and pulled away.

I didn't throw my car in drive and peel out after him. I moved deliberately. I didn't want to draw attention to myself, and there was no reason to hurry. After the Vukov disaster that morning, I wasn't in the mood to tag him with a GPS. Besides, I knew his car, and I had good sight lines on him, so I just tailed him, old school.

"Where are we going, dummy?" I asked.

* * *

For more than an hour, we just drove around. It didn't take long for me to figure out that we weren't really headed anywhere specific. We were driving in a makeshift loop from the streets around Logan Square to the area around Humboldt Park. We passed the soccer field, the baseball field, the boathouse, and the ponds, all without stopping or slowing down to pay any of them much attention. For a second I was worried that he was trying to see if he was being followed. But that wasn't it. The guy was just driving around.

While I followed him, I kept shifting uncomfortably in my seat. My lower back hurt from the beating I'd gotten from Vukov. Maybe I'd pulled something.

I shook my head. What a fuck up. In one morning, I'd managed to piss off a local crime family, the FBI, the Chicago Police Department, and one Croatian housewife.

None of them would be especially forgiving, but it was the CPD that worried me the most. They already hated me. Not long after I'd inherited the business from Dean, I'd taken a spousal surveillance job that had gone bad. Karras was right to say that Dean had always steered clear of the adultery racket, but when I took over the business I thought I'd expand the clientele. One of my first clients was a real estate agent who thought his wife was cheating on him. I'd followed the wife, recorded her hooking up with some guy at the Heart O' Chicago Motel on her lunch breaks, and then gave the recording to the husband. Two days later, he followed his wife to the same motel and shot her and her lover to death.

That would have been a big enough disaster, but the loverboy lying naked and dead on the floor of the Heart O' Chicago Motel turned out to be a police detective named Anthony "Buzz" Bazzano. When the cops found out what happened they tried to get my license pulled. I'd managed to cling to it by calling in favors from people on the licensing board who'd known and loved Dean, but nothing could stop my business from collapsing overnight. Buzz's friends on the force fed stories to the press about my unique combination of sleaziness and incompetence. Clients dropped me. I lost all my long-term security contracts. Worst of all, I lost most of my connections at the department. No more help from the cops, no more inside information, no more referrals for security or investigative work.

The irony of all of this was that now practically the only gigs I could get were matrimonial surveillance. Cheating spouses were my bread and butter. And, yes, the cops were right that sometimes when I got some good pictures, if I thought I could get a better price from the cheater than from my client, I sold them along with my silence. Why not? The law would call it extortion or blackmail. I call it giving the people what they want. It's just a matter of who wants it more.

Like this idiot. I wasn't sure what Dunlap wanted yet or what he'd pay for it. He kept driving in an endless loop, and I kept following—just two guys going in circles. There wasn't a notable presence of sidewalk prostitution in these neighborhoods, so I didn't think he was looking for someone to pick up. Maybe he was killing time before a scheduled tryst, maybe with someone who lived around here. He drove, I thought, the same way a man will twiddle his thumbs. Around and around in the same pattern.

But then I realized the circle was tightening. We were still driving in circles, but the circle was getting tighter, like a falcon spinning in the sky, closing in on the moment it will suddenly drop on its target.

And then he took a new turn. The sun had set hours ago, and we were driving around in the dark when he suddenly turned onto West Augusta Boulevard and parked. A minute later, I drove past and swung onto the next street about a block up and threw my car in park next to a fire hydrant.

Next to me in the passenger seat, I had an equipment bag full of my stakeout gear: GPS trackers, wireless mini-cameras, pliers, lockpicks, my heavy-duty Toughbook laptop. I pulled out my 4K Handycam with infrared, and I ran back to the street and stuck my head around the corner. This stretch of Augusta was mostly small apartment buildings. Most were three stories, maybe six or nine apartments per building. I recorded Dunlap getting out of his car and slipping his keys in his pocket. He checked the trunk of his car to make sure that it was ready—unlatched but not wide open. Then he stood on the sidewalk a moment between two of the buildings, looking around. He wore the same jeans and sneakers as before, but now he'd pulled on a gray hoodie. He walked over to the nearest alleyway, between an apartment building and a row of garages, and disappeared into it.

Well, this is damn peculiar.

I had to decide if I wanted to follow him. He could have walked down the alley and gone in a back door, gone up to an apartment or one of the garages. But he'd also checked his car's trunk to make sure it was open. I assumed he would return in a moment to load something in the back.

Since he'd slipped down the alley, though, I hadn't heard any further footsteps. I hadn't heard a door open. No voices. Nothing.

So I waited. While I did, I looked at the apartment building. Only the lights in the top two apartments were on. Aside from the sound of passing cars out on nearby Humboldt Drive, the night was quiet.

Then further up the block, I heard a door slam.

CHAPTER

6

I DON'T THINK THE woman ever saw him. It was a cloudy, moonless night, and the sky was just a low black ceiling. With one of the streetlights out, the man pressed against the wall in the alley was just another part of the complex of shadows that formed the darkness. The woman was distracted anyway. She came hurtling down the sidewalk, her head down, her purse slapping her thigh, her arms tight around her torso. She stomped along like she was too angry to pay attention to anything around her.

I don't think she even saw Dunlap when he pounced on her. Before she could realize what was happening, he knocked her down. She yelped as she hit the pavement on her hands and knees, but then he climbed over her, swung an arm around her neck and dragged her back into the alley.

Wind stirred the treetops. Cars passed out on the Humboldt thoroughfare.

I took a step, but then I stopped. My hands shook, but I didn't lower the camera.

There was real money to be made here. Not a few thousand from a cheating spouse. What would this man pay to keep *this* quiet? I thought of that nice brick house back in Portage Park. How much equity would he have on that? He would have to pay out. He'd have no choice. I'd recorded him parking, prepping the car, ducking in the alley, grabbing the woman, and dragging her into the dark—and when he emerged from the alley, with the woman or without her, I'd have that too. He would *definitely* pay.

Then something in the shadows stirred.

I almost fell over when I saw that it was the woman who stumbled from the dark and into the light of a streetlamp. She pushed herself out of the alley, one heavy step at a time, holding a knife. Her chest rose and fell. She didn't look at the knife, didn't seem to know she had it in her hand.

She began staggering back up the street, but then she stopped and ducked into the shadows. For a moment, I thought she'd seen me. But no. It wasn't me she was hiding from. A CPD cruiser slowly rolled up the street behind us. If they'd come by three minutes earlier, they'd have stopped the whole thing.

For a moment, the night air was heavy with possibility. All the woman had to do was flag down the cops. I braced myself. Once they stopped, I'd have nothing. Maybe I could sell the footage I had to the news, but did I really want it out there, this evidence that I'd stood by in the shadows doing nothing? No, as soon as they stopped, the footage I had would be worse than worthless.

But then the damnedest thing happened. Instead of waving down the cops, the woman slid back into the dark, just as her assailant had done a few minutes before.

She didn't move. I didn't move. And the cops just rolled on by, oblivious to what was happening in the alleyways and shadows just a few feet away.

When they were gone, the woman sprang out of the dark. She took two steps, stopped, and dropped the knife she'd been holding. Then she started to run up the street.

I had recorded it all, but now I didn't know what to do.

I watched her and clocked the apartment building she ducked into—the same one she'd stomped out of a few minutes before—and I then took a deep breath. Looking up and down the street, I checked the windows of the apartments. Many were dark, some had lights on. None had faces pressed to the glass. I saw no cellphones recording what was happening on the street below.

I jogged over to the alley. There, in a dark pile on the ground, lay Ronnie Dunlap.

I flipped on the infrared again and got footage of him lying there, blood soaking the front of his hoodie, a dark crimson stain that spread out from his neck and across his chest. Spots of blood, already black in the grime and dirt of the alleyway, dotted the concrete around him. It was more or less what I expected, except for one thing.

The son of a bitch was still alive. He was holding his throat, his eyes flickering left and right trying to avoid the camera.

I ran over to his car and looked in the opened trunk. Inside was a body bag, unzipped and splayed open, waiting for a body.

Son of a bitch.

I recorded it, shaking my head the whole time.

Son of a bitch.

I looked around. Empty streets. No time. What should I do? I could let Ronnie die, and then see if I could get some money from the woman who'd slit his throat and left him here. She clearly didn't want the cops involved. Why not? Did she and Ronnie know each other? Is that why she didn't flag down the cops when she had the chance? What would *she* pay to keep this from coming out?

I looked back at him lying on the ground. *Wait a minute, why let him die?* If he died, he was worthless to me. Dead men don't pay. On the other hand, if he lived, I could get money from him *and* the woman. Neither of them wanted this thing to be known. They could both pay.

I had absolutely no time to consider the implications of any of this. I just recognized the opportunity lying on the ground in front of me.

I closed the trunk and hustled back to Ronnie Dunlap. "Ronnie, can you hear me?"

He nodded, pale and shaking.

I reached down and pulled the thick floppy hood of his hoodie around and pressed it into his hand. "Lay there and use this to keep applying pressure to your throat," I told him.

I had to move fast. A car could turn down the alley at any moment or somebody on this block could go for a nighttime stroll, and this whole thing would blow up. The cops and the reporters would show up, and then that would be it for me.

While he pressed the cloth into his bleeding neck, I hoisted him up. I'd never had to carry a full-grown man before. It was harder than it looked.

"Help me," I grunted into his ear. "Use your legs."

I heaved him into the back seat of his car. I had to jostle his feet to get them inside so I could close the door.

"Keys in the car?" I asked.

His eyes, big and bulging, as frightened as they were confused, just stared at me. His head tilted in a *Yes*.

I retrieved the knife and jumped in the car.

I dug out my phone and scrolled down my list of contacts. I had a list bookmarked as RESOURCES. Everyone on the list owed me favors they were obligated to repay.

I pressed the name Lorenzo Muñoz.

"What?" Lorenzo snapped, by way of a greeting.

"Got a wounded man I need you to patch up. It's an emergency. Meet me—"

"Owen Pall, Jesus Christ, man. What are you . . . ? What kind of emergency?"

"Throat wound. Profuse bleeding. There's a fifty/fifty chance he'll be dead by the time I get to you."

"Christ! Take him to an ER, man."

"If I could take him to an ER, Lorenzo, I wouldn't be calling and disturbing your evening. My apologies to your family, by the way."

That shut him up, and except for the labored intake of his breath, the phone went silent for a moment.

Finally he said, "Where are you?"

"Five minutes from your clinic, maybe less if I get lucky with the lights. I know you're even closer, so come right now and meet me. Do not make me wait. If this guy dies because you're still putting on your shoes, we're going to have an even bigger problem to deal with."

* * *

Illinois Immediate Care is one of those walk-in clinics that specialize in cut-rate healthcare for people with shitty insurance plans. Muñoz helped me carry Ronnie Dunlap in through the back, and we laid him out on an examination table next to a cart full of supplies.

As Muñoz muttered curses and tried to patch up the pale, shivering man, Dunlap made no sound. He closed his eyes and lay perfectly still. Maybe he was trying to concentrate on living. Maybe he was hoping to die. It was hard to say.

"What happened to him?" Muñoz asked.

"His throat's cut. Does it matter how?"

"Might help me to know what happened."

"And he might like to know why you're helping him. You're both better off not knowing anything about the other one."

Muñoz stopped for a moment and glanced back at me.

I ignored his steely gaze. "Just concentrate on what you're doing, man," I said. I looked over his shoulder at Dunlap. "Jesus, he looks like shit."

Muñoz turned back to his sutures and bandages. "The wound's not deep. Whoever did this missed the carotid. If they didn't, he'd already be dead."

"So will he live?"

"I don't know, man," Muñoz grumbled. "This isn't really my specialty anymore. I mostly wrap ankles and prescribe antidiarrheals these days."

I told the patient, "I bet that's reassuring to hear, isn't it?"

Dunlap kept his eyes closed.

"Hey, man," Muñoz said to him, cutting off the sleeve of his hoodie with thick bandage scissors. "Can you hear me? What's your blood type?"

Dunlap mouthed the letter B, then crossed his shaky fingers.

"B positive?"

Nod.

Muñoz left to retrieve some blood from a cold storage unit in the back. "We have a very limited supply of these for special cases," he said when he returned with a 350ml bag of blood. "I don't know how the fuck I'm supposed to account for it going missing."

"You'll think of something," I said.

"Once I get him patched up, you got to get him out of here."

"Shouldn't he rest? Can he be moved?"

"I don't give a fuck if he can move or not. He's got to be out of here, and I got to have time to clean up everything before my staff comes in in the morning."

"A few hours to rest, then I'll take him." I started for the door. "I'll be back."

He spun around. "What the hell you mean you'll be back? You ain't going anywhere, man."

I walked back to him. "Take it easy, Lorenzo. I have to go. There's time-sensitive shit going on that I have to tend to. I'll be back, maybe in a couple hours." He started to object, but I shook my head. "Listen to me: I'll be back, maybe in an hour or two, maybe in ten minutes. But I have to go right now. You do your best with him, and no matter what, I'll be back to get him before you have to open. After that, we'll be gone, and you won't hear from me again."

Muñoz took a deep breath. He finally nodded his head. It was just as well that he didn't object further. It's not like the poor bastard had a real choice in the matter.

* * *

I left Dunlap's car at the corner of the alley where I'd found it and jogged back to my own. From where I was parked, I could see the front door of the apartment building the woman had gone into earlier. Only a couple of lights were on, including one on the third floor.

To get Dunlap over to Muñoz, get him settled, and then race back here had taken me nearly thirty minutes. More than enough time for her to call the police and for the police to respond, but the sidewalks were still empty, dark, and quiet. The only change was that the air had turned warm. Rain was coming.

After a few minutes, the woman walked outside. This time a man was with her. I had the Handycam ready, and I got a longer look at her. Early forties, dark hair worn long, coat pulled tight around her thin torso. Her skirt and stockings were torn, and although I couldn't see exactly what she'd put on underneath, I thought something like a T-shirt or a sports jersey was peeking out the top of the coat. The man with her was her age or maybe a little younger.

They were a strange pair. Mismatched. He wore jeans, a T-shirt, work boots. He was built like a roofer, with strong arms and wide shoulders. Despite what had happened out here tonight, he kind of sauntered along, like his good mood was still salvageable. The woman, on the other hand, looked upset. I could almost see her shaking. And yet, there was something else about her. It was the way she held herself, like she was holding on to her dignity with everything she had left.

They walked in the opposite direction of the alley and after a while they stopped at a car under a streetlamp near the end of the block. I got footage of them talking, but I mostly wanted to watch them. They were too far away for me to make out any of what they were saying, but from the coldness of their body language, they seemed to be having a fight. Then the woman got in her car and drove away, and the man ambled back to his apartment building. And that's what seemed to confirm the theory that had been developing in the back of my mind from the moment I'd seen her hide from the police cruiser.

She's married.

I eased out and followed her down the street. It started to rain. There wasn't a lot of traffic, but once the rain started, I could hang back without being seen. We got on I-90, and then she headed for the suburbs. In Evanston, she turned into a nice little neighborhood. When she slowed down to pull into the garage of a two-story redbrick home, I kept driving. At the next street, I swung around and cruised by her house. The garage door was lowering. As I passed by, I observed two details. One, although the garage was big enough for two vehicles, she was there alone. Two, she was holding her side.

Wounded in the fight maybe? Or maybe she's just carrying her torn clothes under her coat?

Up the street, I pulled over to the curb at a corner where I had a view of her home's front windows. I had her license plate number and the address of the house. I could figure out the rest soon enough, but I wanted to see what she'd do next.

No one else appeared to be home. She turned on every light in the house and disappeared into the back. Getting cleaned up, I assumed. After a while, she came out of the house with a plastic kitchen bag and walked to the garbage can at the curb. She stuffed the bag down into the can as far as she could. I almost had to laugh. Anyone watching her, even someone with no idea of what she'd done, would have found it suspicious that she was lifting boxes inside the garbage can in order to shove this bag further down. But I was the only one watching her. I got some nice clear footage of her doing it, even in the dark. Evanston streets, in an effort to exude middle-class safety, are nicely illuminated.

She went back inside, and I could see her sit down on her couch. Gathering her wits, I suppose.

It was not long before her family came home. One boy, high school age, gangly and looking a bit like his mother. And a man, soft around the belly, with glasses. They both wore Cubs T-shirts and hats.

This was what she was protecting, why she'd left the man for dead in the alley and hid in the shadows when the cops passed by.

Her family. Her life.

This is what she'd pay good money to protect.

Later, when they went to bed, I left. It had been a long night, and there was still much to do. But before I left, I got out of the car, strolled over to the garbage can in front of her house, and dug out the bag she'd left there.

CHAPTER

7

MUÑOZ MET ME at the back door of the clinic with his cellphone in his hand.

"My wife is texting me every five minutes wanting to know where the fuck I am," he said.

I didn't say anything to that as I crossed though the darkened back rooms of the clinic to the one searingly bright examination room with an open door.

Dunlap was lying on his back with a padding of clean white bandages taped to his neck. His hands were at his sides, and a wad of cotton was taped to the crook of his arm where he'd been given blood. His eyes were closed, and he did not appear to be breathing.

I caught my breath and was about to say something when I saw his stomach rise and fall. He opened his eyes, tilted his head just enough to look at me, and then closed them again.

Muñoz was beside me, jittery. "Okay, man. I patched him up. So get him the fuck out of here."

"Is he going to be okay?"

Muñoz spread his palms. "I don't know, man. Like I told you, this isn't my thing."

I held up a hand. "This is almost over, Lorenzo. Just take a breath and talk to me like a doctor for five seconds. Tell me the status of your patient."

He took a deep breath and rubbed his face. "Look," he said, "I can tell you that he's not in respiratory distress. That's a good sign. I stabilized the airway first thing, and it seems okay so far. The esophagus isn't injured, and as near as I can tell the major blood vessels look okay. So I think he's out of immediate danger. The larynx and the cartilage took the worst of it. So he's going to have trouble swallowing and talking. He needs to see an ENT surgeon as soon as possible. There could be blood clotting, trouble with the ligaments, permanent damage to his voice, all kinds of follow-up issues. Plus, I don't know how good my suturing job was. I did the best I could with what I had, but I never performed emergency suturing on a throat wound before."

"He looks sedate."

"I got him on fentanyl. That's another thing I'm gonna have to account for, by the way. It's gonna be missed. We don't keep just a ton of drugs around here in the first place."

"I guess he'll be in a lot of pain in the morning."

"I guess he will be," Muñoz said, crossing his arms to let me know he was closed for business and that Dunlap's pain tomorrow was not his problem.

"Okay," I said. "Help me get him to the car."

Muñoz and I slid Dunlap into a wheelchair. The guy was practically useless, just a heavy sack of meat and bones. We finally got him situated in my back seat.

"This is a different car," Muñoz said closing the door. "A different one than the one you brought him in."

I said nothing to that as I walked back around to the driver's side.

His phone buzzed, and he glanced at it and shook his head.

"Thanks for the help," I told him. "Go home to your wife."

"Yeah," he said, "this wasn't *help*. This was settling my account, okay? I don't owe you shit anymore. You said I wouldn't see you again after this, and that's what I expect. I don't care who gets shot, cut, or whatever. You're not getting another Band-Aid out of me."

I just nodded and drove off, leaving him standing there with his cellphone, trying to figure out what lie he was going to tell his wife.

* * *

Dunlap didn't make a sound as I drove him home. I wasn't worried about him, though. Muñoz was far better at this stuff than he said he was. He'd been the youngest vascular surgeon to be board-certified in California history before he'd shit away his life and career on a $15,000-a-day gambling addiction. When it was revealed that he'd been performing unnecessary thrombectomies to "repair" nonexistent blood clots to pay off his gambling debts, he lost his California state medical license and went to jail. Once he got out, he changed his name, relocated to Chicago, and got relicensed here. He got married and took the shitty job at the clinic, but he was lying to his wife and his kids about his past, neglecting to mention his former life, which also happened to include a first wife and a nineteen-year-old daughter who were still in California. I'd stumbled across his secret completely by accident when I was subcontracted to compile background on some guy running a bad-back scam on the pipefitter's union. The guy had come through Muñoz's clinic for treatment for his fake injury, and although all Muñoz had done was innocently prescribe Naproxen for the guy's back, I'd poked around into the doctor's credentials and one thing had led to another, and now here we were, with him indebted to me for keeping my mouth shut.

I congratulated myself on having the good business sense not to squeeze Muñoz for cash back in the day. That move had paid off better than a shakedown would have, especially since I knew his secret couldn't stay a secret forever. It's a bizarre quirk of human nature that a man as intelligent as Lorenzo Muñoz was so self-deluded that he couldn't see that there's no such thing as real secrecy anymore. We all collectively crossed that bridge and set fire to it a long time ago.

* * *

When I got to Ronnie Dunlap's house, I pulled around to the alley in the back, parking in front of his garage door, and texted his wife. She came outside a couple of minutes later, wearing a long nightshirt decorated with sleeping ducks over a pair of hastily thrown-on jeans.

"Oh my God," she said. "What happened to him?"

"Help me get him to the house."

Dunlap was awake and could move his legs, but he was wobbly and had no sense of where he was going. I had to keep him hoisted up and headed in the right direction. When we got inside, Heidi led us through the kitchen and into a hallway. I noticed an open bedroom door in the front of the house, but she directed me toward the bedroom in the back.

"He sleeps back here," she said, chewing her lip. "Please be quiet. I don't want to wake Tobi." Then she asked him, "Are you okay, Ronnie? Are you okay?"

Dunlap, still pretty much out of it, didn't respond to her as I lugged him into the back bedroom. The space had all the impersonality of a guest bedroom, though it also looked like Ronnie slept there full time, with an unmade bed, and clothes piled up in a corner.

After I settled him down on the bed, Heidi bent over him, not touching him. "Ronnie? Are you—" She turned to me, worried and scared. "His throat. What happened to his throat?"

I rubbed my back, which was sore from the beating I'd taken that morning, and which was hurting even more now from all the heavy lifting I'd been doing tonight. I really hoped I wasn't going to wake up with a pulled muscle.

"He got into some trouble."

"Trouble? With who?"

I glanced over at Ronnie. As soon as he'd hit the mattress, he'd sunk back into unconsciousness again. Heidi waited for me to answer her. I'd already decided not to tell her anything. If she found out her husband was an alley-dwelling psycho, her first instinct would be to run to the cops, not to give me money.

"I don't know," I told her. "I found him in Humboldt Park. When I found him he was lying on the ground near his car, cut, bad. His throat. I got him medical attention."

"Oh my God." She looked back at him, seeing his bandages anew. But then she turned back to me. "I don't understand. Did you call the police? Why isn't he in a hospital?"

"I'm not entirely sure what he was up to tonight, Mrs. Dunlap. I think it might have been something illegal. Until we know for sure, perhaps we shouldn't get the police involved just yet?" Yes, *something illegal* was just vague enough to be scary but not scary enough to panic her. *Something illegal* could mean prostitutes or drugs, could mean a million things before it meant *You are married to a psychopath.* I rubbed my back. "Keep him propped up, but let him sleep. I have to go. My night's not over yet."

I headed out to my car, but she followed me outside and caught me as I was walking through the back gate by her garage. We stood in the alley behind her home, and over her shoulder I could see the long row of similarly detached garages, darkened backyards, and sleeping houses extending down the street. The night was silent and cool.

"Please tell me what happened," she said.

"Let's talk tomorrow, Heidi," I replied. "I'm not sure what to tell you yet. I'll know more tomorrow."

"But—"

"Did you really hire me because you were afraid Ronnie was cheating on you?"

She just stood there blinking, which was about what I expected.

"Let's talk tomorrow," I said, and started for my car.

She looked at my Honda. "Wait, where is his car?"

"Right where he left it," I said. I turned around. "By the way, he doesn't know who I am. He doesn't know I was following him. You might want to keep it that way for a while."

As I drove away, I glanced in the rearview mirror. I could see her still standing there in that lonely alley behind her home, growing smaller in the dark until I turned onto the street, and then she disappeared completely.

CHAPTER

8

IF I WAS going to shake these people down, I needed to know who I was dealing with, so I spent the rest of the night back in my office drinking coffee and doing research. The lights were all off in the front of the store, except for the little blue neon sign that read: SECURITY SOLUTIONS that I left plugged in twenty-four/seven. I selected Judy Garland's 1957 studio album *Alone* from Dean's record collection and set it playing on his old Murphy player in the corner next to the coffee machine. After that, I only got up from the computer to flip the record and refill on bean, then I went right back to my research.

I started with the assailant. Like everyone else, his life was scattered across the internet in small pieces of information just waiting to be gathered up like litter on the side of the road. Ronald Dunlap was a Chicago native. He'd grown up in neighborhoods on the North Side, gone to school there, gotten a job there, gotten married there. When he married Heidi Markham, he was twenty-two, she was just nineteen. He was thirty-five now, had a twelve-year-old daughter, and had been an EMT for eleven years. According to the public property records, the house was in Heidi's name. It looked like the previous owners were her parents, so I assumed she'd inherited it. That might complicate things on the financial front, but convincing Heidi to borrow money against the house would be Ronnie's problem, not mine.

More puzzling to me, though, was that my preliminary search turned up no criminal record for Ronnie. I'd checked it just out of curiosity, to see who I was dealing with. What I found was, well, nothing. No documented history of violence, no busts with hookers, no busts for stalking. No arrests of any kind. That wasn't a problem, of course. All I needed was the footage of tonight's attack. But it was strange to uncover zero red flags.

What I found instead was even better, though.

A few months ago, Dunlap and his partner on the ambulance rescued a baby from a fiery car wreck. Both the *Tribune* and the *Sun-Times* published articles about it, and I found some TV news footage of the flaming car, complete with a brief interview with Dunlap—pale, sweaty, and inarticulate—and his exuberant partner the day after the incident. The child's mother had perished in the fire, but the news was quick to label the pair heroes who'd bravely swooped in to save the baby. There was even a brief news story a couple of days later in which the mayor, standing next to the fire department commissioner, called Dunlap and his partner "true Chicago heroes."

So, I had footage of a bona fide "Chicago hero" trying to knife a woman in an alley. Beautiful. This kept getting better. *Ronnie, you and Heidi better call the bank and ask them when you can come in for a talk.*

I got up and refilled on coffee, flipped Judy over, and decided to turn to the victim. Her name was Alice Hardy. I could have found her name going in reverse from her address or her license plate, but I found it even quicker, on a discarded credit card offer in her trash.

First thing I'd done was go through the garbage bag. I found her ripped blouse, skirt, and stockings. All of them contained blood. A spray of countless tiny drops on the blouse, five larger drops on the skirt, and a thick, crusted stain on the right knee of the stockings. The blood on the stockings was probably hers from when she fell, but the blood on the blouse and skirt was undoubtedly Dunlap's.

The rest of the bag was full of kitchen garbage. Egg shells and coffee grounds, Taco Bell wrappers. There was some discarded junk mail. The credit card offer for Alice. A flyer for lawn care services. The normal detritus of a conventional, middle-class life.

I put the clothes in three separate bags and locked them in the office safe next to Ronnie Dunlap's knife and his rolled-up body bag.

From there, the rest was as easy as googling her name. The first thing that popped up was the faculty page of the theology department at St. Ignatius University here in Chicago, complete with a faculty photo, her CV, and her teaching schedule. *Professor* Alice Hardy, then. The rest I pieced together as I kept digging. She was born March 4, 1978, in Schuyler, Nebraska. Valedictorian of her high school graduating class in 1996. Four years at the University of Missouri, with a BA in religious studies. Then a master's degree in theological studies, followed by a doctorate in biblical theology, both from St. Ignatius University.

From what I could tell, she seemed to have found herself while she was at St. Ignatius. In addition to earning her degrees there, she also got married, to a fellow academic named Greg Babbitt. They must have loved St. Ignatius because they both still taught there. Babbitt was chair of the department of Mathematics and Statistics, while Alice Hardy taught in the Theology department. On their university website, I found a list of their latest publications. I didn't understand what any of it meant—she'd published an article with the enticing title "Cognitive Frames of Atonement in the Synoptic Gospels," and he'd written something called *Revisiting Principia Mathematica*—but taken altogether it painted a picture of Alice Hardy and her husband as a couple of uptight intellectuals.

So what were you doing on that street tonight, Professor Hardy? Trying to break free of the life of the mind, maybe. That was going to cost her. Not as much as Ronnie. He'd pay more. But she'd pay something, I could tell.

I searched the public records available online and didn't find any history of altercations with the law for Alice Hardy or her husband. There seemed to be no history of abuse on record, no divorce filings. That made me wonder what story she was telling on social media.

I had burner accounts set up on every social media platform imaginable, so I spent a while poking around, seeing if I could find any connections between my subjects. I needed to know if Ronnie and Alice knew each other, if the attack had personal history behind it, but I found no overlap between them, their spouses, or their children. They all seemed to run in completely different circles. Ronnie's daughter was on TikTok, and Alice's son posted movie reviews on Letterboxd, but none of the adults had particularly big online presences.

Of course, I didn't have time to do a deep dive of every single social media and dating app to see if Ronnie or Alice were actively running around on their spouses or using aliases or their own burner accounts. That would take time. There's a lot of places to hide from your spouse on the internet. To all outward appearances, however, nobody knew each other. That meant the attack in the alley was most likely random.

I knew Ronnie would pay to keep the attack a secret. He had no choice. Alice Hardy was a little more complicated. I'd need to handle her more delicately. If I spooked her too bad, she might still break down and run to the cops. I needed to tell her that I knew the truth. That I knew she was cheating on her husband with some guy who lived over in Humboldt Park. That I knew she'd almost killed a man tonight. That I knew she'd hidden all of this from the police. That I even had footage of her trying to get rid of the evidence. I needed to tell her that the story she was telling the world—about the successful academic, happily married, with a son she adored, and a nice big house in the suburbs—was in danger of falling apart.

I needed to let her know that her happiness was in danger, while at the same time selling her the solution to the problem.

* * *

I was about to move on when I found a picture of Alice. It took me by surprise. Among all the photos of her husband and son on her social media, she'd only posted a single candid picture of herself.

I hadn't really looked at her before that moment. I'd only seen her at a distance or on infrared or in the tiny photo accompanying her faculty page. I hadn't really *looked* at her before.

As I did, she seemed familiar to me somehow.

The photo was a shot of her standing behind her teenage son, him leaning forward, her arms wrapped around his shoulders, both of them laughing. It looked like he was carrying her on his back. Or was she holding him? I couldn't tell which.

I clicked away from the picture, but then I stopped. I clicked back.

Alice with her son.

Then I saw it. Then it was unmistakable.

She looked like my mother.

I sat there with my mouth open.

Of course, Alice Hardy and my mother had almost nothing in common. Alice was a professor with a stable family life. She had a career, money, respect. My mother had never had any of those things.

They didn't even look so much alike physically. They both had large eyes, I suppose, but it was the set of Alice Hardy's mouth, her hesitant half-sad smile, that made me think of my mother. It was the smile of a woman afraid of her own happiness.

* * *

About four A.M., I uploaded my footage of the attack. I gave Judy Garland a rest and turned on the police scanner. It squawked every few seconds, dispatching officers to different scenes:

Shots fired at a party on South Loomis, five people wounded.

Infant abandoned in the Jewel-Osco parking lot in Andersonville.

I pulled up the footage on my monitor, maxed out the screen, hit play. It began with Ronnie Dunlap furtively climbing out of his car. In the Handycam's infrared footage, Ronnie Dunlap moved in and out of focus, but it was unmistakably him. Checking the trunk. Looking around. Disappearing into the alleyway.

The scanner squawked:

Fistfight between four intoxicated individuals outside Wrigley Field.

Shots fired on South Eberhardt, two people wounded.

Onscreen, Alice Hardy suddenly appeared, hurrying down the street, passing in and out of the light from the streetlamps. Stopping and looking around. *Is she lost?* She resumes walking, but she's still unsure. Then she passes in front of the alley.

Her attacker leaps out of the dark like a jungle cat.

He knocks her down and she hits the ground.

Watching the screen, watching Alice Hardy falling to her hands and knees, my stomach dropped.

I ran it back, paused it, and stared.

When I'd recorded this a few hours before, I had been too caught up in the moment to really *see* what I was seeing. Now I couldn't avoid it.

The pain on her face was terrible, vivid, unmistakable. The animal fear. The horror, realized in an instant, in the time it took her to hit the ground, that an act of inescapable violence was about to be done to her, that it had, in fact, already begun. It was like watching someone drown.

Staring at the monitor, I could see my own dim reflection on the screen, translucent and hollow, hovering over Alice Hardy's frozen, terrified face.

The scanner squawked out more updates. Drunks and fistfights and car crashes and shots fired. All kinds of mayhem and tragedy.

But nothing about a woman being attacked in Humboldt Park. Nothing about her stabbing her attacker. With each passing hour, it became less and less likely that Alice Hardy would blow up her safe and comfortable life by reporting the attack to the police.

I was still the only one who knew what had happened. I sat there thinking about that for a minute, staring at my face blurring into her face on the screen.

* * *

I was pretty well exhausted by morning. My eyes felt dry, and I was about to overdose on coffee. I knew I had to stop typing when my fingers wouldn't stop twitching.

I closed everything down and wandered back into the store. I was supposed to open in a few hours, but in the window I hung up Dean's old sign, the one with a cartoon sleuth in a fedora holding up a placard that read **Sorry, We're Out on a Case. Please Call or Come Again.**

I checked the locks and walked upstairs to my apartment to get a little rest. I was still getting used to calling the apartment mine. It had been Dean's for as long as he owned the business. After he died, I packed up my stuff over on Belle Plaine and moved in. So, yes, now it was mine and had been for a few years.

But it still smelled like him. The old cigarette smell in the den, the bacon grease smell in the kitchen. It looked like him too, for the most part. I'd kept everything the same up here, just like I'd done downstairs in the store and the office. I had added a few things of my own, of course. I'd updated the television, hooked it up with a Roku to stream stuff. And the clothes in the closet were mine. But most everything else—the framed movie posters, the books on the shelves, the racks of VHS tapes and the binders full of DVDs and CDs—they were all Dean's. To look at it, you'd think the old packrat was still alive.

I went into the bedroom and plopped down on my bed. This was the only room I'd completely stripped of Dean's presence. I'd brought my own bed with me, and I'd taken everything else out of here and painted it white. Now it was just bare white walls, a bare white ceiling, and white blinds over the windows. Even the door to the closet was white. I suppose some people would find it bleak, maybe even institutional, like a room at the asylum. But I liked it. To me it was a blank canvas. I liked to lay there at night and project my thoughts onto the walls.

Now I just wanted to sleep, to stop the constant churn of that image, of Alice Hardy on her hands and knees, her face a mask of horror.

Thinking about Alice bothered me, so I tried to think of something else. Anything else to help me sleep. The problem was that the only other things I could think about were Dean and my mother and Arkansas. None of that helped me at all.

I never got to sleep that night.

Part III: Friday

Alice Hardy

CHAPTER 9

I WOKE UP FALLING, trying to scream.

I reached out for something, anything, but my hands only found an empty space where Greg had been just a few minutes before. I settled back into my pillow, catching my breath, nodding.

Right. Morning. I could hear the shower going in our bathroom.

I almost closed my eyes, but I grabbed my phone instead. Some sick feeling told me I'd have a message this morning.

From the man in the alley? From Jason? The police?

But I had no messages.

I lay the phone on a pillow and kicked my sheets off. When I did, my knee throbbed to life. It was slightly swollen, and the skin was so discolored it looked like I'd dipped my kneecap in purple and blue paint last night. I sat up and hung my legs off the bed, working my knee to see if the joint still worked. Although it hurt, I could move it.

Still sitting on the edge of my bed, my knee aching, I searched the news updates for Chicago on my phone. There was a story about more luxury apartments opening in River North. News about the Cubs getting routed by the Brewers. And there were three new stories about different shootings on the South Side, all gang or drug related.

But there was nothing about a stabbing last night on West Augusta Boulevard. Nothing about a stabbing anywhere in the city.

What did it mean? I was certain I stabbed that man, maybe even slashed his throat. Even if he could get away on his own, he would have to seek medical attention.

The water in the shower stopped, and a moment later Greg walked out with a towel around his waist.

"Jesus, your knee," he said.

"Yeah," I said. "I told you I fell on it."

"You didn't tell me you hit it that bad."

"Am I supposed to give you a detailed report every time I fall down?"

I don't know why I said that, or why it came out so peevishly, but Greg just frowned and threw off his towel to get dressed. For a moment, he stood there naked as he opened the chest of drawers and dug out his clothes, his hair dripping and matting his hairy little potbelly.

When he'd nearly finished dressing, he asked in a measured voice, "Is your knee okay? Do you need to go see Lavan?"

"I don't need a doctor. It's just bruised."

He nodded, buttoning up his shirt and tucking it in. "Good to hear."

When he'd gone downstairs, I stood up and listened to the sounds of him and Tuck moving around, getting ready. They'd be gone soon. Greg would be off to work first because he had an early class today, and Tuck would be out the door right after him in order to grab a ride to school with Julia. Being alone in the house in the mornings was usually something I enjoyed. I liked to linger over a cup of coffee, listening to NPR and scrolling through the *New York Times* on my phone. But this morning, I dreaded it. I was scared to be alone.

I went downstairs where they were both sitting at the kitchen table, Greg sipping coffee and reading an article on Bleacher Report, Tuck still bleary-eyed as he ate cereal.

"Mom," he said, "I'm tired of cereal."

I poured myself a cup of coffee. "Have a Pop-Tart."

"I'm tired of Pop-Tarts too," he said. "I want bacon and eggs."

I nodded at the refrigerator. "That's the beauty of free will. If you want bacon and eggs, you just have to cook them."

"Yeah, but I just woke up . . ."

"Well, that's the problem of free will."

"I thought you would make them this morning."

"Now I'm a bad mother because I didn't make you breakfast this morning?" I banged my cup down on the counter. I was irritated, so I did it with a little force, but when I did, I caught the edge of the sink and the cup shattered. It startled all of us.

"What the hell, Alice?" Greg said.

Tuck looked like I'd slapped his face.

"I'm sorry," I said. "I didn't mean to do that." Tuck just stared at me, dumbfounded. "I'm sorry," I said again. I showed him my knee. "I'm just upset because I hurt my leg last night. I shouldn't take my bad mood out on you."

He looked at my swollen, mottled knee and said, "Are you okay?"

I stepped over the coffee and pieces of the cup that landed on the floor, and I hugged him in his chair, bending down to kiss the top of his head. "Yes, I'll be okay. I'm really sorry I snapped at you. It wasn't fair."

Tuck drew away from my touch and nodded to let me know he understood, though not enough to grant any kind of forgiveness. Last night, he'd seemed slightly embarrassed by my physical affection, now he seemed viscerally offended by it. He glanced out the window. "Julia's here," he said. "I gotta go. You want me to wipe up the coffee?"

"No, dear," I said, almost choking on my words. "I broke the cup. I'll clean up the mess."

He got up, grabbed his school bag, and left. Once he was gone, Greg, staring at me with both concern and irritation, said, "What the fuck?"

"Everything is okay," I said.

He shook his head. "Is this one of those times where you say everything is okay, but I'm supposed to know everything's not?"

I stared at him. When one of our conversations began with a meta-commentary about my communication skills, I knew I was doomed. I decided to avoid that.

"I'm just . . . my knee hurts and I'm running late. I didn't get those quizzes graded last night, so I'm behind. Now I need to run and get ready for work. I'm just in a rotten mood."

Greg nodded at that, accepting it. I don't know if he believed me, but it didn't really matter if he did. We'd long ago settled into a pattern where he did not deal with my emotions unless I forced him to do so. Since I'd just given him a quick escape route, he took it.

He got up and retrieved his coat and bag from the hallway. "Okay," he said. "Ice your knee and try to stay off it today. And call Lavan if you need to. Don't be stubborn."

I said that I would, waved to him as he left, and then went to the window to watch him back out of our garage and drive down the street.

* * *

Once I was alone, I hobbled around and checked all the house locks again. I peered out windows to see if anyone was outside watching me.

All I saw was our quiet street. The garbage can wasn't at the end of the driveway, which meant either Greg or Tuck had brought it back up to the house this morning after the garbage men came by. I went and peeked inside the garage, and, sure enough, the can was against the wall. I checked to see if it was empty, and, of course, it was. I knew it would be, but I had this terrible fear that the bag of my ripped clothes had somehow fallen to the bottom, where it was waiting to be used as evidence of what had happened last night. Even worse was the thought that perhaps I should have held on to the clothes, just in case.

I skipped my breakfast. I couldn't eat, and I was sure that coffee would only irritate my stomach and make me more jittery. If anything I needed to calm down. After I threw away the broken mug and wiped up the spilled coffee, I showered and got ready for work, packing up my books and notes and the ungraded quizzes. By the time I was ready to go, my hands were shaking so badly I dropped my keys in the kitchen.

I can't do this.

I closed my eyes and took a deep breath. I needed something to steady me.

I'm not a big drinker. I'll have a glass of wine when we go out to eat, but unless I have a bottle left over from a dinner party, there's usually no alcohol for me at the house. That morning, all we had on hand were some of Greg's Daisy Cutters in the fridge and what was left of a bottle of Woodford Reserve in the cabinet.

I had a shot of the bourbon, straight from the bottle. It went down smoothly, but when it hit my chest I had to squeeze my eyes and bite down. On my empty stomach, it made me dizzy, and I had to hold on to the counter.

When I'd regained my equilibrium, I eyed the Woodford to reassure myself that the missing swig of bourbon wasn't noticeable. Then I returned the bottle to the cabinet.

* * *

What happened to him?

On the way to school, I rode in silence. No radio, none of my usual podcasts. I needed the silence, the space to think.

What happened to the man in the alley? Why was there no story in the local news about a stabbing in Chicago last night?

Perhaps he'd gone to a hospital in the suburbs? I tried to warm to that idea because the thing I was really afraid of was that the man had managed to pull himself together long enough to move but then died later, maybe in his car or at home. Maybe he just hadn't been found yet.

Jesus, don't think that. He must be fine. He got up and walked away. You didn't kill anyone last night. That thought's absurd. You got attacked by some bastard. You should deal with that fact, not sit here worrying yourself to death that you hurt him. I hope you did *hurt him, the son of a bitch.*

The most surreal thing about experiencing trauma is that the rest of the world doesn't even notice. I felt like my brain was about to vibrate out of my skull, but next to me at traffic lights people sat in their cars and ate breakfast out of paper sacks, or sang along to music, or stared blankly ahead. No one noticed me at all, much less recognized that there was anything wrong with me. My drive to St. Ignatius was the same as it had always been. I passed the Whole Foods, made sure to slow down at the speed trap on Peterson Avenue, made my turn by the Heart O' Chicago Motel, and arrived at school at my usual time. As I left the parking deck and limped across campus, everything looked normal. Even me. I had on one of my standard teaching outfits—loose maroon slacks and a charcoal blouse with a light gray blazer. I had my bag of books and papers slung over my shoulder. Just another professor on her way to class.

But my knee screamed up my leg and into my back with every step I took, and, worse than that, every bolt of pain reminded me what happened last night.

The only class I was scheduled to teach that day was Semiotics and Biblical Interpretation. When I got to the classroom, a few kids were already waiting. Most, looking at their phones, barely glanced up when I walked in. One girl, perpetually underprepared, had today's text, Frank Kermode's *The Genesis of Secrecy*, open on her desk, urgently trying to comprehend as much of it as possible before the daily quiz I always gave at the top of class.

I greeted everyone with a hello and sat down at the desk in the front of the room. I still had a couple of minutes before we started, and I took out my copy of the book and my lecture notes and tried to jumpstart my brain, to remind myself what we were supposed to be discussing today. It was no use, though. My mind was a blank.

I told myself I would just give them the quiz and then lean hard on my notes during the lecture. *Sorry kids, your teacher couldn't join us today.*

During the quiz, as the students scribbled their answers to the question "According to Kermode, why does the Gospel of Mark frame the messiahship of Jesus as a secret to be kept from the public?" I stood behind the teacher's podium and surreptitiously scrolled the WGN news app looking for anything on a stabbing last night. Maybe something in the suburbs? Maybe an unidentified body that might be my attacker?

But there was nothing. It was as if it had never happened.

When I finally abandoned my futile search and looked up from my phone, I discovered the whole class staring at me, waiting. They'd all been done for a while.

* * *

After class, I shuffled to my office and tried to grade the quizzes. Even in the best of times, trudging through the half-assed guesses and Hail Mary bluffs that sometimes passed for answers among my students made for an arduous ordeal, but today I wasn't up to it at all. I could not stop thinking about what had happened last night. And it wasn't just the attack that made me sick with worry.

I felt sick about Jason. What I'd been doing with him was stupid, reckless. Maybe worse. Maybe unforgivable.

I'd justified it to myself, of course. I'd blamed Greg for being distant, for being preoccupied by the never-ending equation in his head. I told myself he was too comfortable in our lives, too comfortable with me. *I just don't have any unresolved feelings about you*, he'd said. I'd wondered if that was just another way of saying he didn't really think about me at all. In his mind, I was there, next to him, helping raise our kid and make dinner. What was there to think about, right?

But the warm comforts we enjoyed were not the only pleasures in the world. *You come over here to have someone pull your hair while they fuck you.* That was what Jason told me last night before I left.

I had once known that kind of passion with Greg. When we first got together, we had sex constantly. But like fire needs oxygen, passion needs wanting, it needs space to burn. In a marriage, all the available space gets filled, filled with the endless details of life. We had a son to raise, students to teach, papers to grade, meetings to attend, journal articles to write. Greg was a good partner in managing the details of our life together. I cooked, he washed dishes. I supervised the doctor's appointments, he oversaw the college applications. We supported each other, and we gave each other the comfort of family and the room to pursue our own careers.

But, no, we hadn't had sex in a while, and when we did, we certainly weren't on the floor in front of a mirror.

Like Jason.

Jason . . .

I was still disgusted with him for what he said after the attack last night, but now something occurred to me. The attack had occurred in his neighborhood. Maybe he'd heard something that wasn't online yet. Maybe he'd gone back to the alley, seen some blood, seen something. He might have new information that wasn't in the news yet.

I grabbed my phone and called him.

I got a recording. His voice, stiff and formal, saying, "Jason Brennan" followed by a computer-generated female voice saying "is not available. Please leave a message."

I hung up.

My office was on the second floor of Loyola Hall, and when I left for lunch I usually left through the main office, waving at the secretary and whoever might have their office door open on my way to the stairwell. But I didn't want to see anyone at the school right now, so I gathered my things and left by the back door.

I was supposed to go eat, then have my office hours and meet with some students to go over their essays. But as soon as I stepped outside, I knew I wasn't coming back today. I just couldn't.

CHAPTER 10

I DROVE OVER TO Jason's apartment and found an open space right in front of his building. I had to shake my head as I parked. If this space had been open last night, nothing would have happened. A few feet of empty concrete.

I didn't see his truck around, but I went inside and tried the foyer buzzer anyway. It buzzed, but nothing happened.

I walked back outside and stared up at his window as I called him on my cell.

No answer, but I could see Spartacus staring down at me from the window with his sagging, tired old eyes.

When I got Jason's message, I said, "It's me. I'd like to talk to you. I'm at your place. Can you call me back, please?"

I hung up and walked down Augusta, toward the park, and found the alley where I was attacked. It seemed smaller than last night, when it had seemed as big and empty as a black hole. Now it was just a little stretch of potholed concrete between the brick side of an apartment building and the brick side of a small garage. The garage abutted the backyard of another set of apartments. Everything seemed tiny and crammed together.

I don't know what I was hoping to see. Signs of a struggle, maybe. Whatever that would mean in an alleyway. There were numerous dark splotches on the ground, but the ground was, unsurprisingly, filthy—covered in dirt, loose gravel, calcified clumps of blackened gum, and cigarette butts—so, with the naked eye, it was hard to tell if the black spots were blood or just another part of the general grime. I had half wondered if maybe I'd find the knife, thinking that perhaps I'd dropped it in the alley rather than on the street like I remembered. But no. All I found was a dirty alley, unremarkable in every way.

I checked my phone. No call from Jason.

I left to go back to my car, walking past a gray Ford Taurus with a dent in the bumper that was parked by the alley.

* * *

I knew where Jason was working that day. Well, I knew generally where he was working. He told me he was doing a job over in Portage Park by the elementary school. I wasn't entirely sure where that was, but the GPS took me to the school, and I drove around the neighborhood until I saw his truck parked outside a little two-story house on a street of similar houses.

He had a big rooster-red F-150 with a magnetic sign on the door that he could slap on or take off whenever he wanted. Above a phone number and a web address, the sign read:

<u>Brennan Tiles</u>

Quality Materials—Affordable Prices
Expert Installation

I walked up to the front door of the house and knocked. I could hear music inside. Old Crow Medicine Show, his favorite band. I knocked louder. No one came to the door. I rang the doorbell. Even with the music, he couldn't have failed to hear the bell.

I tried the door. It was unlocked. I stepped inside and walked into a big den. The house was furnished with Civil War memorabilia and bric-a-brac. Little figurines of Abraham Lincoln and Robert E. Lee, a display case of old bullets mounted on the wall, a framed recruitment handbill for the 45th Illinois Infantry Regiment, shelves of books. I didn't stop to look at the books, but just glancing out of the corner of my eye I noticed the three-volume set of Civil War history by Bruce Catton that I'd bought for my own father for Christmas one year.

No one appeared to be home, but the music played upstairs.

"Jason?" I called.

He paused the music and called down, "Yeah?"

I walked up a flight of stairs decorated by old family photos and framed handbills announcing a debate between Abraham Lincoln and Stephen Douglas, and I found Jason poking his head out of a bedroom. He wore sweaty work clothes, a tool belt, and a confused look.

"What the fuck are you doing here?"

"Hey," I said, suddenly sorry that I'd done this. "What are you doing?"

"I'm tiling a fucking bathroom. What's it look like? Why are you in these people's house?"

"You didn't answer your phone. I called like three or four times."

He wiped sweat from his eyes with the back of his hand. "I'm *working*, Alice."

I looked around him to see into the bedroom. I don't know why. I didn't exactly expect to find someone laying on her back with her knees in the air, but I had to look anyway. After all, isn't that the way it had started with us?

But there was no one else there. The bedroom was furnished with antiques, including a four-poster bed with a puffy flower quilt and a frilly pink bed skirt. The door to the master bathroom was open, and I could see the unfinished tile work that was underway.

He noticed me looking around and rubbed his stubbled jaw. "Please tell me you didn't come over here to see if I was 'cheating' on you."

"Are we alone?"

"Yeah. Everybody's at work."

"I came over here to see you because of what happened last night. I need someone to talk to about this."

"It couldn't wait?"

And like that, I felt like I was going to explode. "No," I yelled. "I'm losing my mind. A man almost *killed* me last night. I'm supposed to just go on with my life like nothing happened?"

"Jesus Christ, just . . ." He stared at me. "Just calm down, okay. I know you were scared, but—"

"The man had a *knife*," I said. "If he hadn't dropped it when we were wrestling, I don't think I'd be alive right now. Do you realize that?"

He closed his eyes, rubbed the bridge of his nose. "Look, I'm sorry that happened. I am. I really am. It's fucked up. If I could have a go at that dude, I'd knock his fucking brains out for you. I promise you I would. But you're okay. Right? You're alive. You're unharmed, right? How's your knee?"

"It hurts, a lot."

"But it's okay, right? You're walking around on it."

The corner of my eyes were damp. I wiped them with the back of my hand. "Yeah," I said. "Sure."

"Then I think you gotta say, 'Hey, all things considered, I'm a pretty lucky lady.' Right?"

"Sure, Jason. You bet."

"Okay then."

"I went back there today," I told him.

He blinked. "Where?"

"The alley."

"Really?"

"Yeah, I went to see if you were home, and then I went to check out the alley."

"Find any clues?"

The way he said it, the word he chose—*clues*, like we were in an episode of *Murder, She Wrote*—turned me to stone.

"No," I said. "The guy just up and vanished." I stared at him. "I guess I should just forget about it."

"Well," he said, "I mean, I think you should try to put it behind you. Whatever happened to him, it's not your problem now, right?"

"If you don't count the trauma, then, no, I guess not."

He grinned. "You're annoyed with me again. That's always a good sign." He dug his phone out of his back pocket and glanced at the time. "Look, I gotta get back to work. How about you let me call you in a few days, check in on you?"

The way he said made it pretty clear that he was never going to call me again.

"Why bother?" I said.

"Don't be that way. I'll call you."

"I don't want you to call me. As bad as this is, I'd rather deal with it on my own than have to discuss it with you again. You made it clear last night before the attack even happened that you'd pretty much gotten everything you wanted from me."

He stopped smiling. He hitched his thumbs on his toolbelt. Taking a long, deep breath, he said, "Well shit, Alice, as long as we're breaking up, then let's just go ahead and call things what they are, okay? You can act like I'm the one who used you, but *you* came to *my* place last night. And you didn't show up there looking to discuss literature either."

"What the hell does that mean?"

"It means you only text me when you want to feel bad, when you want to slum it and get yourself dirty. And, honestly, that kinda makes me feel like shit. So why don't you go ahead and get out here and let me get back to work. There's an ivory tower somewhere calling your name." He gestured at the door. "Here, c'mon, I'll walk you out."

We walked downstairs as silently as strangers.

When we stepped outside, I turned around.

"I really was attacked," I said, barely able to get the words out. "I just want you to know that. No matter what else happened between us. A man tried to kill me last night, and you acted like I was either crazy or lying about it."

He started to say something to that, but the words stalled in his mouth. Instead, he pursed his lips and nodded. Finally, he said, "It's going to be okay."

I didn't know what else to say. I just turned away.

As I walked to the street, he closed the front door. I heard his music start back up before I even got to my car.

CHAPTER

11

"THIS CITY IS brutal," Megan said. "Chicago will break your heart before breakfast."

"Oh, I know," Todd said, waving his glass around the faculty mixer in my living room. *Chet Baker Live in Paris* was playing quietly on our Bluetooth speaker while a dozen or so academics, clustered in little groups, sipped cocktails and chatted. "Just look at this dystopian hellscape."

Megan smiled at that, but she was never one to be put off her favorite subject, the terror of living in Chicagoland. She'd come from a family of bankers in suburban Texas, and although she'd been here nine years, she'd never quite adjusted. "Well, not to put too fine a point on it, but *this* isn't Chicago. I mean, this just doesn't count. Evanston isn't that much different than Plano or any other suburb. But it's a different situation if you go take a long ride on the Red Line."

Todd sipped his drink and shrugged. "Oh, c'mon, Megan." They'd gone on one date, five years ago, and now he always talked to her like they were an old married couple. "Chicago's got its rough neighborhoods, sure. It's got millions of people running around, after all. But you live and work on the North Side, for God's sake. It's not so scary. You're just upset that you saw that homeless guy jerking off that one time. You never got over that."

"Well, I'm sorry if I think someone . . . *self-pleasuring* in the middle of a crowded train is shocking," Megan said. She turned to me. "Alice, you're the expert here, what do you think?"

"Wait, why am I the expert?"

"Because, of the three of us, you've lived here the longest," she said. Then she laughed and put her hand on my forearm. "You thought I meant . . ."

Todd laughed. "Alice Hardy, the queen of public indecency."

I glanced about the room, looking for Greg. He was by the window, drink in hand, talking with some of the folks from the English department. Aside from a few spouses, everyone at the party was an academic from St. Ignatius. Megan taught French in the Modern Languages and Literatures department. Todd taught in Biology. Most of the departments at school were represented here, either mingling in my living room or refilling their drinks in my kitchen.

I had forgotten that the monthly rotating faculty cocktail party was at our place tonight until I'd come home to find Greg getting ready. I'd begged him to call it off, pleading that I was too tired, but that had only led to a fight. There was no way to cancel on such short notice, he said. Besides, I was the one who'd volunteered us to host it this month. It certainly wasn't his idea.

"But that's right," Todd said. "You've been in Chicago longer than most of us, haven't you?"

"Since grad school," I said, looking down at my glass. "My entire adult life, when you get right down to it,"

"You have a definitive take on it?"

I swirled the ice cubes floating in my drink. "Well," I said, "it's my home, if anywhere is. I love it, and I'm a partisan for it, but it's a tough town. The long winters and the high crime rates are real. And not only on the South Side." I felt my voice crack, so I took a drink. "If this place doesn't break your heart a little bit every day, you're not paying attention."

"Don't get me started on the winters," Megan said, and so Todd did, and as they bitched about the weather I glanced over at Greg again, hoping he'd come save me. He didn't notice me, though, because he was deep in conversation with a creative writing instructor named Paola Nomura. Paola was half Italian and half Japanese—pretty, petite, twenty-eight. She'd published two buzzy short stories in the *New Yorker* right out of grad school, which had helped her land a book deal and a job in the English department at St. Ignatius. She had the sparkle of minor literary celebrity about her, and whenever Greg was around her he seemed a bit in awe. Since he generally didn't take much notice of other people, his interest in her stood out to me.

Greg and Paola were talking with Larry Barst, who also taught in the English department. There was no sparkle about Larry. He'd published an instantly forgotten book of niche literary theory before Paola was even born, and since then he hadn't done much but drink. He was known to have too many bourbons at these cocktail parties and start slurring his way through diatribes about how white men are no longer allowed to have opinions.

Greg said something and both Paola and Larry laughed. Then Larry checked his glass, found it wanting, and headed toward the kitchen. That left Greg alone with the pretty young writer.

I excused myself from the great Chicago debate between Megan and Todd to walk over and join my husband, but Shantell Porter-Hodges, the chair of the Theology department, caught me halfway across the room.

She held a glass of water, which was not surprising, since she only ever seemed to drink water. Trim and toned, she was a vegan who ran marathons in her spare time. While her scholarship focused on the intersection of ascetism and the African diaspora, her interest in the subject of rigorous self-discipline was not purely academic.

She tugged at one of her hoop earrings, something she did when she was annoyed. "Larry came into the kitchen," she said by way of explaining her presence in the living room.

"Ah," I said. "Well, there goes the rest of the booze."

She smiled politely, though I knew her well enough to know that she was not amused by Larry's alcoholism. Some people found him funny, up to a point. Others regarded him as tragic. Shantell, giving no quarter to either his personal weaknesses or his rhetorical flights of grievance, found him insufferable.

"Are you okay?" she asked.

"Why?"

"I noticed you were limping."

"Oh, yes." My knee still hurt, but I'd had two or three stiff drinks now and the pain was almost pleasurable, an occasional little stab of agony amidst the vodka-induced numbness. "I fell last night. Landed on my knee pretty hard."

"Oh no, I'm sorry to hear that. What happened?"

We were not personally close, but I suddenly wanted to lean in and tell her *I've been cheating on Greg and last night I almost got murdered walking to my car.*

"Oh, nothing," I said. "Just tripped taking out the garbage." To change the topic, I nodded toward the corner. "Todd and Megan were talking about the time she saw the homeless guy masturbating."

"Again?" Shantell said, shaking her head. "Good lord. She brings that up at every party. It's the most famous act of onanism since Onan."

"This time it was part of a larger discussion about the social ills of Chicago."

Shantell glanced at my nearly empty glass. "You don't say," she muttered. She ran her fingertip along her long, thin eyebrow. "Well, I guess it's reassuring to know that the social ills of Chicago are getting worked out somewhere."

Larry came out of the kitchen carrying two drinks. He walked up and handed one to me. "Vodka tonic with lime, for the lady of the manse," he said. "I noticed you were running low."

"Oh," I said. "Thank you."

He glanced at Shantell. "You not drinking?"

As she was explaining to him, not for the first time, that she did not drink, I heard Greg and Paola laughing behind me. I glanced back. They'd been joined by Clement, one of Greg's colleagues in the Math department. The pretty young writer and the two middle-aged mathematicians were absolutely guffawing about something, and Paola reached out and touched both their arms. *Oh, you guys.*

Shantell was listening, as patiently as she was able, to Larry describe some fruity drink that she might enjoy because, he thought, it was the kind of thing that a girl might like. "And you're a vegan, right? It's got fruit in it. Vegans can eat fruit, right?"

Megan was still with Todd, but they'd been joined by a couple of other people from St. Ignatius, and the conversation had shifted. She was saying, "Well, in Europe, they contend with their history, wrestle with it. In America, we turn our history into bumper stickers and theme parks. If we can't put something on a T-shirt to sell, we don't deal with it at all. We're not a reality-based culture, you know."

And on and on. People talking, debating, joking. I thought of the man jumping out of the alley at me, his fingers raking my hair, the way his knuckles burned my scalp. I wanted to run screaming from the room.

Instead, I drained my drink.

"Whoa," Larry said, mocking me. "And they say I drink a lot."

He laughed, turning to Shantell, inviting her to laugh along. She just stared at him.

"You do drink a lot, Larry," I said.

"Well," he warned me with a wink, "if you keep knocking back the vodka like that, you're going to get my reputation."

"Not unless I shit myself," I said.

About seven months before, Larry had been arrested for drunk driving, and on the way to the police station he'd passed out in the back of the cruiser and defecated on himself. Everyone knew about it because Todd had gone to bail him out of jail, and Todd has a big mouth.

But, of course, it wasn't normally discussed in public, out in the open, at a faculty party, right to Larry's ruddy face.

He quit smiling. Both he and Shantell stared at me. All around us, things seemed to be moving with geologic slowness until everything simply stopped, and I realized I'd spoken loudly and clearly enough that almost everyone in the room had heard.

I looked over at Greg, who was also no longer smiling. He walked over—to do what, I don't know. To drag me away, to make a joke and try to paper over what I'd said, perhaps. But, with all my friends and colleagues gawking at me, I didn't give him the opportunity. I left.

I didn't run out of the room, but I moved with purpose. I hurried upstairs. Tuck was over at Julia's, of course, so the second floor was quiet and still, like an empty house. I went to my room and shut the door, but I'd barely sat down on the bed before the door opened and Greg walked in.

"What the hell, Alice? Are you drunk?"

"I have had a little too much to drink, yes. Yes, I believe so."

"Great. You've been in a rotten mood all day. And now you get drunk at the faculty party and insult Larry in front of everybody. That's great, just great."

"Like Larry isn't drunk."

Greg took off his glasses and rubbed his face. As he slipped his glasses back on, he said, "Well, actually, I think you've managed to pull off the impressive feat of beating him to the finish line this time."

"Just go back downstairs, please. Just act like nothing happened. I had a little too much to drink, and I said something mean to Larry. It's not that big a deal."

"Are you coming back down with me?"

"I can't."

"You need to. Otherwise it *will* become a big deal. We don't want them talking about this. You want to be a rumor?"

"Greg, I can't go down there right now. Just tell them I feel a little sick. Make a joke about it. The longer you stay up here the more awkward it gets down there."

He sighed and walked to the door, but he stopped before he touched it. He turned around and looked at me and asked, "What's going on?"

I stared at him. I had to swallow the words I wanted to say. How could I tell him? Like this? With everyone we knew downstairs? At that moment, I couldn't help but wish that he'd cheated on me too. It would be so much easier to talk to him if he had fucked Paola or if he'd had some pathetic middle-aged fling with a pretty grad student. I had to stop myself from resenting his fidelity. I would have felt so much less guilty, so much less alone, if he'd cheated on me with someone. But I knew he hadn't. I knew it as surely as I knew his fidelity wasn't based on an overwhelming devotion to our wedding vows either. He was simply too self-occupied to have an affair. He'd long ago settled on the things that interested him—math, baseball, our son—and he didn't have the energy or inclination to make room for anything as time-consuming as an affair. I'm sure it never even occurred to him. He was as dependable as a rock and just as imaginative.

"I need to lie down for a while," I said. "Too much vodka."

He shook his head, but he said nothing more. He went back to the party to put on a good face for our friends.

* * *

I never went back downstairs that night. In time, I heard the party start to break up. Tuck came home, said his hellos, and escaped to his room. Eventually, Greg saw everyone off, cleaned up a bit, locked the doors, set the alarm, and came up to bed. He stood there and watched me as I pretended to sleep, and then he went to our bathroom and brushed his teeth.

When he slipped into bed beside me, he didn't touch me.

He lay there on his back for a while before he said, "Alice."

I said nothing.

"Alice, I know you're awake."

"How do you know I'm awake?"

"Because I've been sleeping next to you for twenty years. I know when you're faking."

I didn't move, staying on my side, clutching a pillow. But I smiled.

He said, very softly, "What's wrong?"

"I'm a fraud."

"What?"

"I'm not who people think I am. I'm faking down there. Faking being some kind of intellectual. Faking being this bougie wife and mother."

"Well, I have no idea what any of that means."

"I know you don't."

"Don't pick a fight, Alice."

"I'm not picking a fight. I'm just saying that you don't come from the middle of Nebraska. Your dad didn't fix cars, and your mom didn't work at Walmart."

He laughed. "Are you about to break into a rendition of 'Working Class Hero'?"

"Now who's picking the fight?"

He sighed. "Look, I don't know where this is coming from, but you have as much right to host a St. Ignatius faculty mixer as the next guy. That's all I'm saying. As for being a wife and mother, I mean . . . you are. No one's trying to take that away."

I squeezed my eyes shut. "Yeah," I said.

"What started all this?"

"Can we just go to sleep? I don't really want to discuss it."

He said nothing to that.

"Okay?" I said.

He sighed. Just being a part of an emotional confrontation was difficult enough for him, but having to be the person to keep one going was basically impossible for him. He turned over, away from me.

"Okay," he said, "but sooner or later, you're going to have to talk to me, Alice."

I said nothing to that and he drifted off to sleep, but the thing is, even then I knew he was right. The only question was whether or not I'd lose my mind first.

Part IV: Friday

Owen Pall

CHAPTER

12

MY FRESHMAN YEAR of high school, my mother got arrested in a bust that made the front page of the county newspaper. At that point, we had been bouncing around the Ozarks, from town to town, my whole life—me trailing after Momma, a backpack full of homework and toys slung over my shoulder, as she raced ahead with a suitcase of our clothes, barely two steps in front of me, trying to arrange somewhere for us to live.

When she got busted that first time, we were living in a house with a couple of drunks named Jim and Bunny. Jim was an ex-Marine collecting disability for some shrapnel that perforated his spine in Vietnam. First thing every morning, he opened a can of Coors and drank all day until he went to bed, sipping his beers through a filthy old Burger King straw. He said it protected his teeth. While he drank, he labored away on a quarterly newsletter he published about the Waco siege called *The Missing Door*. His wife, Bunny, was the only one in the house with a regular job. She rang up groceries at Piggly Wiggly, which is how Momma met her, and at night Bunny'd come home and get smashed on bottom-shelf white wine while she talked about how she needed to stop drinking. I can't say that Jim and Bunny ever set out to teach me anything, but observing them I did learn that everyone is lying to themselves about something.

While Momma and I were staying with Jim and Bunny, I tried to keep out of the way. I read a lot, mostly books we checked out from the library. No matter where we were living, Momma always made sure we had library cards. She was a reader—she got the new Sue Grafton or Robert B. Parker the day they came out—but a lot of times she would just drop me at the library by myself, and then she'd run off somewhere trying to chase down a man or a job. I liked the cool quiet of the library. I'd sit there and read old *Star Trek* novels until she came back to get me. Often she wouldn't come back by the time the library closed, so I'd check out a couple of books and walk back to Jim and Bunny's place by myself.

Then Momma got busted. Police raided a house up on Highway 110 and confiscated a bunch of heroin and guns. The guy who lived there was some wannabe hillbilly Scarface, but the cops also arrested a couple of addicts on the premises. The paper identified Momma by name and wrote, "Geraldine Pall, a local woman, was discovered unconscious on the floor of the back room with a needle in her arm."

The article didn't have a byline, so I don't know the name of the reporter who wrote that line, but they cursed me for life. They must have been proud of themselves for including such a brutal, attention grabbing detail. *Geraldine Pall was discovered unconscious on the floor of the back room with a needle in her arm.* That image of my mother burned into my brain like a brand.

Momma was away for a while after that, but when she returned she looked pretty good. She'd put on some weight, and her skin had cleared up. She hugged me as soon as she saw me, and after dinner she sat close by my side on the couch, her arm looped through mine. She and I had been sharing the same bed since we'd moved in with Jim and Bunny, and she usually hugged a pillow as she faced the wall, but that night she slept curled up with me, her arms around me. She cried a little, and then she whispered that she loved me, whispered how sorry she was, told me in whispers that she'd found new strength in Jesus Christ.

The Jesus stuff really took me by surprise. Momma had never cared for religion. In one of her more lucid moments, she'd once told me, "Never give a dollar to a preacher. Any miracle you got to pay for can't be much of a miracle." But that was before she got busted. Now this same woman was hinging her sobriety—her future, my future, our very lives—on the kind of people she used to mock.

For a while, I guess it worked. We started going to a little Baptist church that was just up the road from Jim and Bunny's place. The preacher, Brother Conrad Miles, was a portly, pink-faced guy with a portly wife and three portly sons. They welcomed Momma and me with open arms, picking us up for church when our car wouldn't start, and having us over to dinner once a week. It was all going well until Momma got busted again.

They found her in some guy's pickup truck outside the rodeo trading sex for heroin. A sad-eyed county judge patiently listened to her pleas for forgiveness, as well as a heartfelt testimonial from Brother Conrad attesting to Momma's faith in the Lord, and then he sentenced her to thirteen months in prison.

Brother Conrad and his family took me in while Momma was away. It was a confusing time, being separated from her and living with this strange new family. The Mileses prayed over every meal, never drank alcohol of any kind, and never watched television except for sports because they considered everything else too worldly. I'd never seen anyone like them.

At home, away from the church, Brother Conrad had a good relationship with his wife and sons. He was strict but gentle, a man of rules who also liked to laugh, and he imparted a powerful sense to all of us that God was always watching.

But then, one day, God turned His head away from me. I came home and found Brother Conrad sitting in the den, an odd look on his face. His wife was at work and his sons were all at band or football practice. I didn't have any extracurricular activities of my own, of course, so I'd come home to the Mileses' house by myself and let myself in with the key they'd given me.

Brother Miles was waiting for me. I guess he hated himself for what he was about to do because he looked like he'd been sitting there for hours, crying. He said he had something to show me in his bedroom, and that's where it happened, where it would always happen, after school before his family came home, in the bed where he slept with his wife every night. I said nothing, did nothing. I just lay there and let him do what he wanted with my body. The first couple of times, he seemed upset afterwards, swearing me to secrecy, telling me that we had to protect his wife and his boys. I didn't say much to that outside of agreeing to keep my mouth shut. I knew if I said anything it would ruin his life, ruin his family, and then where would I go? After Momma had been sent away, Jim and Bunny had made it clear to me that they had no intention of raising me. Brother Conrad seemed to know that too, and after a while, he stopped apologizing for what he was doing. He just did it. It was as if my body was something I owed him, like rent.

And that's the way it remained for a while. It was my initiation into a lifetime of keeping secrets. I'd get sad letters from Momma telling me she missed me, Sister Miles and her sons would treat me like their special project, and Brother Miles would fuck me when no one was around. I read my mother's letters, but I never wrote back. What could I tell her? I kept my head down, and tried to avoid the preacher by going to the library after school. I'd sit there and reread the same *Star Trek* novels and count the minutes until I knew the Miles family would all be home. Sometimes it worked, other times it didn't.

It was that way for most of a year.

* * *

Then one day, Dean showed up. I had walked up to the library after school like usual, and he'd followed me. I hadn't seen him, of course, but he stopped me as I was about to walk inside.

"Excuse me," he said. "Are you Owen? Owen Pall?"

He looked like a high school math teacher. Tall and lanky, he had short gray hair and dark, beetling eyebrows. He wore wrinkled jeans and old white Nikes, with a white button-up shirt under a maroon V-neck pullover. He wasn't really a striking figure until you looked in his eyes. He wore smudged, thick, black-rimmed glasses that he'd gotten in the Marine Corps decades before, and behind them his eyes were puffy, bright blue, and tragic. I would come to know these eyes better than anyone else's, and they always looked like that: as if he was about to inform someone that their loved one had died.

But he wasn't there to tell me someone had died. Instead, he introduced himself and handed me a business card. I was sixteen years old; I'd never been handed a business card before. His read:

Security Solutions

Dean Worrell, owner
Safety Consultations and Private Investigations

I just looked at it and then back up at him.

"Somewhere we can talk?" he asked.

I shrugged.

We sat down on a bench outside the library.

"I understand you're staying with Conrad Miles," he said.

"Yeah," I said.

"Because your mother is in prison."

I shrugged.

"How long have you being staying with the Miles family?"

"I don't know. A few months."

"Almost a year, I thought."

"I guess so, about a year."

He nodded. Gently, he said, "I'm here because I've been hired by someone else who used to live with Mr. Miles. A young man about your age. You ever heard of a kid named Howie Baker?"

I shook my head.

"He lived with the Miles family when he was going through a difficult time a few years ago. This was up in Murphysboro,

Illinois. His parents were divorcing. His father had run off with another woman, and his mother was suffering from depression and had to be institutionalized. The Miles family took in Howie."

I stared at this man with his sad eyes and the outline of a cigarette pack beneath his pullover. I guess I already knew what he was getting at, what he wanted to say, why he was here. But I was watching *him*, wondering about this stranger who had arrived in town to uncover the secret I'd been keeping for a year.

"Do you like living with Mr. Miles?" he asked.

"They call him Brother Miles," I said.

"Right," he said. "Brother Miles. Do you like living with him?"

As he waited for an answer, he sat with one leg thrown over the other, one hand resting between us on the bench.

I glanced down at his hand on the bench and blinked. He was missing a finger, his ring finger.

I must have flinched or something because he told me, "I lost it in Vietnam. Some asshole shot it off." He held up the hand for me to get a closer look. His ring finger was completely gone; not even a knuckle was left. "We were in a firefight, and I was reaching out for the radio to call for backup. Felt like a wasp stung my hand. When I yanked it back, I was down to four fingers. Want to hear the weird part?"

"Yes," I said.

"If we'd kept the finger they could have reattached it. But we were knee deep in hot shit that day, so I didn't have time to look for it. I had to leave it behind. You believe that? My bony finger is probably still over there in some damn rice paddy."

I knew right then, sitting on that bench, that this was the most incredible man I'd ever met.

"About Brother Miles—" he began.

"Did he molest this Howie kid too?" I asked.

Dean stopped cold. He had to sit up straight to keep from falling over. But he never stopped staring at me with those tragic eyes.

"Yes," he said. "I believe he did. And other boys too."

I shook my head. "Son of a bitch," I said.

* * *

Brother Conrad's world fell apart pretty quickly. After I gave a statement to Dean, the police came to talk to me. When Brother Conrad got arrested, I moved in with Jim and Bunny, who were not happy to welcome me back but felt like they had no choice now. "Just until you find somewhere else to hang your hat," Jim told me, strongly implying that I should be actively searching out new accommodations for my hat.

Brother Conrad got out on bail and hired a lawyer, but his wife had already taken off with their boys to stay with her parents. He assured her that he'd been tormented and tricked by the devil, but for some reason she still blamed him. She decided she couldn't go on living in town, not once everyone knew what had happened. Brother Conrad must have felt the same way because soon after that he stuck a 12-gauge shotgun under his chin and blew his tormented mind right into his bedroom ceiling.

* * *

Then Momma came back.

She looked ten years older than when she left. The skin hung off of her like a dress that didn't fit her anymore.

We slept together again, and she cried and cried about what had happened, telling me that if the preacher hadn't killed himself she would have killed him for me.

When she finally fell asleep, I lay there next to her in bed and stared at the ceiling. I knew I had to leave, had to get away. I loved her, but I couldn't stay with her. I couldn't help her or take care of her, and I certainly couldn't count on her to help me. There are some people you either have to leave or you have to die for.

Then I remembered something.

I crept out of bed and dug through my wallet on the bureau until I found the card.

<u>Security Solutions</u>

Dean Worrell, owner
Safety Consultations and Private Investigations

At the bottom, there was a phone number and an address. In Chicago.

* * *

I didn't tell Momma I was going. I left her a note on the bureau, like we were lovers in some old country song. In the note I told her I'd been offered a job in Illinois. I told her there was no reason to worry about me, and I told her I loved her. Only that last part was true.

A friend from school—more of an acquaintance really, just a kid I sat next to in algebra—gave me a ride down to Little Rock, and with all the money I had I bought a Greyhound ticket to Chicago.

When I showed up at Security Solutions, I was unwashed, penniless, and starving. What must I have looked like to the old man? Like a stray dog that had followed him home, I guess.

He was sitting out front in the store trying to explain the plot of *The Big Sleep* to a couple of his cop buddies. When I walked in, my eyes as red as a basset hound's, he blew off the cops and took me to the back office.

He pointed at his chair. "Sit down."

I sat down.

"You smell like greasy French fries and day-old farts," he said.

I nodded.

"When's the last time you ate?"

"The day before yesterday."

He sat down on a box and rubbed the back of his neck. Years later, he told me what he was thinking as we sat there that day. He was thinking, *This boy is fucked unless I do something.* Because what future did I have otherwise? Steet prostitution, maybe. Drugs, probably. Abuse of one kind or another. He knew he either had to take me in or he had to cast me out into a world that had already demonstrated it was more than ready to eat me.

I tried to breathe normally as he sat there staring down at the dirty office floor.

Then he looked up at me. "Can you work a broom?"

* * *

He called me The Kid. Well, I mean, of course he did. As much as he loved all that old pulpy stuff, now he had a real-life sidekick. I was The Kid, Bucky, Tonto, Robin the Boy Wonder.

At first, I literally swept the floors, loaded and unloaded merch for the display cases, and watched the store while he was out working. But it didn't take long for Dean to bring me into the investigative side of things. That old man *loved* being a detective. Loved everything about it, from the long hours to the sneaking around to the morally dubious clients. He couldn't wait to teach me everything he knew, from how to tail someone ("The first rule is, never try to avoid being seen. You only end up drawing attention to yourself if you duck for cover every time somebody turns around.") to why one should avoid divorce work.

"People get divorced because their marriage failed," he told me, "but a failed marriage is never one person's fault, ever. The only reason to bring a detective into it is because you want to blame the failure on somebody else. That turns the detective into an accomplice to a lie. Bad spot to be in. God knows I learned that the hard way."

"You used to do divorces?"

"Sure. Thought I was helping people. Turned out I was only helping people get screwed over."

"They say the road to hell is paved with good intentions."

"Yeah, they say that," Dean said, "but bad intentions will get you there just as quick. Important thing to remember, though, is that the road to hell runs both ways. You can always turn around before you get there."

* * *

For years, Momma kept after me to come visit her. I'd tell her I was busy with work, which was just an excuse but did have the virtue of being true. Still, she'd guilt-trip me anyway.

"You can't carve out a weekend to drive down and see your poor abandoned mother?" she'd ask.

"You could come this way, Momma," I'd say.

"Oh, I can't come to Chicago. It's a ten-hour drive. And all that traffic and crime. The trains and those big skyscrapers. Can you imagine me up there?"

Fact was, I couldn't.

"I don't know how you survived up there," she said.

"Well, it ain't over 'til it's over. Maybe I won't survive up here in the long run."

"Oh, sweetie," she said, letting loose a husky smoker's laugh, "in the long run none of us survives *anywhere*."

I didn't know what to say to that, so we left it there.

And that's the way it stayed, with her in Arkansas and me in Chicago, until I was thirty.

* * *

When the cigarettes finally caught up with Dean, Momma surprised me by coming up to attend the funeral. They had always kept a respectful distance from one another, Dean and Momma, neither wanting to invade the other's territory, but as his coffin was lowered into the ground, she stood next to me and wept the whole time. She'd never even met the man.

She stayed with me a couple of days after that, and when the morning came for her to go back to Arkansas, I carried her stuff out to her car. The sun hadn't come up yet, and the sky was as gray as granite. I waited with her while she smoked a cigarette. When she was done, she flicked away the butt and gave me a hug.

"I'm sorry about Dean," she said into my neck. "I know what he meant to you."

"He saved my life," I told her.

She nodded, coughed, and let go of me, dabbing away tears at the corners of her eyes. "I know he did," she said. She cleared her throat. "Listen, I'm sorry. I'm sorry I abandoned you."

"You didn't abandon me."

"Yes," she said. "I did. That's why I don't blame you for abandoning me later on. I understood why you had to do it." She coughed again and patted her chest. "I just wanted to tell you that I'm sorry. I'm sorry I was a bad mother."

"You weren't a bad mother."

The truth was actually more complicated than that, but the simple version sounded reassuring.

My mother didn't do reassuring, though. Instead, she rolled her eyes. "Yeah," she said, "sure thing."

* * *

She died about thirteen months after Dean. She'd been working as a cashier at Walmart for a few years, and someone from her work called to tell me Momma had collapsed at her register that morning and had been rushed to the hospital. She was in the ICU.

I drove down that night, but by the time I got there, she'd died.

Cryptogenic stroke, the doctor told me. They weren't sure exactly what caused it, but you didn't need a medical degree to know she'd been killing herself since she was sixteen.

I stayed around just long enough to get her buried. She had less than a hundred dollars in the bank, so I had to pay for everything. On her tombstone, I had them carve her name and her dates. I wanted to include something nice like BELOVED MOTHER at the bottom, but they charged by the letter and it cost too much, so I settled for just MOM. As it was, the grave and the funeral cleaned me out. I didn't know a single person at the service. When it was over, I got in my car and came back home to Chicago.

CHAPTER 13

THE ROAD TO *hell runs both ways.*

I woke up soaked in sweat. I hadn't managed to sleep ten minutes at a stretch, and I'd spent my few hours in bed twisting in the sheets, lurching between memories of my mother and half-waking nightmares of Alice Hardy.

You can always turn around before you get there.

I got up, took a shower, got dressed. My mouth tasted like paint thinner. I drank three glasses of water trying to wash out the bitterness.

Then I drove over to Alice Hardy's house. I'd pulled her teaching schedule off the St. Ignatius website the night before, so I knew she had a morning class called Semiotics and Biblical Interpretation starting at 9:30.

I got to her neighborhood and parked at the end of the street as her son was leaving for school. With a backpack slung over his arm, he climbed into a Honda driven by a pretty blonde girl. A few minutes later, Greg Babbitt left for work.

As I watched his car disappear down the street, I knew that now was the time. I could get out of my car, walk over to Alice Hardy's front door and knock. *Hello, Professor Hardy. I have some footage of last night's altercation that I assume you don't want anyone to know about. This footage shows you coming out of another man's apartment, shows you hiding from the police after an assault, shows you attempting to destroy evidence of the attack.*

Wasn't that why I was here?

I shifted in my seat. My back still hurt, but now my head hurt too. I shut my eyes.

The road to hell runs both ways.

I couldn't get out of the car.

Son of a bitch.

Last night, it had all seemed so clear. Squeeze Alice and Ronnie and see what I could get out of them.

But now I couldn't even get out of the damn car. I felt sick. I'd had this conversation with enough people by now—men and women, husbands and wives, fathers and mothers—that I knew the drill. I was familiar with the tinge of guilt you feel when you approach someone to tell them they're going to have to pay for your silence. But now the thought of walking over there and trying to blackmail this woman made me hate myself. I hadn't thought I was still capable of that. A tinge of guilt, sure. It went with the territory. But this was something else.

This was shame.

What, you looked at her Instagram and saw a picture of her with her kid, so all of a sudden she's a real person? Or was it looking at the footage of the attack and knowing you just stood there like a fucking asshole and let it happen?

Well, yes. Pretty much. Last night, all I'd seen was the dollar signs. Now, in the harsh light of morning, with no sleep and no breakfast, I couldn't make myself get out of the goddamn car and walk over there and knock on this woman's door. I couldn't look at her face as I tried to blackmail her.

Turned out, after every shitty thing I'd ever done, I had my limits.

What a time to discover them.

What if you let her go? This woman already had the worst night of her life, what if you don't *come along like a bastard and make it worse?*

I was still pondering that question as Alice Hardy's garage door opened again, and she backed down her driveway.

So what, do you let her go? Do you turn around and head home?

She drove by me. I should have turned away, or looked down, maybe made a show of fiddling around with the radio. That's the way you usually handle it when the person you're following unexpectedly turns your way. You perform casual, unthinking indifference.

Instead, I looked right at her. She didn't see me, didn't pay me any mind at all. Her face was tight and worried, her gaze focused on something or someone far away. I wondered if I could see her now in a way that no one else could. It was like I had a window into her life that no one else had, not even her family. What I saw was someone who looked shell-shocked, like she was still in a daze.

I followed her.

* * *

It's easy to follow someone in Chicago because it's hard to get lost here. For all the chaos on the streets, the streets themselves are laid out in a grid that's as logical as a chessboard. Since I was fairly sure where we were going, it made following her an even easier task. Our drive to St. Ignatius University was uneventful. Traffic wasn't too bad, and I kept a good distance from her the whole way. When we got to the school, I figured she was going to pull into the university parking garage. Sure enough, she did, flashing some kind of parking pass at the sensor on the automated gate. I pulled up to the gate a minute later and took a ticket for non-passholders.

Then I followed her up the ramps. This was delicate work. There were no longer any other cars between us, and she would be driving slowly, looking for a place to park. I let her stay far ahead of me.

She finally found a spot on Level 5 and pulled in. I passed by while she was still sitting in her car, and I drove up to 6 and parked. I got out of my car and walked back down to end of the row, listening for the sound of her door, the setting of her car alarm, the movement of feet. When I heard them, I peeked around the corner and got a glimpse of her. Alice Hardy beside her car, adjusting her bag on her shoulder, slipping her keys into the pocket of her coat, walking over to the elevator.

She stepped inside the elevator, the doors closed, and she was gone.

Okay, so I'd dropped her off safely at work.

Now what, genius? You gonna enroll in classes?

Walking back to my car, I called Heidi.

"How's Ronnie feeling this morning?" I asked.

Her voice sounded like she hadn't been to bed. "He's sleeping."

"Has he woken up at all?"

"Barely, just enough to open his eyes and look around and fall back to sleep."

I told her I had to go but I'd check in with her later. She tried to protest, to rush some questions at me about last night, but I just told her I'd be in touch as soon as I could and hung up. It was rude, and I'm sure she was losing her mind, but I didn't have anything to tell her until I could talk to Ronnie. And I wasn't sure what I wanted to say to him, not anymore.

One thing did seem clear to me, though. Getting money from him now was out of the question. I hadn't helped Alice last night when I had the chance. I couldn't turn around today and profit off of what Ronnie had done. I needed to jettison every plan I'd been making for the last fifteen hours.

I got in my car and sat there for a while. Thinking. Weighing options.

I could just send the video to the cops. That would take care of Ronnie. But it would also expose Alice. My video of her would be all over the news before tomorrow morning. That would be worse than blackmailing her. Besides, even if I sent in the video anonymously, I knew the cops would find a way to track it back to me. And if it became public that I'd made it, I would be ruined. That video wasn't just evidence of someone else's crime, it was self-incriminating, a career ender for whoever was holding the camera.

I considered just destroying it. Just delete it out of existence. But then what would happen to Ronnie? *You just let him go free to recuperate until he's ready to go lurk in another alley?*

I sighed. *Sure, Dean, the road to hell runs both ways. But once you turn around and start walking back, you have to keep climbing that hill.* How could I get Ronnie without using the video, without exposing Alice?

Then, almost as if the old man was answering me, I had a thought.

What if you do some actual detecting? Not surveilling, not bugging. Actual investigation.

Dean always said a detective is just a guy who can't let shit go. I hadn't thought about that in a long time. I'd been too busy planting GPS trackers and taking dirty pictures.

But there *was* some shit about last night that kept bothering me. That open trunk of Ronnie's, for one thing. The body bag waiting there. It was evidence of some kind of plan, evidence of something beyond a sudden impulse to attack another human being. Where was he planning to take her? If rape or murder was the objective, why take her anywhere? It just added to the risk of being caught. If he was taking the risk of putting her in his trunk, did he have other plans for her?

Something else bothered me.

Ronnie was thirty-five years old. From the background check I'd run the night before, I knew he didn't have a criminal record. No arrests for stalking or sexual assault or solicitation. None of the usual red flags you find littering the background of a psycho once he's busted. I hadn't dwelled on that until now, but the more I thought about it, the odder it seemed. Guys don't usually snap one day in their mid-thirties and start shoving women into body bags. That almost never happens. So where was the trail? I could tell I was missing something somewhere.

Think, damn it. You looked at the criminal, you looked at the victim. Where else can you look?

What about the crime itself? Were the police out there looking for a random creep lurking in alleys with a knife? Was there a rash of disappearances being investigated already?

To find that out, Dean would have just called any number of the cops he knew, asked them what they were working on, sniffed around until he found something. That was out of the question for me. I couldn't get most cops I knew to speak to me, much less to help me on a case. I'd have to do this without them.

Luckily, I still had the internet, God's gift to friendless men. I drove back to the office to see what I could turn up.

As I drove, I felt a weird kind of relief. I hadn't done anything this morning to be ashamed of. Now I was on my way to do work, to do *real* work, for the first time in a long while.

Climbing that hill, Dean. Climbing that hill.

My plan to spend the rest of the day on the internet changed, though, as soon as I pulled up in front of the office.

Ronnie's wife was waiting for me.

CHAPTER

14

SHE WAS STANDING out front, cupping her face to the window, trying to see inside. She'd thrown on jeans and a plain green T-shirt. She wore no makeup. Her hair had been washed, but she'd just let it dry itself, and it was frizzy and unruly. She looked more than a little, I thought, like a homeless woman.

I unlocked the door and led her inside. As I turned off the alarms, she looked around at the store, clearly baffled by what she was seeing. People never know what to expect when they come into the place. Dean really set up Security Solutions as three different businesses operating out of one storefront. The first was the investigative and security consulting business, the actual private eye stuff, all of which was handled in the back office. The second was a supply store selling surveillance equipment like drones and spy cameras, prominently displayed in big glass cases by the front windows to draw in customers. The third was the Official Chicago Museum of Private Investigation, which was just a corner of the store with memorabilia from old movies, radio programs, and television shows alongside actual artifacts like a 1922 Pinkerton badge and a 1946 cigarette pack–sized micro camera. The fee for the "tour" of the "museum" was supposed to be five bucks, but Dean had never been able to bring himself to collect it. We'd always just let curiosity seekers peek at the artifacts, and then tried to sell them a Security Solutions T-shirt or button.

"You haven't been here before, have you?" I asked Heidi. I knew the answer, but it seemed like a casual way to begin.

"Uh, no. You and I only spoke over the phone."

When I hit the power switch, an old reel of radio highlights—Howard Duff in *The Adventures of Sam Spade* and Sydney Greenstreet in *Nero Wolfe*—started playing on a loop. Heidi stared up at a poster on the wall for the 1953 Mike Hammer movie *I, the Jury*, which advertised "man-woman violence in 3-D," and I could tell she was wondering if she had hired a crackpot. Once, I'd tried to tell Dean that the ambiance of the store wasn't professional enough, but he'd only blown cigarette smoke at me and said, "Who gives a shit about ambiance?"

Heidi said, "Can we . . . can we talk?"

"Yes. Would you like to come back to my office?"

I locked the front door and hung the "We're out on a case" sign in the window.

"Just opened and now I'm closing again," I said with a smile. "I'm never going to make my fortune at this rate." I showed her to the office in the back. "I need to hire someone to watch the front while I'm out doing the actual detective work, but I can't seem to find time to do it."

The office was not what people expected either. I suppose they thought it would look like something out of one of the detective movies out on the wall. A big desk in front of a window, a flashing neon sign, maybe a filing cabinet with an office bottle.

Instead, it was mostly a storage room. Product for the spyware store stacked to the ceiling. Hand-dated filing boxes so packed with documents that there were tufts of paper sticking out the sides. The dates on the boxes went back decades.

I did have a desk, though. It was pushed into a corner, cluttered with paperwork and firearm catalogs. My rugged laptop, one of those heavy-duty kinds made for construction sites, was perched on a stack of paper. Next to it was the office safe, the coffee pot, Dean's old record player, and his collection of vinyl albums.

I cleared away a couple of boxes of Wildfire Pepper Spray and Sleuth Gear Hidden Cameras from a folding chair by the desk, and I asked her to sit. Then I sat in my desk chair and said, "So, Mrs. Dunlap, how is Ronnie today?"

She twisted her hands in her lap. Her voice shook as she said, "He's . . . his throat. It's been *cut.* It was *cut open* last night. He can't even talk, can't say a word. He has to write on a pad."

"Are his stitches okay? Is he drinking, eating?"

"He won't even try solid food, and I'm scared to give him any. He's been drinking tomato soup and chicken broth through a straw. Along with water. I crush up the pain pills we have in water, and he takes them that way."

"That's good."

"He needs to see a doctor, but he won't do it. He told me to get him the soup and some stuff, bandages, antiseptics. But he said no doctors. No hospital. His old partner from the ambulance, Erik, was a paramedic. He's the only one Ronnie trusts. He's supposed to come over today." She stopped twisting her hands and for the first time, I saw a flicker of light in her eyes. She looked mad. It was nice to see some life in her. "No matter what he says, though, I'd get him a doctor, except that you said he might have been into something illegal last night when this happened. And since I'm paying you to *tell me things,* I don't understand why you won't tell me what happened."

I murmured a bit, trying to do some quick calculations. If I told her the whole truth, she might fuck things up for me, go to the police or the press too soon.

She said, "Just tell me one thing, did he try to kill himself?"

I blinked at the question.

I leaned forward and said, "The way you asked that seems to imply that he's tried it before."

"Twice," she said. "Well, at least twice that I know about. There might be more. You never know with Ronnie. But I know of one time he tried when he was a teenager. Barely a teenager. Thirteen. He tried drinking this cleaning stuff his mother had under the bathroom sink. It put him in the hospital. The other time was maybe a year ago."

"What happened that time?"

"An overdose. Tobi and I weren't at home. It was Erik who found him."

"The fire department didn't put him on some kind of sick leave after that? Require him to do counseling?"

Heidi closed her mouth. She shut her eyes. Then she bit down, squeezing her eyes shut tighter as a few tears escaped and rolled down her cheeks. After a moment, she blew out a breath and wiped away the tears that had pooled at her chin. She opened her eyes and looked at me.

"Erik talked me into not telling anyone. Said Ronnie'd lose his job if anyone found out about it. Ronnie's supposed to be seeing a therapist, but how do I know if he goes to the appointments all the time? And when he does go, who knows what they talk about? He'll never tell me anything. Says it's private. Everything's always private with Ronnie."

"And—"

"No," she interrupted, "you tell me what happened last night. Did he do this to himself?"

I took a deep breath. I didn't want to tell Heidi about the attack because I didn't know what she'd do yet. I settled on telling her part of the truth. "I followed him from your house to a restaurant. He had dinner, alone. Then he drove around for a while. I lost him for a bit, and when I caught up to his car, it was parked. This was over by Humboldt Park, in that area. I found him lying in an alley by himself, his throat cut. The knife was beside him."

"Did he . . . Do you think he did it himself?"

"His car was parked at the end of the alley, the trunk open, and inside was a body bag."

I watched her reaction to that information.

"A body bag?" She shook her head. "What are you saying? What the fuck is going on?"

I spread my palms.

She ran her hands through her hair. I saw now why it was messy.

"Maybe he hurt himself?" she said. "And he planned to get into the body bag? Or . . ." She shook her head. "Is it something else?"

I leaned in closer. I could tell the idea was in the back of her brain, trying to get out. I just needed to nudge it a bit. "Like what, Heidi? What are you thinking?"

She sat forward in her chair. Her eyes were a washed-out blue, like the bottom of an empty swimming pool. "Maybe . . ." She turned up her hands. "God forgive me for saying it, but . . ." She shook her head and took a deep breath. "I have to tell you something, Mr. Pall."

"Okay."

"I found some . . . some horrible dark pornography on his computer once. Violent stuff. Rape, murder fantasy type things. I was so freaked out, so furious and scared."

"Did you confront him?"

"Yes. But he talked his way around it. Like he always does." Her hair hung down and she tugged at the ends of it, pulling out strands one at a time. "I'm not a strong person, Mr. Pall. Maybe you've already figured that out about me. He said it was just a website he stumbled onto. Said it didn't mean anything. But he agreed to go to a couples' therapist with me after that and talk about it."

"Did he actually go with you?"

"It didn't last. He told her, the therapist, what he'd told me—that it was just a mistake, that it didn't mean anything—and then his mouth slammed shut. He's *impenetrable* when he wants to be." She shook her head and ran her hands through her messy hair again. "But if you found a body bag in the trunk of his car . . . God, maybe he was trying to . . . to actually do something . . ."

"Like what?"

"Maybe he was attacking someone with the knife, to put them in the bag. *Oh, God.* But maybe in the fight, *they* wounded *him*. I mean, is that possible?"

"That's what I thought," I said. I paused as if I was considering the possibility. What I really thinking, though, was that this was shaping up better than I could have hoped. If I stuck to the story of finding Ronnie in the alley, then Heidi could hire me to investigate. If I could find some kind of evidence that he'd done this before, we could hand him over to the police without bringing Alice Hardy into it, and without implicating me as an opportunistic bystander to her attack. I might even emerge from this whole mess with my reputation restored.

Heidi chewed her bottom lip, coming to the exact conclusion I wanted her to come to. Maybe her husband was a violent psychopath. Maybe *someone* should investigate.

But then she jumped too far ahead.

"Then maybe we should go to the police together right now," she said. "If Ronnie is . . . is this kind of person, if he's dangerous, we should call the police. They can take him into custody, investigate. That's what they're there for, isn't it?"

"Well—"

"I mean, a *body bag*. Jesus Christ . . ." Heidi put her face in her hands. "Jesus Christ."

She was like that for a while, not crying, just hunched over holding her own face. When she looked up, she said, "What are you telling me about my husband? That he's some kind of . . ." She couldn't even finish the thought.

"I honestly don't know, Heidi. That's what I want to find out."

She rubbed her neck again. "Lately, he's been going out more and more, staying out late with no good explanation. That's why I hired you, because I was suspicious that something was happening. God, I was just hoping it was another woman." Suddenly she stopped, and I watched her face as she realized that the words she'd spoken were true. “Some part of me was praying that he was cheating on me,” she said. “What does that say about *me*?”

“I’ve been in this business a while, Heidi, and I’ve never been hired by anybody who was happily married. Even in good marriages, people sometimes cheat, but in a good marriage you can just come out and ask, ‘Are you cheating on me?’ You can talk about it, sometimes you can even work it out. You only hire a detective when you can’t have an honest conversation with your spouse anymore. That’s a bigger problem than the infidelity. I’m revealing trade secrets here, but by the time somebody hires a guy like me, the marriage is all but over anyway.”

She only half heard what I said because she was still being hit with the realization that the truth about her husband might be even worse than she’d feared.

“If you really saw what you say you saw last night, then maybe he’s done this before,” she said.

“I had the same thought. That’s why I’d like your permission to keep investigating, to keep looking and see what there is to find out.”

“But why not just go to the police right now?”

“Because right now we don’t have any proof Ronnie has committed a crime. Without that, the police won’t do anything. They’re not going to commit time and resources to an investigation without evidence of a crime. Let’s find out what there is to find out before we get the cops involved. And, listen to me, what you need to understand is that once the cops *do* get involved, then it’s out of our hands. You don’t want to find out the truth from a bunch of cops, with a pack of reporters on your front lawn, with all the traffic on your street choked off by police cruisers and news trucks. You want to find out before everybody else, so you know what you’re going to be dealing with. Just give me a few days to find out. If I can turn up something, then we’ll take it to the police. I know people on the force, and we can take it directly to them, to the guys we know we can trust.”

She pondered that.

While she did, I said, "You want to be able to sit down with your daughter and tell her the truth, don't you?"

She looked down at her hands. "Of course, I do."

"Then let me find the truth. No matter what it is."

She looked up at me. "And what about you? What do you want out of this?"

"I want the credit, Heidi. I'm going to be frank with you right now. The cops in this town, they think I'm no better than a peeping tom. If there's a bigger story here, I want everybody to know who cracked it. If I have to watch some idiot from the CPD get handed the case on a silver platter and take all the credit for it, I'm going to throw myself in the Chicago River. This is my job. This case could make me."

I said all that just to convince her, but the moment I'd said it, I realized it was true.

She pondered what I'd said, but I could tell the main thing she was thinking about was what she was going to tell her kid.

"Okay," she said finally. "I can wait a few days."

"Good."

"But in the meantime, I can't stay with Ronnie. I can't have Tobi around him. If he's suicidal, or if he's . . . if he's *this*. Whatever this other possibility is. We can't stay with him." She shook her head, convinced. "No, of course not. No. I'll go home and pack up some stuff for me and Tobi. Then I'll go pick her up at school."

"You have a place you can stay?"

"My sister and her wife. I know they'll let us stay with them if it's just for a few days."

"Where do they live?"

"Andersonville."

"Okay. I'm going to go with you to pick up your stuff."

"I would appreciate that. I don't want to be alone with Ronnie. I mean, he's too weak to move, much less to hurt anyone, but still I'd feel safer if someone was with me."

"Of course. Would you mind waiting out in the store for a moment? I need to lock up."

"Okay," she said, getting up and wandering out, still in a daze.

When she was gone, I opened the safe and took out one of the guns. I chose the little SIG P365 and grabbed its concealed-carry holster. I didn't think I'd need the gun, and I wasn't much of a shot anyway, but I brought it along just in case. As I clipped it to my belt in the small of my back, I remembered something else Dean had said once.

"I never had to shoot anybody while doing this job," he told me. "But I sure made some people stop and reconsider their options."

CHAPTER 15

There was an old faded red Dodge pickup parked in front of the Dunlap house when we got there. As she was walking across her front lawn, Heidi nodded at it and told me, "That's Erik's truck."

When we walked inside, Ronnie Dunlap was lying in pajamas in his bedroom in the back of the house. Tending to him was a trim man of military bearing a few years younger than Ronnie himself. He rose from beside the bed, standing ramrod straight, and stared at us coming down the hall. He wore silver-rimmed glasses that made him look like a scholar, but his pale hair was cut high and tight, and he wore a ratty white T-shirt with filthy dungarees shoved into cracked combat boots.

"Ah, Mrs. Dunlap has returned," he told his patient.

Tilting his head, Ronnie gazed up from the bed through bleary red eyes.

Neither of them was looking at Heidi, though. They were both staring at me.

The man in spectacles and combat boots stepped forward and extended his hand to me. "Erik Reid. I used to be Ronnie's partner on the ambulance."

I took his hand. His grip was firm, strong, and he didn't let go right away.

"And you are . . ." he said, still clutching my hand.

"Owen Pall. I'm the one who found your partner last night."

He let go of my hand. "Yeah, God, thank you for saving his life." He shook his head. "Hell of a thing. Ronnie can't tell me much about it. Do you know what happened?"

I ignored him and turned to Heidi. "You had something you wanted to say, Heidi?"

She took a deep breath, gathering her strength, and looked past Erik Reid. Addressing her husband, her voice shook. "Ronnie, I'm leaving. I'm taking Tobi."

The wounded man on the bed blinked at her. Then he turned and looked up at his partner.

Erik Reid smiled at Heidi and then spoke to her like a spoiled child. "Whatever strife there may be in the marriage, do you really think this is the responsible thing to do, to leave an injured man like this?"

Heidi said, "Is this any of your business? Are you his lawyer?"

"Well, the man's throat's been cut, Heidi. He quite literally cannot speak for himself, so let's say I'm advocating for him." He tilted his head at me, and told her, "Apparently, you brought along an advocate of your own."

Staring at him, I spoke to Heidi. "Heidi, do you have anything else you want to tell Ronnie while we're here?"

"No," she said.

"Then if you want to go get your stuff, I'll hang out here with the guys."

Ronnie gazed up at us, still loopy with painkillers. He wouldn't be worth talking to for another day or so, and I'd want to talk to him when he was alone.

Erik Reid crossed his arms and asked Heidi, "Are you going to tell him where you're taking his child after you slink out of here and leave him confined to a bed?"

"He can call me or text me," she said. "We can discuss it then when he's ready."

"Well, are you at least going to tell him *why* you're leaving?"

"He knows why," she said. "What I want to know is how he got hurt last night. You can tell him that for me when he's ready to wake up."

She turned and headed back down the hall and up the stairs, leaving me and Erik Reid to stand there and stare at each other.

"Well, she's pissed," Reid said with a smile. "Ronnie probably deserves it, though, dumb bastard. I assume living with him isn't a barrel of laughs." He looked down at the man in question, who had drifted off. "Yep, he's asleep again." Reid shook his head and turned back to me. "So what did happen last night?"

"Didn't Ronnie tell you?"

Instead of answering, Reid kneeled beside the bed to examine his patient. He nodded to himself and drew up a small rolling oxygen tank by the wall and affixed the breathing tubes into Ronnie's nostrils. He checked to make sure the straps were secure, then turned on the oxygen.

"Eases the stress on respiration," he explained, standing up. "Yeah, like I said before, Ronnie couldn't tell me much. Said he ran into some trouble on the street. I told him, 'Don't go walking around Chicago at night, you dumb fuck. At least not without some protection.' You never know what's waiting around the corner."

"No," I said, "you don't."

"You found him?"

"I did."

"See what happened?"

We stared at each other.

"I saw enough," I said.

"And then you went and got him fixed up. Where'd you take him?"

"A guy I know."

"Why didn't you call 911?"

"I didn't think he'd want me to."

"Why not?"

"You ask a lot of questions."

"Well, I'll tell you, Owen, this whole situation is a bit of a headscratcher. My buddy gets his throat cut in a dark alley in the middle of the night, and his wife just sticks him in bed without taking him to the doctor or calling the cops. And then she shows up the next day with some stranger and announces she's leaving him? It's all a bit curious, to say the least."

I nodded. "*You* call the police?"

"No."

"911?"

He smiled and nodded at Ronnie. "We *are* 911."

"Take him to the doctor?"

Reid kept smiling. "I'm not his wife. I'm not the one who's supposed to be taking care of the man." He pointed at the ceiling. "She's the one who promised to love, honor, and obey this dumb bastard, in sickness and in health." He shook his head. "I don't know what this world is coming to, Owen. I truly don't."

"Given your concerns, it would make sense for you to call the authorities."

I was gambling, almost daring him to get the police involved. But something about Erik Reid bothered me. Given the situation as he'd described it, why *wouldn't* he call the police?

"Maybe I will," he said.

We stared at each other for a while, while Heidi Dunlap ran around upstairs throwing things in bags. We could hear the opening of closets and drawers, and we both recognized the frantic pace at which she was moving.

"What do you do, Owen?" Reid asked. "For a living."

"I'm a private investigator."

He stopped smiling. "No kidding?"

I nodded.

He glanced at the ceiling, as if looking through it so he could watch Heidi.

"Ah," he said.

Heidi came downstairs with two large suitcases. She left them by the front door, and said, "I'm almost ready. Just need a few more things."

"Okay," I told her over my shoulder.

She ran back down the hall to her own bedroom.

"So what now, Owen?" Reid asked me.

"Now Heidi's going to go."

He nodded and waved a hand. "Well, good riddance to her as far as I'm concerned. We never really hit it off. I'm sure Ronnie will be heartbroken, though. He dotes on her and the kid both, you know."

"That wasn't the impression I got," I said.

"Well, there's two sides to every story, Owen. Don't ever forget that. But I wasn't really asking 'what now' about Heidi. What now for you?"

I shrugged. "I'm an investigator. I'll investigate."

Reid smiled. "I really hope you have that printed on a business card."

Heidi came back with another suitcase and a backpack.

"I'm ready," she said.

I didn't say anything more to Erik Reid. When I got to the front door, I picked up a couple of suitcases and looked back at him. He hadn't moved. He stood between his wounded friend and the window, his eyes obscured now by a glare of sunlight on his glasses, still smiling to himself.

* * *

I pushed the suitcases into the back of Heidi's car and closed the hatchback.

"You going to be okay?" I asked.

She nodded. "I called the school on the way over here and told them I was coming to pick up Tobi. They'll have her ready when I get there. I called Leighann, my sister, too. She wasn't thrilled to know we were coming, but she said we could stay with them as long as we needed to."

"What's the address?"

She told me.

As she climbed into her car, I looked back at the house.

"How long did Ronnie and Erik work together?" I asked.

"About two years. Until Erik quit a couple months ago to take care of the old lady who rents him his apartment. He's like her nurse now."

"Are Ronnie and Erik still close?"

"Yes. Well, as close as Ronnie is with anyone. They definitely grew closer after Ronnie tried to kill himself. That was last year."

"You said it was Erik who found him?"

"Found him. Saved his life."

"What happened?"

"It was the middle of the week. I was at work, Tobi was at school. Ronnie took a whole bottle of Ativan. Erik just happened to swing by."

"He married?"

"Erik? God, no. Erik's impossible. You saw the way he is. Always acting superior, acting like he knows it all. He can be a real asshole, even to Ronnie." She stopped and looked back at the house. "You didn't see him last night, did you? With Ronnie? I mean, you're not suggesting . . ."

"No, I didn't see anyone else," I told her. "Not suggesting anything. Just curious about him, that's all." I stared at the license plate on Erik's truck until I had the number memorized. "Just curious."

Part V: Before

Erik Reid

CHAPTER 16

ONE NIGHT A couple of weeks before Ronnie got his throat cut, I climbed into my truck and drove over to Logan Square. As I passed the Logan Theater, I saw some girls coming out of Intelligentsia carrying cups of coffee. I slowed down and followed them as they drifted over to the park. It's a little cluster of trees and lawns sitting at the center of a roundabout. In warmer weather, it's a popular place to hang out. Groups of teenagers, mostly. Laughing, yelling, jumping around, lounging on picnic blankets. The guys trying to be cool for the girls, the girls being cool for each other. But even in colder weather, people still congregate there. As traffic swirls around them, they huddle on benches or on the steps of the tall marble monument in the middle of the park.

I circled the park, watching the girls I saw leave the theater. One white, one black. Tight jeans, shiny puffer jackets. They sat on a bench, talking, sipping their steaming coffees.

I circled. They just sat there, talking.

How long could I do this until somebody noticed? My truck, almost thirty years old, red, and scratched up, is pretty distinctive, especially in Chicago. You don't see a lot of old pickups around here. Not as many as you see out in the redneck parts of Illinois, anyway.

But those girls sipping their coffee never noticed. They sat there on that bench as oblivious as cattle, discussing whatever they were discussing, for thirty minutes. I circled the park the whole time, and they never noticed me at all.

* * *

Eventually the girls left. They stood up and walked over to the CTA station across the street and disappeared down the stairs to catch a train. Too bad, but I saw more girls walking. There are always more of them. Sometimes with men, sometimes together.

And sometimes alone.

I saw one walking down the sidewalk. Young, white, maybe only twenty or so. Black jeans, pink parka. Brown hair pulled back.

I slowed down to follow her. It was dark now, but she had earbuds in, listening to something as she walked along like she didn't have a care in the world.

I slowed to a crawl behind her.

It took her a while before she glanced back and saw the truck. At first, she just kept walking. Maybe she was trying to ignore me. Act like it wasn't happening. Like maybe I was just a guy looking for an address.

But I just kept crawling along behind her, not even going five miles an hour, staring at her through the windshield.

She glanced back. I saw her curse, shake her head.

She stopped. She turned around.

I stopped.

She expected some catcall. *Hey, baby. Nice ass.* Something like that.

But I just stared at her.

"Fuck you," she said, and gave me the finger.

I just stared.

Now she spun around and started walking fast.

I crawled after her, picking up a little speed to stay with her.

She walked faster. Not just faster but stronger. I had her blood pumping now. When she looked back over her shoulder she wasn't pissed anymore, she was scared.

Now my blood was pumping too. Whether she wanted it or not, she and I were locked in the moment together.

But then she did what most of them do these days, she reached for her phone. She was going to call the cops, or maybe record me and post it on the internet, shame me, make me go viral. But she was too scared, and she fumbled with the phone. By the time she could press record, I was gone.

* * *

As I drove home, I thought about that girl fumbling with her phone.

It made me smile, made my heart thump faster. I had to catch my breath.

What if I'd pulled over and gotten out?

It had been a while. Two long years since my last one. I always tried to do it out of state. The girl drawing pictures at the sand dunes in Indiana, that was the last one. I sunk her in the water, but they'd found her after only a day or so. Before that, I'd gone all the way to DC. The jogger running with a baby stroller in the park. I'd put her in the back of a rental van and left the stroller on the trail. They found the baby, but they never found the jogger. The first few I'd done had been even further away than that, in Afghanistan. Two sisters just outside a shit village in the middle of nowhere. The Bagram prostitute I left in an open field under the sun. I could remember every one of them.

But now it had been too long. Two miserable years. I was ready to break my own rule about only doing it out of state. Doing it in Chicago meant I'd have to be extra careful, and I'd been planning for two years, making sure everything was perfect.

I'd followed so many of them down the street. Young ones and old ones. Teenagers. Young mothers with kids. Small ones in tight jeans. Big ones in flowing dresses. Healthy ones in running shorts. Sometimes in pairs or in groups, but mostly alone. I'd followed some to their cars. Sometimes I'd followed them back to apartments, to houses. I never stopped following them until they saw me. Being seen by them, getting their blood racing, was the whole point.

Some cursed me, reached for their phones. One or two might have even managed to record me before I got away, but I doubt it. I'm fast and they're scared. But the question kept gnawing at me.

What if I really did it? What's to stop me?

But everything wasn't perfect. Not yet. Not quite yet.

CHAPTER

17

I WAS STILL THINKING about it when I got back home that night. I locked the garage door, and as I walked across the backyard, I saw that the light was still on in the flat upstairs. I braced myself. The old woman would want to talk.

Sure enough, as soon I opened the back door of my flat she rang her bell. Even though I was the one who'd installed it so she could ring it when she needed me, I hated that fucking bell. It was like I was her servant.

I climbed the stairs up to the top flat and unlocked her door with my key. The lights were off in her den, but I could still see its faded pink walls and blue trim in the glow from her bedroom doorway.

"Erik?" she called from her bed. "Is that you?"

"No, it's the Boston Strangler," I said.

"What?"

"Of course, it's me, Mrs. Holding. Who else would it be?"

Her flat smelled old, exhausted and gray, like the woman herself. I stopped in her bedroom doorway and stared at the vision of hell waiting there for me. Gigantic and immobile, she lay metastasizing in her crumb-covered bed, the greasy remote controls for the television and the streaming services still in her thick, spotted hands. When I came in, she muted the true crime show she'd been watching. She was always watching that shit. There was nothing she loved more than an everyday horror story.

She lifted her sagging jowls in a toothless smile. "I was wondering where you were. I thought you weren't working tonight."

I crossed my arms. "I told you I was going out tonight."

She looked pained. "Oh, that's right. I'm sorry. That's right. You told me that."

"Was that all you wanted, to check up on me?"

"Please don't be cross with me, Erik. I get lonely."

"That's not my fault, Mrs. Holding. Quite the opposite, in fact. If you think about it, I'm the only reason you're not lonelier than you are."

"I know, Erik," she said. She tried to force another smile onto her unhappy mouth, but it wouldn't stay put.

I just stared at her and waited.

She said, "Please be nice to me, Erik. You don't know what it's like when you get to be my age and everyone you know is dead and gone."

She wasn't really that old. Although she was crippled with rheumatoid arthritis, diabetes, and heart disease, she was only seventy-nine, which was young enough to still have some friends and family left, provided you had friends and family to start out with. But after burying some long forgotten husband decades ago, she'd run off everyone else she'd ever known with her overbearing neediness. Now she was living out the last gasping years of an empty, lonely life.

I didn't say any of that, of course. I just said, "Well, you got me."

"Yes," she said. "And you know I thank God for you every day, Erik."

"I know you do." I shook my head in wonder. Imagine living a life like hers and still thanking God for anything. "Do you need anything before I go?"

"Yes," she said, "could you sit down for just a moment? I want to talk to you about something."

"I'm tired, Mrs. Holding."

"Please, Erik. It will only take a minute."

I sat down in the chair next to the bed. I tipped it back and leaned against the wall.

"What is it?"

"Well," she said, gathering her strength, "how would you like to stay with me?"

I stared at her.

"We discussed this, Mrs. Holding. I don't do that anymore. I have my own bed."

She nodded. "That's not what I mean. I want you to work for me. Not just helping out. I mean, officially. Full time. I've been thinking about it. I can't really go out anymore. Even with the stairlift, it's hard for me to get up and down the stairs. And I don't really want to go outside anyway. There's nothing left for me out there. You're the only link I have to the outside world. You know that. I know it too. Why don't we make it official, then? You could name your salary and you could be my . . ." She didn't want to say *nurse*. "My caretaker."

"I already have a career, Mrs. Holding. I haven't even locked down my pension yet."

"I wouldn't just pay you," she said. "I would give you the place."

I lowered the legs of the chair to the floor.

"What do you mean you'd *give me* the place?"

"I'd leave it to you in my will." She nodded, sure of herself. "Yes, I would. You already have the run of the place. Now it could be yours, yours to do with it as you please. I know you want to redo everything downstairs. Now you could. You could do whatever you want. I'll leave the place to you. I'll leave *everything* to you—my gift to you, for all that you do for me." She tried to smile again and almost started crying. "My only friend."

* * *

After I left her, I hurried down to my flat and checked the transparent tape at the corner of the door. Still secure. I peeled it off, unlocked the door, and ran inside.

I was so jacked up with adrenaline, I could barely make my rounds in the apartment, but I managed to calm myself long enough to take care of business. I checked the windows, made sure my security tape was undisturbed, and saw that the curtains were drawn and fastened down.

Inside my bedroom, I stripped naked. I folded my clothes and put them away. Then I opened the closet door. I'd installed a panel up top, like a fake ceiling, and I slid it back and pulled down the cardboard box behind it.

I carried the box out to the living room and took out the body bag and the knife.

I unrolled the bag. I'd bought it for ten dollars at a medical surplus auction in Indiana. It was black vinyl, ninety by thirty-six inches, with four handles. Totally leakage proof. It would hold up to four hundred pounds with no strain. I spread it out on the floor.

I laid the knife on top of it. It was a Mossy Oak survival knife with a ten-inch blade and a rubber grip handle. I'd bought it with cash at a hunting goods store in Wisconsin. I'd had it longer than I'd had the bag. They'd both been waiting. Like me. Waiting too long.

With the knife in my hand, I unzipped the bag, laid down inside, and zipped it close over me. It wasn't easy, zipping and unzipping from the inside, but I managed with a little effort. After a moment, the bag settled against my naked flesh.

I'd been developing the idea for two years now. Reconnoitering possible hunting grounds, assembling the tools I'd need. Thinking, planning. I wanted to take more time with the catch than I had in the past. One thing that had always eluded me was a place to take it to dress it. My desire was to use Mrs. Holding's basement, of course. The guy who'd lived here before me had used it to microbrew beer, and there was a little narrow room in the back that had a metal table, a small plastic tub, and a spigot with hot and cold running water.

The old woman herself was an obstacle, but she hadn't been down there in years. At this point, she wasn't even physically able of getting down the narrow stairs. Besides, I'd figured out a way to get her out the picture. I'd long since been keeping track of her pills, and sometimes at night I'd slip her a couple milligrams of her Lunesta instead of her beta-blockers. Mostly, I did it for fun. I'd knock her out with the sleeping pills, and then sit there and curse her to her drooling face. That was cathartic. But I was also testing her drug resistance, seeing how deep down the well she went when she was on the stuff. And I knew for a fact that I could knock her out and she'd never know the difference.

But even with all of that, I was cautious because the place still technically belonged to her. That's why my flat was still painted the same horrific pink and blue as her flat upstairs. She still had final control over the building, and as long as she did, I was hesitant to take the final leap.

Now, however, that had changed. With one touching gesture of love and devotion the old biddy had bequeathed the whole place to me. I would get that in writing tomorrow and then I'd go quit my job.

Once that was done, I could do whatever I wanted down here. Down here, and down in the basement.

But I knew I didn't want to do it alone. First off, I couldn't use my truck. It was all wrong. A truck was impractical, to begin with, and an old red pickup in Chicago was just a little too distinctive. I needed a boring midsize car, something that blended in with all the other Altimas, Malibus, and Impalas on the road. Something invisible with a good-sized trunk.

Something like Ronnie's Taurus. A car as bland as the man himself.

Of course, I didn't just want him because of his car. Some hunters like to hunt alone. Others like to bring a dog along. Part of my planning over the last year had been my steady prepping of Ronnie, binding him closer to me. We'd been talking around the subject for months now, inching closer and closer to it. I'd been working on him a little bit every day, chipping away at objections and moral impediments, like clearing woodland one tree at a time until you're ready to build yourself a house. He was almost ready. I'd known as soon as I met him that he had the same womanhate I did, but his was buried down deep where he couldn't get at it, buried under a lifetime of pussification and self-loathing. I'd known I'd have to dig it out for him, but at first I couldn't figure out how.

Then one day last winter the big dumbass himself showed me how to do it.

CHAPTER 18

HE TRIED TO kill himself.

I found him laid out in his bedroom, the one at the back of the house where Heidi keeps him like a pet, lying there on his bedsheets fully dressed next to a note telling Heidi he hated her and hated himself and he couldn't go on living in this world any longer. The note didn't even mention the kid. I laughed when I read it. I stood next to his bed and stared down at him lying there quietly slipping away.

I felt his pulse. Still there, but weak. I thought about letting him die, just to see how it would feel, but I knew he didn't really want to die. No one ever wants to die, not really. A guy like Ronnie, lost and rudderless, so ready to obliterate himself, was just looking for a master. And I knew that if I saved him, I could become that master. I could make this formless blob of a man into my slave.

So I yanked him up, yelled at him to wake up, and dragged him to the bathroom. I flung him over the side of the tub and then went to the kitchen to grab a big plastic spatula with a flat handle. While I ran cold water over his head, I pushed the handle of the spatula into his mouth. At first, his teeth snapped down on the handle, but then he gagged, coughed, and puked.

When he finally came to, he curled up on the floor of the bathroom like a fetus, shaking and wet. He opened his eyes, blinking against his dripping eyelashes, and the first thing he saw was me.

I bent down and patted the hair slicked back against his scalp. "Ronnie," I said, "listen to what I'm about to tell you, okay? Suicide is just misdirected rage."

He coughed out some more bile and started crying.

I patted his head some more.

"You should direct that rage at the people who deserve it," I told him.

The front door opened. Heidi was home.

I gave him another pat. "We'll get to that later," I said.

* * *

Heidi freaked out when she saw him on the bathroom floor, of course. But I talked her out of calling 911 by assuring her that Ronnie would lose his job and probably wind up in a psych ward if we told anyone what he'd done. I slipped his suicide note into my coat pocket without her seeing it. I figured she'd only freak out more if she read it.

We took Ronnie to the bedroom and got him settled. By the time I left a few hours later, he was sitting up in his bed, still groggy, but talking and starting to eat again.

When I got home and took off my coat, I found the suicide note. I was about to throw it away when I stopped myself. I read over it again. Then I slipped it in a ziplock bag and put it in an empty drawer. I can't say that at that moment I developed some master plan for how I might use it. I just knew it was something that could hurt Ronnie, which meant it was something I might want to hold on to.

You never know when you might need to hurt someone.

* * *

We didn't discuss his suicide attempt for a while.

I eased into that conversation with him carefully, very gradually. At first it was all about our supervisor, Coral. That bitch thought she could talk to us like we were children. I didn't respect her at all. Why would I? I'd been to war. I was patching up wounded soldiers in Nangarhar while she was still giving blowjobs to frat guys in Carbondale, so when she tried to tell me what to do, I mostly ignored her. Ronnie hated her worse than I did, though, because she'd chewed his ass out for clipping the side of a car as we were going through an intersection one night. The accident wasn't his fault; some idiot had tried to make the light as Ronnie was taking us through. Coral, though, had acted like Ronnie was a dipshit who didn't know how to drive. After she jumped all over him for that in front of the rest of us, he hated her. He absolutely hated her.

"If I thought I could get away with it, I'd drop her in a fucking well," he'd told me one night, snow smacking the windshield. "I'm not joking. I'd fucking drown her."

We'd gone out on a call—a guy had supposedly had a heart attack in the lobby of a movie theater, but when we got there, the guy was gone. Just up and left. So we were riding back empty-handed, and Ronnie was still fantasizing about killing Coral.

"I'd tie her up and drop her in and listen to her choke on the water."

"No, that would be over too quick," I told him. "You want her to suffer, here's what you do."

I outlined a torture session that would last as long as she did, probably for days if you staunched the bleeding and gave her enough water to keep her alive. I went graphic, far beyond the bounds of the usual revenge-against-the-boss fantasies, but what I was really doing was watching Ronnie.

I kept waiting for him to shake his head, laugh nervously, shudder and tell me to knock it off.

He didn't.

It kind of developed from there, night by night, as one vile fantasy fed into another, until the focus was not just Coral but all womandom. Eventually, it was the only conversation we were having when it was just the two of us.

It didn't take us long to get around to Heidi.

He hated her for trapping him in their marriage by getting pregnant and refusing to get an abortion. That was years ago, but he'd only become more bitter about it. He told me he was bored with her five seconds after he came in her for the first time, and now he was tied to her for the rest of his life. Worse than that, he was reliant on her. She made more money than he did, and they lived in her family home, which she'd inherited and was in her name. The dumb bastard's whole life was dependent on her, and he despised her for it.

We really got down to it one night, heading back from the hospital after dropping off a nineteen-year-old with three bullets in his chest and the words FUCK and LIFE tattooed on his knuckles. Even after seeing something like that, all Ronnie could do was rail about Heidi.

Just that afternoon before work, he told me, she'd found his porn on their computer. Now he was humiliated.

"I'm a man, what does she expect?"

"What'd she say?" I asked.

"Nothing. That's not her way. Plus, she knows I won't put up with any of her bullshit. But it's there in her stupid silences. She's all hurt, betrayed. What, she thinks I don't beat off? I beat off every time she walks out of a room. I jack off more now than I did when I was fifteen."

"But you hide it from her. You don't tell her about it, right?"

"Of course not."

"That's why she's surprised. She thinks you're sitting at home in a jar, like some fucking bug she caught out in the yard. They're all like that. They complain about how men want a 'trophy wife,' right? But that's bullshit. *They're* the ones who want a trophy. Heidi caught you, and now she wants to gut you, stuff you, and hang what's left of you on a wall. That's all a woman really wants, something that looks like a man but's empty inside."

He pondered that while freezing winds shook the ambulance and flung snow against the windshield.

"Thing that really upset her," he said, "was what I was stroking it to."

"What was it?"

He shrugged, darting a quick look at me out of the corner of his eye. "You know . . . kinda violent stuff. Fantasy stuff."

When he told me that, I was giddy. I could have screamed *I knew it.* But I didn't. I played it cool. I just told him, "Well, there's nothing weird about that, man. Lots of guys like that kind of thing."

"Yeah?"

"Dude, of course. That's why that shit exists, you know what I mean? It's an emasculated world we're living in, but we all know how men really are. What are you watching? Torture porn? S&M? Rape fantasies?"

He shrugged.

"Shit," I said, "that stuff's been around forever. You know what kind of fucked up shit archaeologists have found painted on the walls of caves?"

"Yeah, I guess that's true."

"Sure," I said. "We all do what you were doing. I know I do."

"You do?"

"Sure. Like I said, lotta guys do. Either a little or a lot. I guess you do it a lot."

"I guess," he said, still uneasy talking about it out loud. "Where do you go online? DarkFetish? Places like that?"

"No, that shit's too tame for me."

"Too tame! It's some fucked up shit on there."

"But it's all playacting. You know what I mean? It's the trophy animal thing again. A bunch of people pretending. I was on there for a while, but they kicked me off for violating the 'community standards.' If you can believe that. Said I'd crossed boundaries. But the whole idea of boundaries is bullshit. It's just another bit of brainwashing. No, man, if you want something really fucked up, you got to go somewhere where there's not a 'community' to transgress against. You got to go to the dark web, to a place like Defiler. You know that one?"

"No."

"That's the most fucked up shit in the world. And it's real. Which is the thing. It's *real*, man. It's real. We live in this stupid plastic world. Plastic and make-believe. That's all civilization is, really. Just animals pretending to be 'civilized,' which is just animals pretending to be people. Truth is, in this world, you're either predator or prey."

"I guess you figured that out pretty quick over in Afghanistan, huh?"

"No, man. I mean, yeah, you see it on stark display over there, like you do in any war. But, no, I had the world figured out from day fucking one. Any fifth grader on a playground can tell you that the world comes down to predator and prey."

"I know that's right."

"But if you're a man, everything you're taught is designed to beat that out of you. Teach you to obey, to do what you're told. Why? So women can feel safe. Why should *they* feel safe? The world *isn't* safe. You feel safe? Of course you don't. You're a man. You don't get to feel safe. You're the one who's supposed to tackle the burglar as he's climbing through the window. The woman gets to run the other way while you're protecting her. Think of all the shit you and I see every night. People fucked up from gunshots or drugs or car wrecks or heart attacks or choking on a fucking hot dog. From whatever. Everything can kill you. You know there's no such thing as safety. I know there's no such thing as safety. But women get to live in this fantasy world where bad things won't happen to them. That's why they freak out more than we do when anything does go wrong."

Ronnie was shaking his head in wonder, marveling at the truth of what I was saying.

"Predator and prey," I told him. "That's all there is. And guys like us, we're fucked up because we never get to act on our desires. We've been stuffed and mounted."

"You're right," he said. He stared at me. "You realize that you're actually right?"

"Goddamn right I'm right. If you don't mind me saying, Ronnie, I think that's why you took those pills, man. It's why you tried to kill yourself. You're turning all that animal aggression and rage on yourself. You're still doing it too, slowly killing yourself in order to spare everyone else. But why should you? Did anyone ever earn that kind of mercy from you?"

He sat with that thought.

I told him, "One of these days, man, one of these days we gotta do something. We really gotta do something. Some *real* predator shit."

"Me and you?"

"If not us, then who? Everybody else has had their balls cut off, man. I don't know about you, but I'm sick of being prey."

Ronnie didn't say anything to that, just turned and stared out the window, watching the traffic lights in the snow, trying to sort through his own thoughts. But I knew. I knew the bait was in his mouth, and that when the time was right, I could set the hook and reel him in.

* * *

It was only a couple of nights later that we got the call that changed things between us.

Three AM, a wreck over at Milwaukee and Cicero. A car had hit an ice patch and smashed into a big snowplow parked on the curb. The guy in the snowplow had bailed out, but his vehicle was on fire. Soon the car would go up too. Police and fire were on the way, but Ronnie and I were coming back from the hospital on another call, and for once we got there first.

We told some onlookers to stay back. As we approached the smashed car, glass crunching beneath our boots like ice, we heard a baby howling in the back seat. She was strapped into a safety seat, screaming but unhurt.

In what was left of the front of the car, the baby's mother was impaled on the steering wheel, her face spiderwebbed in blood from where she'd flown up and hit the windshield on impact. The windshield was gone now, scattered all around us, but she was stuck on the wheel, her face full of glass. She was alive, but she was dying in front of us.

I glanced around at the spectators standing far behind us, back on the curb, separated from us by a knee-high wall of plowed dirty snow.

I had my gloves on already.

Ronnie said, "Should we—"

"Now's our chance," I told him.

He stared at me. "For what?"

The woman was gasping for breath, blood running out of her face, neck, and torso.

"Practice," I said.

He wiped sweat off his forehead. "Are you serious?"

"She's dying anyway," I said. "Shame to let the opportunity go to waste." I looked at him. "Tell me not to do it, and I won't do it."

His Adam's apple jerked in his throat. He just stared at me.

I nodded at him and leaned into the car. Her neck was bleeding. I slid my thumb and forefinger in the soft wet wound. I opened it wider.

Ronnie turned back around. The spectators on the curb kept watching us. The baby in the back seat screamed. Snow drifted in through the shattered window.

"Jesus Christ, man," he said.

I didn't look at my partner. I watched the woman. I watched her eyes go from alive to dead, from bitch to meat, as her blood slid down my glove.

Ronnie stood behind me, sweat dripping off his face. But he didn't say anything. He was terrified, but he wasn't outraged. He just watched, his tongue flicking at the snow melting on his lip.

Flames kicked up under the car. The cops and the television trucks rolled up, people jumping out, yelling. I stood up, peeled off my gloves, hurried around to the back of the car and pulled out the screaming baby.

People gasped when they saw me carrying the baby away from the burning car. I handed her to Ronnie. The cameras got the rescue in clear, bright detail. We led every local newscast for the next twenty-four hours. One of the spectators snapped a picture of me handing the baby to Ronnie, sold that photo to the paper, and we were on the front page of the *Tribune* in the morning. At the firehouse, they framed it and hung it on the wall. Me looking handsome and heroic in the glow of the fire from a totaled car, Ronnie standing beside me, looking schluby and stunned.

All the news reports mentioned that the mother had died before we could help her, but the rescued baby was the real story. Even the mayor and the fire department commissioner said so.

I texted a screenshot of the front page of the *Tribune* to Ronnie.

We're heroes, I told him.

CHAPTER 19

AFTER THAT, RONNIE didn't speak to me for days. Even around the other guys we worked with, he was quiet, almost shell-shocked. This went on long enough that I started to get worried. Worried that I'd misjudged him, that he might pussy out and go to the police. I even started to wonder if I needed to do something about him.

But, in the end, I didn't have to worry. He was just letting it sink in.

The night of my farewell party, he finally wanted to talk about it. At the end our shift, they brought out cake and punch at the station, and then everyone slapped my back and told me to enjoy being some old lady's nurse, and they all went back to work. Ronnie and I walked outside.

He'd been acting normal for the first time since the wreck, joking around and being himself, so I suggested we swing by my place to have a couple of beers. It was about five in the morning, and there's nothing like having a drink while the rest of the world is barely awake. Even Mrs. Holding was still asleep. I brought out a couple of Old Styles, and he drank one while he sat on my couch and complained about his wife.

He'd had yet another fight with Heidi, this time because she was nagging him about being "emotionally unavailable." I had theories, of course, about women's concepts of emotional availability—namely that the term actually meant "emotionally submissive"—and I was regaling Ronnie with those theories when he suddenly laughed.

"What?" I said, leaning forward in my La-Z-Boy to put my beer on the coffee table. "Did I say something funny?"

He shook his head. "That one in the car," he said.

I nodded.

"I wish I could do that to Heidi," he admitted. "I mean, I couldn't get away with it. Husband is always the first place they look. But I wish I could do her the way you did the one in the car."

"Sure," I said. "I don't blame you. You could tell her, 'You want to see my emotions? Well, here they are.'"

Ronnie laughed at that, hard. He cackled like an idiot. He *was* an idiot, to tell the truth, but he was my idiot.

"I can't believe we did it," he said. "That one in the car. We killed her, man. We actually got one. Real predator shit. Every time I think about it, it makes my heart pound."

I was glad to hear him use the word *we*. But I'm also a paranoid son of a bitch. Paranoia is nature's radar. That's why I monitor my apartment to make sure I don't have intruders, why I switch out my phones, why I use a burner laptop and Tails. I'm not trying to become prey for some other predator.

So I leaned forward and just asked him straight out, "You're not wearing a wire, are you, Ronnie?"

"What? What are you talking about?"

"This is the first time you've mentioned anything about the wreck, and you bring it up in a weird way? Like, 'Hey, remember that time we dot dot dot?' Weird."

He stared at me. "I didn't say it like that, man. I just thought you'd want to talk about it."

"You haven't answered my question, Ronnie. You go to the police? You wearing a wire?"

"Dude. Of course not. Don't be ridiculous."

I nodded. "Of course not." I picked up his cellphone, which he'd taken out of his pocket and left on the coffee table between us when he sat down, and checked to make sure it wasn't recording. It wasn't, but I shut it off anyway, just to be sure.

"Really," he said. "You got to believe me. What we did the other night . . . . It's all I can think about. I think we should do it again. *That's* why I brought it up."

"That's nice to hear," I said. "Hang on a second, man."

I got up and went to my bedroom and got the Mossberg 9mm from my bedside table. I walked back into the den. I sat back down in my chair and put the gun on the table next to my beer.

Ronnie stared at it like it might bite him. I saw his Adam's apple spasm in his throat. "What's that for?" he asked.

"Protection," I said.

"From what?"

"Well, man, from you. If I need it."

"Why would you need protection from me?"

"In case you prove untrustworthy. In case you're dangerous."

"Jesus, I'm not dangerous, man."

"Well, let's make sure. How about you stand up and take off all your clothes so I can make sure you're not wired up?"

He just stared at me. "Are you kidding?"

"C'mon, Ronnie. Think about what we're discussing here. This really seem like the time and place for me to start joking around?"

"I'm not going to take off my clothes, man."

"Sure you are," I said. Not being mean or threatening. Just being matter of fact. He *was* going to strip down. I nodded at him to start. "C'mon, as naked as the day you were born."

He stared at me, trying to look tough, for a while. Then he cursed and shook his head and reached down to untie his boots. He kicked them off, peeled off his socks, and then stood up and stripped. With his clothes in a pile, he sat back down, bare-assed on my couch.

I got up to poke through his clothes and look in his shoes. While I did, he sat there cupping his dick and balls in his hands. When I was done, I sat back down.

"Okay," I said.

He shook his head, grabbed his underwear and started putting it back on.

"I gotta go, man," he told me.

"Don't get pissy," I said. "I had to make sure."

"Yeah? Well, why don't I make you strip down?"

"If you think about that, you'll realize how dumb it is," I said. "I'm the one killed that bitch while you stood there with a hard-on and watched. I'm the one with the reason to be suspicious."

He just shook his head again as he was pulling up his pants.

"Want to see something?" I said, standing up.

"Another gun?" he grumbled, putting on his boots.

"No. You'll like this, I promise."

I took him to the pink basement door and unlocked it. We walked downstairs. I'd already soundproofed the passageway and stairwell with black acoustic studio foam. Soon, I'd finish the rest. For now, the basement was a long gray room with exposed gray brick walls, a concrete floor, with a door at the south end.

I led Ronnie to the door and unlocked it. Inside was a little square room, six feet by six feet, with cast-iron sink and a metal table attached to the wall. On the wall above the table hung a carpenter's handsaw, a hacksaw, a gut hook skinning knife, and a surgical bone saw. On the table, waiting for us, was my cardboard box. I picked it up and carried it back into the larger room. Then I pulled out the body bag, unrolled it on the cold concrete floor, and placed the Mossy Oak survival knife in the center.

He stared at it.

I smiled up at him.

"Sometimes I ride around with this stuff in the truck," I said. "More of a thrill, knowing I have it right there if I wanted to use it."

"Really?"

"Yeah. I cruise around Logan Square and Humboldt Park, pick out some prey on the street, and follow her around."

"And what?"

"So far, that's it. Just test runs. So far. But I think it's time to go to the next stage."

Ronnie pressed his fist to his lips and looked back at the saws hanging on the wall in the little room.

Finally, he took a deep breath and felt his chest. "My heart is beating so fast," he admitted.

"That's how you know it's real."

He took another deep breath. "I need . . . I need to think about this."

"I didn't bring you down here and show you this shit to have you think about it, man. If you didn't really want to do this, you would have run out of here already."

"Yeah, but what we're talking about, it's . . ." He licked his dry lips. "There's no going back from it."

"No."

"The one in the car, she was dying. She was going to die anyway, probably, no matter what we did. It was the perfect cover. But this," he nodded at the knife and the bag, "there's no cover for this."

"No. There's not. This is me and you leaving the world behind. You were ready to leave it all behind when you tried to kill yourself. But there's no reason for you to take out your frustration on yourself, no reason for you to be alone."

"What you're talking about . . . That's crazy, man. That's fucking crazy."

"Is it? Is it really so crazy? We're just animals. Animals kill each other. All day every day."

"Yeah, but—"

"But, yeah, of course it's crazy. In this world, any guy who isn't castrated and anesthetized is crazy. You want to be crazy with me, or you want to stay a lonely ball-less zombie?" I went in for the kill. "I never had a family worth a damn, Ronnie. Neither did you. This would make us closer than any two brothers could ever be."

He ran his hand through his hair. I thought he was going to cry.

"I know. I know, but . . . You just gotta give me time, Erik."

"Time for what?"

"To get my head around this."

"Why? You said you wanted to do it. This," I pointed at the stuff on the floor, "*this* is what we've been talking about."

"Yeah . . ."

"So, what is it? What's the problem? Don't tell me it's the whole moral thing? You can't still be hung up on that."

"No. It's not that." He ran both hands through his hair now, as if to assure himself that he was still intact. "I'm scared, man. It's a scary thing. You just got to give me time." He turned toward the stairs to go.

"Hey," I said, rolling the bag up with the knife and putting it back in the box. "I get it. It's hardcore. It's real. So it's scary." I gestured upstairs. "Don't worry about it. We'll sit down, finish our beers." I stood up and gave him a brotherly slap on the shoulder. "It's okay."

* * *

But I was pissed at him, mainly because his failure to commit to the final stage suddenly made him dangerous. He'd watched me kill the one in the wrecked car. If he was going to come in on this with me, I had to know I could trust him.

I shouldn't have worried, though. I should have known that once I quit the ambulance, it would only take a few days, a few weeks at most, for him to go into a panic without me. He had no other friends, either at the station or in the real world, he hated his wife, and he didn't give a shit about his kid. He was a boat without a sail.

One night he just showed up at my door after work and said, "Okay, man," as if we'd been discussing it all along. Which, I suppose, means he had never stopped thinking about it. "Let's do it. Final stage. Predators. Let's do it."

I brought him inside. "I thought you were scared."

"I am. Be stupid not to be, right? But I want this. I really want this. I guess I always did. But I was afraid to want it. I was afraid—this is stupid—but it was like I was afraid someone would read my mind. Like if I even thought about it, someone would find out. So I didn't even let myself think about. Until I met you."

"Okay," I said. "But now that's not good enough."

He stared at me. "What's that mean?"

"It means you need to be initiated."

"But that night, the one in the wreck—"

"That was *me* breaking the seal. Now *you* have to do something."

"What do you want me to do?"

"You need to go grab one off the streets," I said. "Do her with the knife, zip her in the bag. For your first time out, it's too risky bringing her here alive, even drugged and gagged. So do her first, then bring her to me, and we'll take her apart in my basement. Then we'll go dump the pieces."

"But why . . . why do I have to go get her alone?"

"To prove you're a man. Simple as that, Ronnie, to prove you're a man. You've never been to war. Hell, you've barely been out of the North Side. You need to go get one and bring her to me to prove you can do it. To prove I can count on you."

I'll admit, having Ronnie go get her and bring her to me was an ego thing. Like I was Dr. Frankenstein and he was Igor. When I was a kid, my stepmother had a dog that would catch squirrels and leave their mangled bodies on the back porch of our apartment, just to prove himself to us. I didn't tell Ronnie I was turning him into my dog, but that's what I'd been doing since the day I saved his life. In some ways, I'd been doing it since the day we met. I'd *own* him after this, my very own slave, something I'd always wanted.

"How do I do it?" he asked, finally.

"You go down to the South Side. Somewhere you can find one that won't be missed much."

"I don't want to go all that way. I don't want to have her in the car that long. And I want a white one. One that looks like Heidi, if I can find one. I should go to Logan Square and Humboldt Park, where you cruise around."

"Smarter to go to the South Side. It's chaos down there. I mean, don't go to Englewood, obviously, or you'll never come back. But try Washington Park. You can slip in down there and pick up a whore without getting noticed by anyone who's going to talk to a cop. Take her to an alley or an empty lot. Somewhere dark. Don't do her in the car. Blood, DNA, all that. Make her get out of the car and then do it before she knows what's happening. If you don't want to go all the way to Washington Park, maybe just go down around Midway. The whores hang out on Cicero between Forty-Seventh and Archer."

"A whore . . ."

"Sure, they'll get in the car with anybody, go anywhere with anybody."

"I don't know, man."

"Trust me. It makes the most sense. You want a high crime area the cops have more or less abandoned, and you want to grab somebody who won't be reported if she goes missing. Or, if she is reported missing, the cops won't really do anything to find her."

"I don't know," he said again, but he was pondering it, I could tell.

"You'll know," I said. "Trust me, you'll know."

"But then once I do her, then what?"

"You bring her to me. You can park in my garage. I'll park my truck out front on the street. I have a big fifty-five-gallon commercial garbage can with wheels on it. We move your kill from your trunk to my garbage can, then we wheel her to the house and take her down into the basement."

"No one's gonna notice?"

"Notice what? It's a garbage can. I do maintenance and yard work around there all the time. They're used to seeing me toting shit back and forth. Someone asks, I'll say squirrels got into the vents again and fucked up the insulation and we're having to tear it out. But, hell, no one's gonna ask."

"Then what?"

"Then we take her apart in the basement. Drain her, chop her into manageable pieces, wash the blood down the drain. We'll bury the carcass in a spot I got picked out. I figure it's a good idea to get it outside of the city, so we'll jump over the state line and dump it in Indiana. Gary's a godforsaken shithole with even worse crime than we got here, and only about a tenth of the police resources, so we'll bury the carcass in the marshes there. That way, even if it's found, it's less likely to lead back here."

He nodded, taking it all in.

"When are you going?" I asked.

"I'm off tomorrow . . ."

I nodded. "I'll get the stuff for you."

"Jesus."

I smiled. "I had a feeling tonight was the night, man. Soon as I heard the knock on the door. I know you. I *know* you, Ronnie."

Quietly, as if he was stunned by the truth of it, he said, "I know you do."

I got the box and carried it out his car. He popped the trunk.

"Nice and roomy," I told him.

He placed the box in the trunk.

"Jesus, I'm nervous," he said. "I'm shaking already."

"I know," I said. "But you're going to be fine. Tomorrow night. I'll be waiting for you. Don't use the phone. No calls, no text. Have a normal evening. Tell Heidi you're going out to a movie. Go somewhere like Logan Square, have a bite to eat, then maybe go to the theater and buy a movie ticket. Use your debit card so there's a history of your purchases, just in case you ever need to prove where you were. Then, quietly, slip out and go down to the South Side, grab one, do her, put her in the bag in the trunk. Have the bag open and ready."

He drew a deep breath. "Then what?"

"Then bring her to me."

CHAPTER

20

THE NEXT NIGHT, he never showed up.

After a few hours, I figured he'd chickened out. I spent most of the night peering out my window. Although I'd told him not to call or text, I kept checking my phone too.

Nothing.

I almost got in my truck to drive over to his place and see if he was still home, but I didn't want to run the risk of missing him, so I waited. All night. I kept the Mossberg on the coffee table in case the cops started banging on the door. I wasn't worried, though. Worry is a womanly disease, passed on from mother to son, from wife to husband. I won't tolerate it. I was enough of a realist, however, to at least consider the possibility that Ronnie had fucked up and gotten caught. That's why I had the gun. If something had happened, if the CPD came to my door, I wanted to be prepared to deal with them. I had no intention of going to jail.

I'd wasted the whole night waiting for Ronnie like that, watching the news, monitoring the police scanners. Waiting for the dog to bring me the rabbit he'd caught.

Nothing.

Finally, at about five in the morning, I kicked off my shoes, rechecked my locks, and laid down on the couch to catch some sleep.

A few hours later, I was awakened by the pinging of my phone.

Im hurt bad, he wrote. *You got to come see me.*

I wrote him back that I was on my way. That's it. Simple message. I'm on my way. I didn't say anything more, didn't ask any questions. Part of me was reading the messages through the eyes of cops and prosecutors. So far, nothing incriminating. Just a guy telling his friend he got hurt, and the other friend saying he'd come help.

* * *

I grabbed one in Humboldt Park, he scribbled out in the notebook he was using for communication.

"I told you to go to the South Side," I said.

He tilted his head. He knew.

I wanted a white one, he scribbled.

I shook my head at him. "This is what you get for being a racist, Ronnie. Was she at least a prostitute?"

No I wanted one like <u>Heidi</u>, he wrote.

"It doesn't matter now," I said. "What happened?"

I dropped the knife, he wrote.

She got hold of it

Somehow

Cut me

To be honest, I wanted to get up right then and leave. I'd never misjudged anyone so bad in my life. Ronnie was as submissive as a dog, sure, but some dogs are too dumb to train. Not only did the dumb fuck go to the wrong part of town and pick the wrong kind of target, he was so inept she'd almost killed him.

"She saw you? Did she get a good look at you?"

He hung his stupid head. Obviously, she'd seen him.

"Jesus Christ, man. Where's my knife? Where's my bag?"

He shook his head.

"What do you mean?"

I don't know, he scribbled.

I closed my eyes when I read that.

"Who patched you up? What happened?"

Some guy. I don't know.

I thought I was dead but he picked me up.

Took me to some doctor. Patched me up. Brought me home.

"And you have no idea who this guy was?"

He shook his head.

"Is your car here?"

He shook his head.

"Do you know where it is?"

He shook his head.

"So my stuff could be there? The knife and the bag, it could be in the car."

He shrugged.

"What does Heidi know?"

He shook his head at me.

I leaned over to him. "Don't shake your head at me, you dumb fuck. Tell me. Write it out. Tell me what she knows."

I didn't tell her Nothing.

I pondered all of that for a while. Then I looked up and asked, "Who is the woman? The one you attacked? Where did you grab her?"

W Augusta, near the park. Just some woman. I don't know.

"Why didn't she call the police?"

He shook his head.

I gathered his sheets of paper, ripped them up and flushed them down the toilet.

Then I went back to him. "We need to find your car. We need to find the guy who picked you up. And we need to find this woman you attacked before she decides to go to the cops. You've left me quite a mess, Ronnie. And I do not appreciate it."

He was staring at me, dizzy and weak and afraid, when the key turned in the front door.

"Ah, Mrs. Dunlap has returned," I said, as Heidi walked through the door with some man I'd never seen before.

* * *

Later, after Heidi and her new protector were gone, I sat by Ronnie for a while, watching him sleep, and doing some thinking about the current predicament.

First things first, I needed to find Ronnie's car and recover my knife and bag. I'd cleaned them both thoroughly before I handed them off to Ronnie, making sure the knife had no prints and the bag hadn't retained any spare hairs or fibers from me. And since I'd left no paper trail when I purchased them, I didn't think they were traceable back to me. But I didn't want to take the chance. I needed to recover them and get rid of them.

Then I needed to check out this Owen guy. Owen Paul? I took out my phone and googled the name and got nothing I could use. Then I threw in "private investigation" and got what I was looking for. Owen *P-a-l-l.* He ran a place called Security Solutions over on Irving Park. I shook my head. Heidi must have hired him to follow Ronnie.

"What does this guy want?" I asked the slumbering imbecile to my left. "What does he know?"

Ronnie kept on sucking in oxygen. I had half a mind to strangle him right there in the bed. He'd ruined this beautiful thing for both of us, ruined it before it really even began. I guess it just goes to show that no plan is foolproof. A fool will always find a way.

I let him sleep.

"Oh, by all means keep sleeping," I told him. "Let me take care of this."

At least I knew who Owen Pall was now. I could figure out how to take care of him. But the woman from the alley, the one who'd seen Ronnie and could identify him, who the hell was she?

Part VI: Saturday–Sunday

Alice Hardy

CHAPTER

21

THE MORNING AFTER the faculty party, I woke up with a hangover and an email in my school in-box from the chair of my department. My regular life, which I'd put on hold for as long as possible, had finally caught up with me. In her email, Shantell thanked me for hosting the party the night before and asked if I was feeling okay this morning. As she was closing her email, she delicately reminded me that I was next in line for the rotating chairmanship of the Theology department, a responsibility, she wrote, that she had always felt I was more than ready to assume. I'd deciphered enough faculty emails to know that, between the lines of this one, Shantell was gently implying that I needed to make sure the rumor didn't get around that I'd become an alcoholic who made scenes at parties. If I did, I could kiss the chairmanship of the department goodbye.

I wrote her back thanking her for her email. Then I composed a short, strategically chipper message for everyone at the party, thanking them for coming last night and apologizing for my absence at the end of the evening, an absence I blamed on the recurrence of a migraine. I wrote Larry a separate email, short and light, making fun of myself, patting his ego, apologizing if I'd said anything "dumb."

I had other emails to answer. Questions from a colleague about a symposium, "Organized Religion in the 21st Century," that we were supposed to host at St. Ignatius next year. A request for a meeting from a student in my Religion and Gender class. And a reminder from HR that I was behind on my mandatory sexual harassment training. Every faculty member, the email reminded me, needed to complete the requisite number of hours of up-to-date training on recognizing and reporting sexual harassment before the end of the semester.

The thought of sitting through an online training program for sexual harassment while my knee was still sore from being attacked in an alley was too great an irony to bear. I decided I'd take care of the training later. Instead, I went downstairs.

Greg was in his office. Saturdays were typically his days to catch up on work. He had his own papers to grade, articles to write, emails to return.

Silently, I left him working and went and found Tuck on the couch. He was wearing shorts and the Fritz Lang *Metropolis* T-shirt I'd bought him for his birthday. I told him, "Grab your coat, we're going to the movies."

He looked up from his phone. "Now?"

"Yeah, why not? Music Box is showing a Joan Crawford matinee at 11:30."

"Which movie?"

"*Sudden Fear*," I said. Then, knowing my audience, I added, "They're showing it on 35mm . . ."

He thought about that, clearly tempted. "I don't know. I was supposed to go over to Julia's."

I shook my head. "Bring her. I haven't gotten much Julia time lately. C'mon, text her and let her know we're coming to get her."

That's how Tuck, Julia, and I wound up in the darkened theater with a handful of other people an hour later. The movies were our thing, mine and Tuck's. His father handled the season passes to baseball games; I made sure to renew our membership cards to the Music Box.

The movie was a fifties melodrama, with Joan Crawford as a woman who marries the wrong man, played by Jack Palance, who sets out to kill her with his girlfriend. The kids seemed to enjoy the movie, though as soon as it became suspenseful I realized that I wasn't in the right frame of mind for it. In the climax, as Palance chased Crawford through the streets of San Francisco trying to kill her, I quietly got up and went to wait in the lobby.

When the film was over, Tuck went to the restroom, and Julia and I stood outside under the theater's big illuminated marquee. The day was cool, and she wore a white coat with caramel-colored fur trim, black jeans, and fur-trimmed boots. Her tousled hair was chestnut-blonde and her face was high pink. As usual she didn't look at me. Julia was the kind of teenager who seemed to have never had a conversation with an adult in her life.

"How did you like it?" I asked.

She blushed. She always looked surprised when I spoke to her.

"Oh, uh, it was okay," she said with a smile. She scrunched her nose. "Kind of cheesy? Tuck likes old movies, over-the-top stuff."

"He got that from me, I guess," I said.

She shrugged and took out her cellphone, an indication that our conversation was over.

I nodded. So much for bonding with Tuck's girlfriend.

* * *

I dropped the kids off at Julia's house, and then I went home.

Greg was in his office working.

"Hey," I said.

"Hello," he said, his eyes darting back and forth between two books open on his desk and a 3D graph on his computer screen. "How'd it go?"

"Fine. Julia said about three words to me."

"Well, that's not terribly surprising," he said, turning a page in one of the books. "Making conversation with her elders does not seem to be Julia's strong suit."

"What are you working on?"

"Oh, you know. Same old, same old." He glanced up at me. "I could explain it to you, but then I'd have to resuscitate you."

"I appreciate that," I said.

He nodded. "You okay?" His tone carried the implication of *Because if you don't need anything, I should really be getting back to . . .*

"Yep," I said. "I need to catch up on my own work stuff."

He glanced up at me again. He didn't say *You embarrassed both of us last night with your inappropriate behavior, but I have neither the time nor the inclination to discuss it right now, so please leave me alone.* He just nodded. "Okay," he said.

I started for the door.

"Hey," he said, "how's the knee?"

I turned around. "'How's the knee?'"

"Yeah."

"It still hurts."

"You need to ice it."

"I will."

He said nothing to that in reply. He turned another page in of one of his books, rested his chin on his fist, and went back to reading.

In the kitchen, I shook some ice into a plastic ziplock bag and carried it upstairs. Then I sat down on my bed, with the ice on my knee and my laptop on a pillow. I opened my school email and immediately pushed the computer away from me.

My son, my husband, my job. I couldn't concentrate on any of them. My family and my career, the twin pillars of my identity, had never seemed more distant. I could take my son to the movies. I could send emails to people at work. So what? What did any of it add up to?

All I could think of was him.

The man in the alley.

He'd looked at me like he hated me his whole life. Like I was going to pay for what I'd done to him.

It didn't matter how insane that was. It didn't matter that I was a complete stranger to him—no more than it mattered that I had a life, a family, a career, that I liked to read, that I liked to sit in a dark theater and whisper facts about old movie stars to my son.

None of that mattered to the man in the alley. He'd decided that I was the one who needed to pay whatever he felt the world owed him.

I sat back against my pillows and adjusted the ice on my knee. I tried to do the same thing I'd been doing since Thursday night. I tried to think of something else, of anything else, except that man—that horrible, broken, insane man.

But it didn't do any good.

CHAPTER

22

I WAS STILL THINKING about him the next morning when I woke up grinding my teeth and clenching my fists.

How could you let him get away? The police were right there. All you had to do was raise your hand. But you hid . . .

I'd hidden in the shadows. I'd hidden in order to protect my life, to protect my family, to protect my reputation.

But after I tried to hide what had happened in that alley, something even more terrible happened, something I hadn't expected.

It worked.

I'd gone home and gone to bed and when I woke up the next day, my life hadn't changed at all. My son, my husband, my friends and colleagues. They were all the same. The only thing that had changed was me. I'd saved my life, but now I was too furious to live it.

Now all I could concentrate on was that man from the alley.

Who was he? Why had he done this to *me*?

That's what I wanted to ask him, what I wanted to scream in his face: *Why me?*

Next to me Greg lay curled around a pillow, sleeping on his side. I checked the time on my phone. It was barely seven. Slipping out of bed, I tried to be quiet as I limped into the bathroom. After I peed, I climbed into the shower and washed my battered body.

The scratches on my hands were sensitive to the hot water, and while the swelling on my knee had gone down, the bruises were turning bright purple. The nastiest mark on my body was decades old, though, a small but deep gash on my left breast where I'd fallen off a wooden fence and cut myself at summer camp when I was fourteen. The worst part of *that* injury had been the embarrassment, the fact that my budding breasts were a fleeting topic of conversation among all the kids and counselors. Now I wondered if my knee would retain some similar scar, some small permanent mark of what had happened to me in the alley.

As I was getting dressed, Greg woke up, turned over, and reached for his phone.

"Hey," I said, pulling on jeans.

"Hey yourself," he said, scrolling through headlines.

"I'm going to the library today to do some research for my *New Testament Studies* article. I'm behind on it, and I really need to spend some time in the stacks."

"Okay. When will you be home?"

"In time for dinner. Before I leave, I'll take the pork chops out of the freezer to defrost. We can have those with the brussels sprouts."

"Okay," he said. Some article had caught his eye and he'd stopped scrolling and started reading.

"Hey," I said.

"Mm-hmm?" He didn't look up.

I stared at him. After a moment, he put the phone down. He stared back at me, and I realized he was still mad about Friday night. Maybe he was waiting for me to bring it up, to apologize. Maybe I wanted him to ask me what was wrong, to express concern rather than judgment. Either way, we were both irritated that the other one wasn't going to say anything. The difference between us was that his irritation would disappear the moment I was gone. I knew that as soon as I left the room, he'd pick up his phone and go back to reading whatever he'd been reading.

"Yes?" he said.

I took a breath. "You need to make sure your son sends an email to that guy at the Office of Student Living at USC."

"Okay."

"He needs to do it today. It should have been done last week. We all agreed that he needs to make the arrangements for check-in himself. That's his responsibility, and we need to hold him to it."

Greg gave me a thumbs-up. "I'm on it."

I nodded. His foot was sticking out of the sheets. I gave it a little pat.

"I'll see you tonight," I said.

"Good luck with the research," he said, picking up his phone.

* * *

Although I was supposed to be going to St. Ignatius, I drove over to Jason's place instead. Not to see him, certainly. In fact, I dreaded the idea of running into him. But I needed to look at the alleyway again. Perhaps I thought that if I looked at it enough in the daytime, I would see it differently. I was tired of thinking about it as a gaping black hole.

When I got there, I parked and got out of my car. As I crossed the street, I noted, with some relief, that Jason's truck wasn't around. The morning was bright and clear and getting warmer by the minute. The top of the Hancock tower was visible five miles away. Sparse traffic glided by on Humboldt Boulevard.

I walked over to the alleyway. Nothing had changed from the day before, of course. The same potholes pocked the same filthy concrete. The mouth of the alley, always smaller than I remembered it, ran between the brick side of an apartment building and the brick side of a small garage in someone's backyard.

I walked around to the plate glass front door of the apartment building and looked at the mailboxes. There were six units. The names for each unit were handwritten on tiny slips of paper next to the buzzers. Most of them were just last names: Lambertson, Kellar, Orts, Neybert, Sise.

I buzzed each one. The first two didn't answer. The third one did, but an irritated voice only crackled at me incoherently.

"Hello," I said. "I was hoping you could help me?"

The voice crackled again and the line went dead. I tried it again, but there was no answer.

I tried the next name, Neybert. No answer.

I tried Sise and I heard a door open. I peered through the glass and saw a big man padding down the dimly lit hallway in a tank top, boxer shorts, and slippers.

He opened the door and stuck his head outside. "You the one buzzing everybody?"

"Yes, I'm sorry. I was hoping—"

"It's eight-thirty in the morning, lady. On a Sunday, people are in bed."

"I know. I'm sorry. I'm hoping I could ask you a quick question."

He sighed. "You better not be a Jehovah's Witnesses."

"I'm not."

"Or from whatshisface running for alderman."

"I'm not here for anyone. I'm just trying to find out if you might have heard or seen anything strange Thursday night."

"Jesus Christ, lady," he said. "It's eight-thirty on Sunday morning. My one day to sleep in."

Before I could reply to that, he slammed the door in my face and padded back down the hallway.

There was one name plate left, written out by hand in purple ink: Aoife Murphy.

I pressed the buzzer.

"Hello," a young voice crackled after a moment.

"Hello," I said, trying not to sound frustrated or desperate. "I was hoping I could ask you a quick question, uh, about the neighborhood?"

"Uh, I'm about to leave for work," she said. "If you want to wait, I'll be outside in a minute."

She walked out the door ten minutes later, an auburn-haired, green-eyed girl in maroon nurse's scrubs. Maybe only a year or two out of college, she wore white sneakers and carried a pink vinyl backpack over her shoulder, and she instantly reminded me of some of the nursing students I'd had in my classes over the years.

She smiled brightly at me. "So you wanted to know about the neighborhood?" she said, slipping her keys into a pocket on her backpack. "You thinking of moving here?"

"Uh, no, not exactly. I was actually interested to know if you were home Thursday night."

Her smooth brow crinkled. "Thursday? No. Why?"

I hesitated. I didn't want to scare her, to make her afraid of stepping out of her apartment, but it seemed to me she needed to know.

"I was attacked here the other night."

She leaned closer to me. "Oh my God," she said. "Where?"

"Here, right around here," I said, pointing toward the alley. "A man jumped out of that alley as I was walking down the street."

My voice cracked when I said the words, and I thought, *Do not cry in front of this poor girl. You're only going to scare her.*

"Jesus," she said. She looked over at the alley as if there might be some glaring evidence of the crime still there, some giant obvious thing that she'd simply walked past. When she looked back at me, she asked, "Are you okay?"

"Yes, I'm fine. Well, I mean, I'm not hurt physically."

"What happened?"

"He got away. I think I wounded him. There was a struggle, but I got the knife away from him and I think I wounded him."

She put her hand to her mouth. "Oh my God," she said. "Thursday night, you said?"

"Yes."

"What did the police say?"

I didn't know how to answer that. I didn't know how to tell her that I hadn't notified the police. I just said, "They're working on it."

"Well, God, I wish I could help, but I was working Thursday night."

"I see. But you haven't heard anything? None of your neighbors said they heard anything that night?"

She shook her head. "No, I'm sorry. I haven't heard anything from anybody." She pulled a cellphone from her pocket and checked the time. "Well, look, I'm going to miss my bus. I have to go."

"Of course. Thank you for talking to me."

I was surprised when she stepped forward and gave me a hug. I just stood there awkwardly and let her squeeze me. "I'll say a prayer for you," she said.

I felt something like a smile stumble onto my face as I told her, "You're very kind."

With that, Aoife Murphy wished me luck and left for work.

When she was gone, taking her effervescence with her, I just hovered in front of the apartments for a moment. As I stood there, alone now, the building felt large, cold, and indifferent.

I turned back toward the alley and drifted over toward the detached gray-brick garage on the other side. It sat at the end of a fenced-in backyard, behind what looked like a spacious two-flat. I smelled cigarette smoke. The garage door faced the street, and I walked past it to look at the yard. When I did, I found an older, potbellied man sitting in a plastic lawn chair, leaning against the garage, smoking. He stared at me like he'd been waiting for me.

He said, "I bet you're looking for that car that was parked out here the other night."

CHAPTER 23

I BLURTED OUT, "WHAT car?" It wasn't the most graceful of openings, but that's what came out of my mouth.

"The one that was parked out here Thursday night." He shook his head. "Some crazy shit going on that night."

I grabbed the top of the chain-link fence. "If you were here Thursday night," I said, "I'd really like to speak to you. It's very important."

The man was down to the filter on his cigarette and leaned over and dropped it in the mouth of a beer bottle. The bottle, I noticed, was full of cigarette butts. The fresh bottle beside it, however, was full of beer at eight-thirty in the morning. The man picked up his drink and stood and walked into his garage. After a moment, I heard the garage door unlock and he pushed it open.

Inside the garage was a weight bench and a stack of weights, a treadmill, a bar for pullups, and a big system of dormant speakers.

The old man made his way through the workout equipment, mumbling to himself, and scratching his bald head. He wore a tight black White Sox T-shirt and blue jeans, and he shuffled out onto the sidewalk in a pair of dirty brown house slippers.

He rubbed his stomach and didn't look at me. "What you wanna know about Thursday night?" he said.

"You were home that night? Late. Around ten or so?"

"Sure I was. Where else would I be? I look like a man with a social life?"

"Did you hear anything?"

"Nope."

He still wasn't looking at me. He took a drink of his beer.

I said, "Okay, but you, you saw something?"

"Saw a gray Ford Taurus parked out here that night. Some guy left it. I noticed it because no one's supposed to park here, blocking our garage. I mean, I'm not an asshole about it, because my son-in-law, he keeps his exercise stuff out here. So we don't use the garage for parking, but, still, no one's supposed to park here."

"Did you see the man who parked the car?"

"Not too well. I was in the back room, and I looked out the window, and I saw a man getting out of the car. It was dark, and I saw him from the back window, and I only saw him for a second. So I didn't see him good. He was just a guy. Kinda big. Had on a hoodie. That's about all I can tell you."

I had to catch my breath at the mention of the hoodie.

I stared at the old man, or rather, I stared at the side of his head. He hadn't looked straight at me since he'd stepped out of his yard.

"Later on," he said, sipping his beer, "I come out to smoke—my son-in-law doesn't like me smoking in the house, and he pays the rent so I let him have his way—but I come out to smoke and the car is gone. Okay. So I figure, 'Good, it's gone.' But then, I don't know when, maybe twenty or thirty minutes later, the car came *back*. I saw a guy park it right where it had been, right in front of our damn garage, and then he ran up the street. *Ran*. And jumped in another car and drove away."

"That is a little strange."

"Well, and the strange thing about it is, I don't think it was the same guy as before. This guy looked smaller and he didn't have on a hoodie."

I was trying to process this information, when the old man coughed and cleared his throat.

"Want to hear the strangest part?" he asked.

"Yes, I do."

"The next day, I was sitting out here and *another* guy came and got the car. *That* guy I saw real good because I was right here," he pointed at the yard, "and I had words with him. Told him, 'Hey, you can't park here.'"

"What did he say?"

"Said he was picking up the car for a friend. And I believe it too, because I'm pretty sure he wasn't the same guy I saw the night before."

"You mean, this was a third man?"

"Yeah, like that old movie. No zither music, though." He laughed, coughed, and had another sip of beer.

"So just to be clear: you saw a big man in a hoodie park his car in front of your garage about ten o'clock on Thursday. Sometime later, you looked out and realized the car was gone, but then you saw another man bring the car *back*, run up the street and jump into another car and drive away. Then the next day, Friday, you saw a third man come and pick up the car."

"Yep. That's what happened."

"What did this third guy look like?"

"I don't know," the old man said with a shrug. "Just a guy."

"White?"

"Yeah."

"Tall?"

"Not really. About as tall as me, so about five-nine or so."

"Young?"

"Hell, everybody's young to me now." The old man sighed, settling into the fact that I wanted an actual description. "I guess he was in his thirties. He was wearing glasses, dungarees, and combat boots. Had short brown hair, and with those boots on, he looked kind of military to me."

"Did he—did he or these other men you saw—were any of them wounded? Maybe a throat wound?"

"Wounded? No. Not when I saw them, anyway."

"Would you be able to identify them?"

"The guy with the glasses I talked to, sure. Those other two, I doubt it."

"And what was your name, sir?"

He turned to look at me now, for the first time. He had aching whiskey-brown eyes, pale and bloody from booze, and he had gray stubble on his chin.

"I'm Glen," he said. "Glen Samuels."

"Well, thank you for talking to me, Mr. Samuels."

"What's your name, hon?" he said, extending his hand.

"Alice," I said, shaking with him. "Alice Hardy."

He held on to my hand and said, "Heard you tell that nurse next door that you were attacked. That true?"

"Yes."

"Thought I heard you tell her you called the cops."

I gently pulled back my hand. "Yes."

He shrugged. "I didn't hear any attack, but I could have missed it, easy. I was up in my room, watching the Cubs get killed. Love watching the Cubs get killed. My two favorite teams are the White Sox and whoever's playing the Cubs. So I was celebrating," he held up his beer bottle to indicate the form his celebrations took that night, "and I was probably out of it a little, but I *am* pretty sure the police didn't come around that night."

I didn't know how to reply to that, so I didn't.

Glen Samuels turned away from me again, peering down the street like he was looking for something. "I'm pretty sure," he said, "they haven't come around here at all, in fact. Not in the last few days, anyway."

"I haven't notified the police yet," I admitted. "I just didn't know how to tell that to the girl next door."

He nodded and put his beer to his lips. "They say most crimes go unreported. Don't know how they know that if people aren't reporting them. But, hell, I believe it. People have their reasons to keep things quiet sometimes, I guess. And no one likes talking to cops. But I'll tell you what, hon, if you send the police my way, I'll sure tell them what I saw."

* * *

I drove to St. Ignatius and parked in the parking deck. Then I walked to the library, swiped my faculty ID at the entrance, and went down into the research stacks. Down there it's a silent maze of wire-caged study carrels, soft lighting, and floor-to-ceiling bookshelves. I had a dedicated spot, with a desk and chair, in the section on foundational ethics and ancient religious practices. It was my favorite place to be lost, a shadowy place of refuge from my ordinary life. I'd hidden here many times before, hidden from Greg and Tuck, from my job, from students with questions, from administration requests and departmental service requirements. I'd even hidden here in the early days of my affair with Jason.

Now, as I sat down in my study space, I didn't take out my laptop, didn't pull any familiar volumes from the shelves. Instead, I took out my phone, opened the Notes app, and made some quick notations:

Glen Samuels Notes

- Saw three men
- 1st man dropped off the car (Ford Taurus)
    - Man was big, wore hoodie
- 2nd brought it back later
    - No description
- 3rd picked it up
    - White, approx. 5'9", 30s, glasses, boots, dungarees, short brown hair, possibly military?

Okay. Three men in the alley. A car that kept moving. Since only one man attacked me, his friends must have been nearby, waiting in the car.

But Samuels never said he saw these three men together. Perhaps there were only two men in the car. The one who attacked me, and his friend to take him to the hospital. But why bring the car back? They couldn't have known that I wouldn't contact the police. Why return the car to scene of the crime, only to send the third man back to get it the next day?

I heard a door creak open somewhere off in the stacks. Two girls, laughing and joking. "Jesus Christ," one girl said, "look at this place. Does Dracula live down here?" Her friend laughed and said, "Where the fuck is philosophy?" Their laughter trailed off as they moved away. Then another door opened, and they were gone.

Although the stillness and silence of the stacks returned immediately, the sudden intrusion by the girls was a jarring reminder of where I was and why I was here in the first place. I studied old texts for a living. I wrote articles, gave lectures, and graded essays for a living. I could barely get my students to turn in their work on time, how was I supposed to find a criminal? Determining who exactly had committed the crime that took place in the alley at the intersection of W. Augusta Boulevard and Humboldt Boulevard was outside my range of skills. And if, by some miracle, I did find that man and his accomplices, what then?

Stop torturing yourself. Just own up to the truth. Tell Greg what happened. Tell Tuck. Then go to the police. Stop being a coward.

I turned back to my Glen Samuels notes. Stared at them, read them over and over.

Three men, a car parked by the alley.

One of the men matched the description of my attacker. The big man in the hoodie. He was out there, the man who had done this to me. I'd almost killed him in that alley. I was almost sure of that now. Had he planned to put me in the car? Was he planning to take me somewhere?

But those other two men. Who were they? How were they connected to this?

Part VII: Saturday–Monday

Owen Pall

CHAPTER

24

SUNDAY NIGHT, I poured myself some coffee and put on *Alone*. Judy sang:

I'll go . . .
I'll go . . .
I'll go my way by myself
This is the end of romance
I'll go my way by myself
Love is only a dance

I sat down at the computer. Dean had taught me the importance of keeping detailed notes on a job as you went along, just like a cop. You never knew what would help you out later on down the road, and you couldn't trust your memory, so it was best to open the case file at the outset and add to it as you acquired new information. Given the explosive nature of this particular file, I had it double encrypted and hidden away on an external hard drive that I kept locked up in the safe when I wasn't using it.

I opened the master folder I'd titled HARDY. Inside, the files were titled HARDY&BABBITT and DUNLAP.

Now I started a new file: REID. I started recording what I'd spent the weekend uncovering.

Erik Thomas Reid was thirty-one years old. He lived in a Greystone two-flat at 1627 W. Golden Grove Avenue, where he had been for two years. Before that he had lived briefly with his stepmother in Pilsen after being discharged from the army.

Normally, it's hard to get hold of a military service record unless you're next of kin, but I know a guy named Rob Wysocki at the National Personnel Records Center in St. Louis, and he hooked me up. Wysocki likes gadgets, and I was fully ready to bribe him with one of the arial drones I keep in stock, but lucky for me he's also the kind of guy you don't really have to bribe. He'll pull a record just to show you he can.

What I learned from Wysocki is that Erik Reid had gotten an Other Than Honorable discharge from the army. While an OTH discharge is not quite as punitive as a Dishonorable discharge, Reid was, to use a phrase from the unofficial nomenclature of the United States Army, a shithead.

In particular, he was a creep. He'd been officially reprimanded on three separate occasions for unwanted attention directed toward female personnel. He was a stalker, basically. He had a history of zeroing in on women he worked with, following them around, calling them, leaving inappropriate messages. He seemed possessive and potentially violent.

Wysocki said the records got vague the closer they got to the heart of Reid's discharge. He'd behaved inappropriately before, but then an "incident" occurred between him and a Private First Class Liz Rusnok that had gotten his ass kicked out of the army. Wysocki didn't know what the incident entailed, but he said it's never a good sign when the army goes out of its way to declare that you're something other than honorable.

When I tracked her down late Saturday afternoon, Liz Rusnok was more than happy to tell me about the incident between her and Reid. I found her living in a small clapboard house down a dirt road about two and a half hours west of Chicago, just outside of Galena. A threadbare American flag, the colors faded to brown and gray, swayed in a breeze at the corner of her low-slung porch. When I got there, Liz was in her backyard smoking weed and painting birdhouses.

As soon as I explained that I was a detective from Chicago doing a background search on Erik Reid, she said, "Oh, that motherfucker. Well, first thing you need to know is he's a fucking psycho. Did you know that? He tried to kill me."

"Jesus, really?"

Every detective has their own style of interviewing people, but I learned mine from Dean. He told me, "The best way to talk to people is like you're sitting around bullshitting in a bar. That thing in detective novels where the guy's a smartass who goes around insulting everybody, that's fun to read, but it would never work in real life. People would either clam up or they'd tell you to go screw yourself. You wouldn't get anywhere. The thing to remember is that everybody *wants* to talk, and if you give them a friendly ear, most the time they'll tell you more than you even want to know."

"Hell yes, really," Liz Rusnok said. She wore a sweaty tank top and baggy khakis, with a black do-rag covering whatever hair she had, which didn't seem to be much.

"What happened?"

She plopped down on a purple lawn chair and motioned me to take the empty one next to it. A hip-hop song I didn't know was playing from a cellphone on an upturned bucket behind her. As I sat down, she took out a chrome Zippo and a red, white, and blue glass pipe.

"That piece of shit," she grumbled, lighting the pipe. It bubbled for a moment while she pulled in smoke. "What'd he tell you about me?"

"Nothing. I found out through somebody else."

"Who?"

"Liz, I ain't gonna lie, I got a hold of his military records. I saw that he got an OTH discharge. Your name was listed in a complaint. The record said the complaint had been 'resolved.'"

"*Resolved*," she said with a sneer. "Son of a bitch should have been lined up against a wall and shot."

"What'd he do?"

She sighed. "I didn't even like him, okay. There was no 'relationship,' no matter what anyone said. I never liked him, but, hell, no one liked him. Erik's an asshole. A know-it-all, a sexist, a bully, a bigot. But he's the kind of asshole that even other assholes don't like. He's just . . . angry. Weird angry. He's mad at the world, the whole world. *Especially* chicks. I mean, I never met a dude who hated chicks more than that guy.

"So I avoided him. But one night . . . one night, I got lonely. I don't want to go into it. It involves another guy, and there's no reason to bring him into this. Suffice to say, I was upset. I was lonely. I'd been drinking too much. We weren't supposed to have any liquor, but I'd got hold of some *and* . . . anyway. Like I said, I was upset, lonely, and drunk. And I can't handle my liquor. That's an important part of the story. Why I switched to weed. I cannot drink. But that night I was drunk, and I thought, 'What the hell, I'll fuck this guy. I don't like him, but he's not bad looking and I hate myself right now, and I want to degrade myself, so why not?' So that's what I *thought* was going to happen when we went into that tent, but when we laid down, he unlaced his boot. I'll never forget it. Real calmly, he unlaced one boot, pulled the lace all the way out and then he wrapped it around my neck. And you got to understand, you can make a perfectly good ligature out of an ordinary shoestring, but this was the lace from a standard issue hot weather combat boot, okay? It's heavy-duty fiber built to last, to last in the desert. So when I tell you he started choking me with it, it's important for you to understand, it was like being strangled with a wire. I thought I was going to die."

"Jesus, Liz, that's horrible."

"Yeah."

"What happened? Did you fight him off?"

"I tried, but I couldn't. He was on top of me. He had my arms pinned down with his fucking knees. There was nothing I could do, and when I looked in his eyes . . ." She shuddered. "I can't explain it. I've been in combat, okay? I've seen people get shot. I saw a jihadist blow himself up right in front of me. But I never thought 'I'm going to die' until I looked up at Erik's face and saw his eyes. He looked furious and . . . and *joyful* at the same time. Like he was getting revenge on me for something horrible that I'd done to him. Even though I barely even knew him.

"But, anyway, no, I couldn't really fight him off. What happened was I was twisting around, and I kicked over this crate. It fell over and made a bunch of noise, and when people came to see what was up, they found us."

"Why wasn't he thrown in jail?"

"Because they didn't believe me. Simple as that. He told our superiors we were doing kinky sex shit and since we got caught I was just trying to smear him to save myself from getting court-martialed. They believed him. I was the one who had bought the contraband liquor, and I was the one who snuck into the tent with him with the intention having sex. I never should have admitted any of that. Once they heard that, nothing else I said mattered. No one liked him, but they still believed him over me. Or, at the very least, they didn't believe me over him. He said, she said. We were both kicked out for the same thing. For the liquor, for the improper sexual conduct on duty, for the conduct unbecoming. I think if I hadn't raised a fuss about it in the first place, hadn't said, 'This guy assaulted me,' they would have just slapped us on the wrist with an Article 15. But I couldn't let it go, so they discharged us both. Like flushing a toilet, just get rid of the whole mess."

"And that's the last you saw him?"

"Last I saw or heard about him until this very moment, yeah. You said you're doing a background check for the hospital?"

I'd fudged my story a little.

"Yes. He's a paramedic in Chicago. I'm doing some background research on him that should have been done before."

"I'll say it should have been done before." She grunted as she sat up in the lawn chair. She took a deep breath and stood up. "I got to get back to my birdhouses."

"Okay," I said. "This helps. I want you to know this helps a lot."

"Doesn't help me any," she said, walking over to inspect one of the birdhouses. She shook her head. "You know, all I ever wanted from the time I was a little girl was to be in the army. 'GI Jane,' my family used to call me. Now, because of that fucking asshole, I'm labeled *other than honorable*? It's not fair."

"You ever think about getting a lawyer, maybe seeing if you could get it reversed?"

Liz Rusnok gently poked the roof of the birdhouse and then rubbed her thumb and forefinger together. "It takes money to get your honor back. Money and time and passion." She picked up her paintbrush and dabbed at the wood. "I ran out of all three a long time ago."

* * *

Sunday afternoon, I paid a visit to Wendy Sharber, Erik Reid's mother. She was a bartender at Carol's Pub, a honky-tonk over on North Clark Street where Chicago yuppies, transplanted rednecks, and lesbians in blue jeans gather together to drink beer and listen to live country music.

"Actually," Wendy told me when I gave her my card and explained who I was, "I'm Erik's *step*mother. Or I was, for a while."

"How long?"

She pointed me to the other end of the bar, away from the day drinkers, where large, framed drawings of Dolly Parton and Willie Nelson hung on a brick wall beneath a mounted set of longhorns. I waited next to an empty darkened stage. The live music didn't start until later. On the speakers overhead, I recognized George

Strait singing "Fool Hearted Memory," which, a lifetime ago, had been my mother's favorite country song.

As she came around the bar to talk to me, Wendy Sharber asked a balding guy in a purple sweater, "Mikey, you good?"

The man looked up. He had watery yellow eyes. He consulted his beer, judged it adequately full, and waved her away.

She smiled thick red lips at me. "Oh, the humanity," she said. She wore a lot of bronzer and had a pile of yellow hair, all of which gave her a kind of sun-cracked golden luster, even though we hadn't had more than two straight days of sunshine in the last three months. When she smiled, her eyes crinkled. "So, what can I tell you?"

"How long did you say you were Erik's stepmother?"

She leaned against the wall and crossed her arms. "Oh, about two years," she said. "Two years and some change."

"How old was Erik at the time?"

"Sixteen?"

"Did he have siblings?"

"No, just him. That was enough, believe me."

She slid a pink-tipped fingernail up the sleeve of her black T-shirt. When she did, I saw a tattoo of a weeping heart bannered by the words FANCY DON'T LET ME DOWN.

"Sixteen-year-old stepson," I said. "I bet he was a handful."

"Yeah. A handful. That's one way of putting it. A pain in the neck is another way to put it."

"Why was he a pain?"

She laughed. "Because he hated my ass. I don't know why. Wasn't like I was the evil stepmother or anything. But, boy, he sure thought I was."

"What about his father?"

"Tommy? He was alright. He was kind of . . . he was a mild man, you would say. I have four ex-husbands, and Tommy was the mild one. Just went to work, came home, ate dinner, and watched TV until it was time to go to bed. Never had an ambition in his life. I think Erik always resented him for being weak. Which I guess he was, but he was nice enough to me."

"If you don't mind me asking, why'd y'all break up?"

"Because I met my *next* ex-husband," she said with a *what-are-ya-gonna-do* shrug.

"Did Erik get into any kind of trouble at school?"

"All the time. Most of it was because he wouldn't do his homework. Said it was stupid. That was the thing about that kid, he thought he was smarter than everybody else. And he always was kind of bright, but I used to tell him, 'Nobody's so smart they couldn't stand to learn something.' He loved *that*, let me tell you."

"Any other kind of trouble?"

"Well, hell, he got expelled. He slapped some girl in the middle of the cafeteria, in front of God and everybody. I don't remember why. She said something he didn't like. I don't know what all it was about. But he slapped her. A girl! He got expelled, and we had to get him a whole new school to go to. That was a pain in the ass. Tommy whipped him for it, of course. Normally I think corporal punishment is wrong, you know, but Erik tested my faith in that theory."

I nodded. I'd been looking into Erik Reid's past for two days, and I'd already found two instances of him assaulting women.

"What about after he graduated? Any trouble then?"

"Oh, I don't know. Tommy and I had already split up by then and I lost track of them. Erik went in the army. I can tell you that much because when he got out, he lived with me for about five minutes. That's the last time I really saw him."

"I'm surprised he'd stay with you, and surprised you'd let him stay, considering the way you two didn't get along."

She shrugged and scratched her tattoo again. "Well, he asked nicely, and he said he'd help out with rent. But the niceness didn't last past the first day or so, and I never saw a nickel out of him. When he left, he called me a dumb *c-u-n-t.* Screamed it at me, right there on my back porch, if you can believe that. I don't know why I let him stay in the first place. Guess I thought I owed it to Tommy for the way I ran off on him."

"Tommy still alive?"

"No, he died a few years ago."

"Did Erik tell you why he got kicked out of the army?"

She pushed away from the wall so quickly I thought she was going to grab me. "He got *kicked out*?"

"He did."

She scoffed. "Well, he neglected to mention that to me. Must have slipped his mind, huh? I thought he just didn't reenlist. What'd he get kicked out for?"

"He assaulted a woman he was serving with. She says he tried to kill her."

Wendy Sharber shook her head and looked down at the floor. After a moment, she turned around to glance at her customers at the bar.

"You don't seem surprised," I said.

When she turned back to me, I could tell that she'd been thinking. "Well, I am and I'm not. I had no idea something like that had happened. Like I said, he neglected to tell me he got kicked out of the army. But now that you tell me, you want to know what I think, right? Well, all I can say is, that boy always had a meanness in him. Nothing I could do with him. It was like he was convinced of something terrible."

My mother's George Strait tune had ended, followed by a pop country song of a newer vintage. I didn't recognize it, which wasn't surprising. I'd stopped listening to country as soon as I left home, so I probably didn't know any country song recorded after 1997.

Wendy Sharber jerked her head at the bar. "I need to get back to work."

"Sure," I said.

We walked back down the bar. I thanked her and was about to leave when I remembered something else I wanted to ask her.

"Wendy, do you know anything about Erik's birth mother? Is she still alive?"

She leaned over the bar and laced her fingers together. I noticed a pinkie ring in the shape of a tiny broken heart. "Oh, no," she said, "his mother died about a year before me and Tommy even met. That was the thing, you know. Why I married him. Here's this nice guy with a broken heart, wife dead of cancer, and a boy who needs a mother. I thought I was gonna step in there and save the day. Didn't work out that way."

"Do you know what Erik's relationship with his mother was like?"

"Not really," she said, pushing herself back from the bar. She opened another beer for Mikey. "But I guess he loved her. Most boys love their mothers, don't they?"

"Yes," I said.

* * *

Sunday night, getting late.

There's nothing left for me, Judy sang
Of days that used to be
I live in memories
Among my souvenirs

I needed to go to bed, needed sleep. I closed the file on Reid, but then, on an impulse, I opened the one on Alice Hardy. I clicked on the JPG I'd swiped from Alice's Instagram page, the photo of her with her son.

I just stared at it for a moment, not really thinking anything. Just staring.

Then I closed it.

I turned off the record player, shut down the office, and went upstairs. There was some leftover orange chicken and rice in the refrigerator. I heated it up and ate it standing at my counter. Around me was all of Dean's stuff. His pots and pans, plates and utensils. His posters on the walls of the den. His bookshelves full of his books and tapes. I stared at it all while I ate. Then I washed up and went to bed.

Lying alone in the blank whiteness of my bedroom, I chased sleep, but my mind was too wired, too worked up and wide awake, preoccupied with Erik Reid and Ronnie Dunlap, with Heidi Dunlap and Liz Rusnok and Wendy Sharber.

And Alice Hardy. I fought off the urge to go over to her place, stake it out, check up on her and make sure she was alright.

I was doing the work. I was following my leads. I was assembling a case.

Leave it at that. Go to sleep, man.

I shut my eyes, tried to will myself to rest, if not to sleep.

CHAPTER 25

THE DOWNSTAIRS BUZZER went off first thing Monday morning. I was still in bed, watching the window shades glow brighter and brighter with the morning sun. When the buzzer went off in the kitchen, indicating that someone was at the front door of the store, I pulled on a pair of pants and hurried downstairs in a white T-shirt and bare feet to see who it was.

I leaned out the doorway and found Kat Salazar waiting for me.

"Hey, kid," she said. "You left a message for me yesterday?"

Kat was a veteran police dispatcher. After my search of the news reports hadn't turned up any promising leads yesterday, I'd given her a call. I'd found her name and number in an old file Dean had marked "Salazar Daughter." It was a case going back almost ten years. Kat had hired us to help find her runaway teenage daughter, something none of her friends in law enforcement had been able to do, and Dean had delivered big time, tracking down the girl to some shithole in rural Indiana, where it turned out she was living with a forty-six-year-old long-haul trucker. Kat was so eternally grateful that, even after the rest of the CPD had turned its back on me, she would still take my calls.

I asked, "You got a minute to talk?"

Kat was a short, compact woman in dark jeans and a sleeveless black tank top. Her hair was dyed such a deep shade of mahogany it looked like she'd done it with furniture stain. She shrugged and said, "Sure, that's why I'm here."

I asked her to wait a moment, and I ran upstairs to put on shoes and a proper shirt. Then I hustled back downstairs to unlock the store and let her in.

She shook her head as she appraised the place. The Mike Hammer posters on the wall, the replica of the Maltese Falcon propping open the front door, the advertisements for concealed carry permits. She smiled.

"This place. Jesus. You kept it just the way he had it, huh?"

"It draws in foot traffic," I said with a shrug.

"I remember the first time I came in here to hire Dean. I thought, 'What the hell is this? Is this guy a kook?'"

"Then you found out he was."

She smiled sadly. "He was a character, God rest his soul. How long has he been gone?"

"Almost five years, if you can believe it."

She nodded and checked her watch. "Well, time marches on, I suppose. Speaking of which, I only got a few minutes I can give you. Don't want anyone on the force to see my car out front."

"Sure. Well, I appreciate you swinging by. I'm working on something, and I thought you might could help, if you're still doing dispatch."

"I am. What do you want to know?"

"I'm wondering if you've noticed any patterns lately. Last six months or so, maybe a year. A rise in assaults on women. Street stuff, guys jumping out of alleyways, that kind of thing, especially on the West Side."

She leaned against one of the glass cases and crossed her arms. "Are you kidding? We get assaults, sure."

"Anything like a pattern, though, a serial offender?"

"Oh, I don't know if I could say. I just take the calls. Muggers, rapists—that stuff happens every day. My job is nothing but that shit, you know. If I'm dispatching a unit somewhere, then someone's either having a bad day, or they're having the *worst* day."

I nodded. "Just wondering if anything stood out. Anything reoccurring."

She shrugged. "Same old bullshit, as far as I can tell. Drunks, fights, shootings, car wrecks. The usual." She poked her bottom lip with her forefinger. "You know what, though? Now that you mention it . . . Okay, so there hasn't been some upswing in assaults, but I have noticed something weird the last few months. I've gotten like three or four calls—about once or twice a month maybe?—of women complaining about being followed down the street. When I've dispatched officers, it never amounts to much. The asshole is never around when the unit gets there. He never stops, never says anything, never gets out of his vehicle, but it does sound to me like it's maybe the same creep."

"Any description?"

"Young, white, glasses. Pretty nondescript beyond that. Like I said, there hasn't been any contact, and he doesn't even get out of his vehicle. And before you ask, no, no one got a look at his license plate."

"What's he drive?"

"Oh, yeah," she said with a laugh. "I guess that would help, wouldn't it? He drives an old red pickup truck."

* * *

All my information gathering and sorting had consumed the entire weekend, and I hadn't sat down to eat a hot meal since Friday. I was sick of standing at my kitchen counter scarfing down takeout and leftovers, so when Kat left, I hopped in the shower, washed all my relevant parts, and then headed up Irving Park to eat at my favorite breakfast place, a little family-owned restaurant called Shilas.

I slid into a booth, and when the waitress came around, I ordered my usual, black coffee and a breakfast burrito with a side of fruit. While I waited for my food, I took stock of where I was at with the case.

I had thought that my best chance to get Ronnie without dragging Alice into the spotlight would be to find some actionable proof that he had done this before. After all, I knew I had a criminal; I just needed to find a crime I could bust him for. So far, that had been a dead end. None of my research had given me any reason to think there was an unsolved series of murders or disappearances going on that could be traced to Ronnie. Aside from his suicide attempts and disturbing porn preferences, nothing even helped me in assembling a compelling background profile. He had no history of violence on record, no criminal record of any kind. Until he'd grabbed Alice Hardy in that alley, as far as I could tell, his rage had all been turned inward.

But then there was Erik Reid. He was the one with a history of violence toward women. The discharge from the army for trying to kill Liz Rusnok. The expulsion from high school for assaulting a girl. It was Erik who fit the psychological profile of a killer.

And now I'd learned that he matched the description of a creep—white, eyeglasses, driving a red truck—who'd been following women around for the last few months.

So how did this—what I knew about Ronnie and what'd I'd discovered about Erik—fit together? Erik certainly seemed like the dominant partner in that relationship, "the only one Ronnie trusts," Heidi had told me. He'd saved Ronnie from a serious suicide attempt, and he'd talked Heidi into keeping it a secret.

I could almost hear Dean telling me to take it easy. Assemble the facts. Make as few assumptions as possible.

I reminded myself that none of the information I'd uncovered meant that Erik was Ronnie's accomplice. It was all circumstantial. If Erik was Ronnie's accomplice, then why wasn't he there with him that night? Hell, Ronnie might not even have an accomplice.

Maybe he was going to take Alice Hardy somewhere all by himself. And maybe Liz Rusnok was a liar and Wendy Sharber was an evil stepmother. Maybe Erik Reid, like everyone else in Ronnie's life, was just someone who happened to know a psychopath.

But the old man had also taught me that the detective's primary investigative tool—the one that steered all the others—was stubborn, irrational instinct. It was the thing that made you wait five minutes more, that made you turn left instead of right, that made you distrust someone even when his story seemed to check out.

Something about Erik was off. I'd known it the moment I met him. The way he tended to Ronnie the morning after the attack. It was possessive without being affectionate. I thought about what Liz Rusnok had told me, about the way he looked at her *furious and joyful* at the same time as he tried to strangle her to death. That's what I'd seen in his face as he regarded Heidi packing up her things to go, smirking and cold-eyed, a man amused by his own simmering rage.

He has to be involved. I don't have any real evidence yet. But I can feel it. I know he's involved in this somehow. I fucking know it.

Of course, there was only one way to know that for sure. Only one person besides Erik himself who could confirm it.

The waitress brought over my food and refilled my coffee. As I unrolled my knife and fork, I resolved to give the best breakfast burrito in Chicago the attention it deserved.

But I knew where I was going after I ate. It was time to brace Ronnie.

* * *

On my way to his house, Heidi called me to check in.

"I've been talking to my connections on the force," I told her. "I've talked to four different cops. So far, I don't have a solid lead."

She took that in. "So what are you telling me? He hasn't done this before?"

"I can't be sure yet."

She let out a breath. "Jesus," she said, almost panting. "That would be such a relief."

"Where are you?"

"At my sister's. I'm about to go to work."

"How's Tobi?"

"Confused about why we're staying with Leighann. But she's used to Ronnie and me fighting, so she's rolling with it. She stays on her phone all the time anyway. Instead of hiding in her bedroom and texting, she's hiding in my sister's guest room and texting. But this can't go on much longer."

"Have you talked to Ronnie since you left?"

"Just a couple of text messages. Friday night he texted to ask if we were okay. Just like that, 'Are you okay?' I wrote back 'Yes.' That was it. I know I should have asked him if he was okay. He's still my husband. He's still Tobi's dad. If something happened to him while we were gone, I don't know what I'd tell her. But I'm scared to talk to him. You know what I mean? I want to check on him, but, at the same time, I don't want to."

"I'm on my way to talk to him now. I'll let you know his condition."

"Okay. But you haven't found anything yet?"

I could have told her what I'd found out about Erik, but Dean had always warned me never to tell the client more than absolutely necessary, especially in the middle of an investigation. An investigator can process new information objectively, methodically; at least, that's the goal. The client, on the other hand, is always more emotional. I didn't want to tell Heidi about Erik, only to have her go running off to the cops without me.

"I'm still looking."

She said, "Okay, well, look, I appreciate you being thorough and all. But if you're not finding anything, then maybe Ronnie really did hurt himself. Maybe this was another suicide attempt, and what I should be doing is seeing about getting him some psychiatric help.

I think I need to see about getting Ronnie committed. My daughter and I need to be back at home, and Ronnie needs to be . . . somewhere else. Somewhere he can get some kind of professional help. Leighann can help me arrange that when the time comes."

I didn't argue with her. I assumed this newfound resolve had come about through a consultation with her sister, so I didn't press the point. It was much easier to accept that Ronnie had hurt himself than to believe that he was out on the streets hunting women. "Okay," I said. "I understand. Can you just let me see what I can find out today? Let me finish up my work, and I'll give you my report tomorrow morning. That way you can make your final decision with as many facts as possible."

She drew a deep breath. "Okay," she said. "But today is the last day."

* * *

When I pulled up to the Dunlap home, the street was quiet. The sun was out now, and the days were getting warmer. I even heard birdsong from the trees.

When I stepped up to Ronnie's door, the shades were drawn. Despite the sunlight on the windows, the place felt cold, lifeless. I rang the bell a few times but got no answer. I knocked. No answer. I tried to peer through the curtains, but there was no gap in them. I walked around to the back of the house. Locked. No answer when I knocked again. Curtains drawn, blinds lowered and closed.

I walked back to my car. I had a couple of lockpick sets in my gear bag. One was a big thirty-two-piece set in a foldout leather case. It could get you into a goddamn bank vault if you didn't mind the whole world knowing what you were doing. I took the other one, a small jackknife that fit in the palm of my hand. It only had six picks, but I'd found that if I couldn't get in somewhere with it, I was usually doomed, anyway. I strolled up to Ronnie's front door, used the jackknife's snake rake pick, and popped the door in under a minute.

The house had that deep stillness and quiet that only comes from emptiness. I didn't have to look around to know that no one was there, but I checked every room anyway. In Ronnie's room, I rifled through his closet and drawers. I didn't really know what I was looking for. Clues, I guess. A serial killer journal where he detailed all his crimes would have been nice. But all I found in his drawers were clothes, a couple of dogeared EMT guides, and bits of junk like old headphones and batteries. His closet yielded up a few more clothes, an empty suitcase, and a box of more crap—parts of a broken camera, an old watch, a couple of issues of *Sports Illustrated* with the Blackhawks on the cover.

Then I looked in the den. There, on the coffee table, lying side by side, was a cellphone, a wallet, and a suicide note.

The note read:

Heidi,

Do you know you ruined my life? I hate the man you made me into. It was always your house wasn't it? It was always your life too. Well you can have the house and you can have the life all you want because I don't want either one anymore.

Ronnie

I don't know how long I stood there staring at it, but I got lightheaded and had to sit down on the couch.

The son of a bitch was going to kill himself. But where was he?

I got up and walked out the back door and went to his garage. Empty.

I went back into the house. I found an old note from Ronnie to Heidi stuck to the fridge, reminding her to get beer when she went grocery shopping. I compared it to the suicide note. I was no expert, but it sure looked like the same handwriting.

I sat down and stared at the suicide note some more.

No confession, no mention of the alley or the attack.

Assuming it was authentic, assuming Ronnie had written it, what did it mean? He wasn't in the house. Where was he?

I shook my head. Something about this was wrong. I couldn't explain it. Something about this was just wrong. Ronnie and Erik were together in the attack on Alice Hardy. I had no proof, but I was sure of it. Just like I was sure that Ronnie didn't just up and decide to kill himself by wandering off into the night. It made no sense.

And where the hell was Erik?

Almost in answer to that question, I looked up. Something else was missing.

I looked around. I searched every room again. I looked in all the trashcans.

Ronnie's notepad. The one he'd been using to communicate with since Thursday night. It was gone. Why would he take it with him? Why were there no discarded notes lying around? Requests for food or drink, answers to questions. Why get rid of those? If Ronnie was going to kill himself, why would he go through the trouble of cleaning up after himself?

The more I looked around, the more I realized that there was no evidence at all that Erik Reid had even been here.

And right there, at that exact moment, I should have called the cops and told them the same story I told Heidi. That I'd followed Ronnie, found him wounded, and brought him home. I could have showed them the suicide note. I could have shared the background I had on Erik. It was more than enough to warrant them going over to his place to question him. There was nothing to point to Alice here. I could turn everything over to the cops and let them figure out the rest.

But I couldn't let it go. I couldn't let some fucking cop figure it out. I hadn't slept sixty straight minutes in the last four days because I was chasing down leads on these two guys. Now Ronnie disappears, and Erik's presence is wiped clean from the house? What was I supposed to do, go home?

The one thing I knew for sure was that I wasn't calling any cop. This case was *mine*. I was going to break it, and I was going to get the goddamn credit for breaking it.

A detective is just a guy who can't let shit go.

Damn right.

I took a picture of the note just to document it. Then I made sure everything was as I'd found it and I left.

I ran outside and drove straight to see Erik.

CHAPTER 26

CHICAGO IS A city of brick and mortar. Sure, it has its famous skyline—and God knows the developers keep throwing up architectural wonders of steel, glass, and concrete on the Gold Coast that no one can afford to live in—but the real Chicago is in the neighborhoods, where all the single-family bungalows, two-flats, three-flats, and horseshoe-courtyard buildings date back to the era after the great fire, when Chicago was rebuilding itself as a working-class city made to last. That's where Erik Reid lived, in a red brick two-flat with white trim and big bay windows, on a block of identical flats and clean sidewalks, with trim plots of grass in the front, and larger yards and detached garages in the back. The only thing that set Eric's home apart from all the others was that his curtains were pulled shut.

I didn't see his truck, so I swung around back and cruised the alley behind his place. His garage door was closed, the yard empty, the curtains all drawn. I drove back around to the front, parked on the street, and walked up to the door. It had a big plate glass panel with embossed white floral decoration. I knocked. Nothing. I waited and knocked a couple of more times. According to the mailbox, Reid was downstairs in Unit 1. His landlord, Mary Margaret Holding, lived upstairs in Unit 2. I cupped my hand and peered between the decorative swirls and flowers on the door pane and saw a foyer with the door to Reid's flat next to a flight of stairs going upstairs. I tried the front door. Locked.

I walked around the building and climbed the back steps to Reid's back door. I still had the jackknife lockpick set in my pocket, and I had the door open in about a minute.

I knew that entering Reid's flat like this was moving me deeper into legal jeopardy, but I didn't ponder the implications of that for very long. I'd been operating well outside the law for five days now. And if Erik Reid was what I thought he was, I didn't really have a choice. I closed the door behind me and crept into his flat.

The place wasn't exactly what I expected. I'd sort of assumed Reid lived in something that looked like a dungeon at Guantánamo Bay. But the walls of his flat were painted birthday cake pink and trimmed in baby blue. It was so surprising that, for a split second, I was afraid I'd broken into the wrong flat.

A couple of bills with his name on the kitchen counter reassured me that I was in the right place, though. Despite that, the place barely felt occupied. Those pink and blue walls were bare. The dining room didn't even have a table and chairs, just bare hardwood floors beneath an old, mounted ceiling fixture. In the front room, a plain brown couch, an old beige armchair, and a rickety-looking coffee table faced a flatscreen television. The bedroom yielded up a bed, neatly made with dark sheets. A flea-market dresser with a few clothes, folded and stowed away. His EMT uniform and some shirts and pants hanging over an empty hamper in the closet. A lamp using a wooden chair as a bedside table.

What I didn't see anywhere in the apartment was any sign of a personality. Reid didn't have a single picture of himself, his friends, or his family. He owned no books, no movies, no video games. If he owned a computer, he had it with him. Otherwise, there was no indication that he had any hobbies or any preoccupations—any interest, really, in anything at all.

There was also no sign anywhere of Ronnie.

I stood in the empty dining room pondering all this nothingness for a while. Then I realized that I hadn't found any kind of documents, not even any documentation from his time in the military. What was I missing?

I went back into the kitchen. A few plates, pans, glasses, and utensils. His refrigerator wasn't exactly bursting with food, but, in truth, it was better stocked than mine.

In his walk-in pantry, among a few cans of beans and corn and boxes of macaroni and cheese, I finally found his documents. Routine stuff mostly, some health insurance information, some old tax forms, some papers from his time in the military. All of it neatly organized in different folders in different boxes, none of it of interest to me.

But coming out of the pantry I noticed the door. It was pink and blue-trimmed, and it fit so seamlessly into the rest of the hallway that I'd walked right past it. I tried the handle.

Locked.

"Well, that's fucking interesting," I said.

I tried to pick it, but it didn't spring as quickly as the back door. I had to get down on my knees to work on it for a bit. When I did, I noticed something easy to miss at first glance. A small piece of transparent security tape at the bottom of the door, the kind of thing a paranoid guy would do to make sure no one was going into his stuff when he wasn't around. I got up and checked the back door where I'd come in. Sure enough, it had been taped too. I'd broken the nearly invisible security seal when I'd come in.

I ran back to the pink door. I didn't worry about breaking the seal. It took a minute, but I finally sprang the lock.

Wooden basement steps, the walls of the stairwell layered in some kind of black foam.

There was a string for the lightbulb. I pulled it and light illuminated the concrete floor at the bottom of the steps. I walked down. It was like walking down into another world. The basement ceiling and walls were black, covered in the same black soundproof foam. The floor was cold and gray. At the end of the room was one last door. One last lock. One last seal at the bottom of the door.

When I got it open, I couldn't find the light switch for the little room. The light from the basement behind me shone in.

Inside, mounted on hooks on the wall, hung saws and knives. Four in all, clean and sharp, glinting in the light. Beneath them, a gray metal table next to a cast-iron sink. Tied to the legs of the sink, two pieces of rope spilled onto the floor.

I stared at the ropes. The saws. The knives.

When I tried to pull my phone out of my pocket, my hand was shaking, and I fumbled it. The phone dropped to the floor with a loud slap.

I spun around.

Nothing. Just an empty basement, cold and silent. The door open at the top of the stairs was quiet.

I bent down in front of the saws and knives and picked up my phone.

Behind three locked and sealed doors, Erik Reid has a little room in a soundproofed basement filled with tools for vivisection.

As I stood up, blood rushed my head. My heart beat itself into a blur.

Okay.

Okay.

Take it easy. Breathe. Assemble the facts. Make as few assumptions as possible. Record everything.

Once I had video of the entire basement, I locked up and got out of there. Fuck the seals; let him know someone was here. I was back in my car in less than five minutes, staring at the footage I'd recorded.

The basement looked even creepier on video, like a dungeon.

This cannot be what I think it is.

Maybe Reid was a deer hunter. *I didn't see any hunting equipment.* Maybe he just liked to butcher his own meat. *In a soundproof basement? And why the ropes?* I wasn't sure where to go or what to do next. I wasn't sure who to talk to next. This was either nothing at all or it was the most insane fucking thing in the world. I'd wondered where Ronnie was going to take Alice Hardy the night he attacked her. What if he was going to bring her here to Erik's little room in the basement? I'd either found some guy's harmless hobby, or I'd found evidence of murder and madness.

I turned on the ignition.

CHAPTER

27

I'D BEEN DRIVING around for a while, just trying to reassemble my brain, when I realized someone was following me. I'm not sure where I picked them up, but I was making a turn onto Devon when I caught them in the side mirror. Three cars back, making the same turn. An atomic silver Lexus SUV. Suddenly, I wasn't in a such a daze anymore.

I'd followed hundreds of people in my years as an investigator, but I'd never had anyone follow me before. That, coupled with my current state of mind, made me wonder if I was really being followed or just being paranoid.

So I got onto Sheridan and then made a quick swing onto Lake Shore Drive. The Lexus followed. Of course, the driver might just be going that way. So were a lot of other people, but the Lexus hung back no matter how slowly I drove. So we cruised on for a while, the waves of Lake Michigan crashing in the sun on our left as the city slowly rolled by on our right—first Lincoln Park and the harbor, then the luxury hotels and apartments on the Gold Coast. The Lexus stayed back there. Two guys in it.

"Okay," I said. I'd been carrying the Sig with me since Friday. It was in the glove compartment, and I took it out and slid it out of its holster. I left the holster on the seat beside me and slid the gun into the pocket of my jacket.

I turned off Lake Shore Drive at Monroe. There wasn't enough traffic between us, so the Lexus was only one car length behind me now. It stayed right with me, even when I suddenly swerved onto Columbus and plunged down into the underground parking garage beneath Millenium Park.

The driver of the Lexus tried to keep up with me while still playing it cool, but now he wasn't sure what to do. I zipped up to the toll gate, whipped out my parking pass, and zoomed right through. I had parking passes for damn near every garage in town. I was betting this guy didn't. Sure enough, as I was descending deeper into the garage, he was still stuck back at the toll gate trying to figure out how to get in.

The garage beneath Millennium Park is a low-ceilinged concrete labyrinth, one of the largest underground structures in the world. I'd gotten lost down there once trying to follow someone on a surveillance job, and Dean had chewed me out so bad I went back and drove around the place for three hours until I understood all its twists and turns. It's divided into a north side and a south side. The north side goes up six levels and comes out on Randolph Street, up on the ridge behind the pavilion in the park. The south side, on the other hand, *descends* three levels and comes out down the hill by the Art Institute.

The main entrance to the structure is in the middle, on level three, which connects the two sides. I turned left into the south side and descended further down into the depths of the garage. I went all the way down to level one, the lowest level. On days when there are no big events going on, no parades or protests or Bears games, the south side of the garage has plenty of open spaces. Down on level one, it's sometimes completely empty. That was the case now.

I could have just gotten out of there, slipped out of one of the garage's ancillary exits, and lost the Lexus. But I needed to know who was following me and why, and since they were lost and I wasn't, I had the advantage down here. I decided to stay and wait.

I drove to the far end of the garage and parked next to the stairwell. There were fourteen stairwells all over the garage, but this one, number eight, was the one most likely to be empty.

I steadied myself, checked the gun in my pocket, and got out to go hide in the stairwell.

I waited.

The garage was cold, and because a mist hung in the air just below the low concrete ceiling, the place smelled of wet cement. Cameras blinked away in dusty, webbed corners.

I needed to piss. I hadn't needed to until now. Funny, the way nerves work.

I heard the angry screech of tires echoing down the ramp from the upper level. After a moment, the Lexus swung into view, spotted my car, and raced toward it.

I slipped back into the stairwell and drew a long slow breath.

The Lexus pulled up beside my car. I'd parked close to the stairwell but not too close. Doors opened, shoes slapped pavement, and a couple of voices grumbled in what sounded a lot like Croatian to me. A car alarm beeped on the SUV, and the shoes hurried toward the door to follow me upstairs.

I stepped out and pointed the gun at them. They stopped.

Josip Vukov. The guy with him was like a smaller version of him. They both wore tracksuits, expensive sneakers, and gold chains over hairy chests.

"Raise your hands," I said. I would have liked to have gotten quippy with them, but I was too scared. I had to concentrate to keep my voice steady.

The men stopped. The small guy looked at Vukov.

They raised their hands.

"Why are you following me?" I said. "What do you want?"

Vukov just glared at me.

"Turn around," I said.

Vukov kept on glaring.

"I *will* shoot you both," I said. "Turn around."

He looked up at the camera in the corner. "On the camera, you'll shoot us?"

"You're a known criminal who beat me up last week in front of the police, and now you're on camera following me into an empty parking garage. I bet I can get away with claiming self-defense, especially if you're carrying guns."

Vukov breathed through his nose and glared at me with escalating fury, but he turned around. His buddy followed his lead.

"With your left hands, take out your guns and put them on the ground. Both of you."

Each man took out a piece from a shoulder holster under his tracksuit and put it on the ground.

"Now toss me your keys over your shoulder."

"What?" Vukov said, starting to turn around.

"Don't turn around, goddamn it. Throw me the keys to the Lexus."

The smaller guy looked at Vukov, who finally nodded. The smaller guy dug out his keys and lobbed them over his shoulder.

I picked up the keys and used the fob to unlock the SUV.

"Go sit inside," I told them. "And Vukov, I don't know why you still have a hard-on for me, man, but just so you know, I'm completely off your case. I'm on to something else, a whole other case, and I haven't given you a thought since Friday. So you go your way, and I'll go mine. Understand? If you leave me alone, I'll leave you alone."

He said nothing to that. Didn't acknowledge it at all. He didn't even turn his head to look at me. He just walked over to the Lexus with his buddy following him and climbed inside.

I hurried to my car, jumped in, and tore out of there. I was barely to the ramp before I saw Vukov leap out of the SUV to scoop up the guns.

I raced up the ramp, waved my parking pass at the tollgate to get out, and sped out the Columbus Street exit. A couple of minutes away, I said, "Holy shit," out loud and wiped the sweat off my face. Then I rolled down my windows and tossed the Croatian's car keys out into the traffic on Michigan Avenue.

CHAPTER 28

I WEAVED THROUGH THE traffic with my heart still beating in my ears. Christ, what a day. I had to shake my hands a few times because the adrenaline pumping through me made it difficult to hold on to the steering wheel.

I was frankly shocked by Vukov's persistence. He'd already kicked the shit out of me, and like the cops had said, that ass-kicking had pretty well gotten his point across. I really hadn't given him a moment's thought since Thursday. So why follow me around now? For that matter, how did he find me? He didn't even know who I was last week.

I wondered if it was possible that Karras or Styrczula had dropped my name in front of him. That would have been negligence to a profound degree, even by the standards of the CPD, but it was one possible explanation.

I didn't have a personal contact number for either of the cops on my phone, but I thought Dean might have something on Karras back at the office. Besides, I needed to sit down and regroup and really consider what I'd discovered at Reid's apartment. Given what I'd found there, now might time to bring the police into the Dunlap case.

So I drove to the store. I opened up and turned on the lights, but I didn't turn on any of the signs. I went to the back and opened my computer. Years ago, to cut down on the amount of time I'd have to spend digging through boxes and stuffed manila folders, I'd converted a lot of Dean's old contacts into one huge spreadsheet. It was hundreds of names long.

Before I looked up the cop's contact information, though, I made a detour. Over the last five days I'd become accustomed to switching on my computer and going immediately to the files on the Dunlap-Hardy-Reid case. It was like muscle memory at this point. So I opened them up out of habit, and I decided to upload the video from Reid's basement before I did anything else. I'd just started uploading the files when the front door dinged.

I adjusted the Sig in the holster in the small of my back. I got up to go tell whoever it was that we weren't actually open, but as I walked through the office door someone hit me in the mouth with a baseball bat.

I swallowed my front teeth as I stumbled backward into the office and toppled over on the floor. I felt the Sig slip loose of its holster and heard it skitter across the floor. Tasting blood and aluminum, I was trying to get up when the little Croatian stepped over me and cracked me in the kneecap with the bat. When my hands jerked up to my kneecap, he hit me again and shattered my right wrist.

Vukov said something to him in Crotian and the little guy backed off.

Vukov knelt next to me, careful not to get any blood on his shoes. He took a cellphone out of his pocket. He aimed the camera at me.

"A picture for my wife," he told me. "To show her what happens."

I gagged and coughed up a bloody wad of meat and teeth.

"I see you again, I'll kill you," he said.

He stood up. The little guy leaned over me and rooted through my pockets.

"Where are my keys, motherfucker?" he demanded.

I tried to tell him, but my front teeth were gone, my lips were blown apart, and my tongue was already so swollen it filled my mouth.

"What?" he said.

I babbled again.

Vukov barked something at him in Croatian.

The little guy answered him in English. "I only got spare for Lexus, man," he explained. "I need keys to my apartment." He turned back to me. "Where are my keys, motherfucker?"

With what was left of my mouth, I tried to explain that I'd tossed them. I don't know how much sense I made. I don't know if he got mad because I'd thrown his keys away, or if he got mad because I wasn't making any sense at all.

But either way, he stood up, lifted the bat and beat me until the world slipped away.

Part VIII: Friday–Monday

Erik Reid

C H A P T E R

29

After Ronnie's wife packed her bags and walked out the door with her detective, I drove over to West Town to pick up his car.

I cruised by the spot once to scout out the situation, and I saw his gray Ford Taurus with the dent in the bumper. It was parked in front of someone's garage. He was lucky it hadn't been towed.

I drove past and kept going for a while. When I was far enough away, almost to Ukrainian Village, I parked on a side street and walked back. When I got to the car, I took out the spare key I'd gotten from Ronnie. I was about to open the door, when someone said, "Hey, that your car?"

I looked up. An old bald man wearing a Gale Sayers jersey was leaning on his chain-link fence in a yard next to the garage. He had a beer in his hand.

Assuming he was about to complain about the car being parked in front of his garage all night, and not wanting to invite a debate, I gave him a wave and tried to sound friendly as I said, "Just picking it up for a friend."

"Well, you tell your friend he can't park there," he said. "Blocking my garage."

I gave him a quick salute and climbed inside. I had the spare with me, but Ronnie's key was already in the ignition. Jesus Christ. The dumb bastard was lucky the thing hadn't been stolen.

I sped away, with the old man still glaring at me from his yard. I drove straight back to Ronnie's, pulled into his garage, and popped the trunk. Nothing.

I went inside and woke him up.

"Where's the knife and the bag?"

He stared at me, drugged and dumb, and shook his head.

"Did the detective take them? Think. Did you see him take them out of the car?"

He blinked slowly. Then he shrugged even more slowly.

Fucking idiot. It didn't matter. I could assume Owen Pall had the stuff. I could assume that he had everything. So what was he waiting on? Money? From who?

Maybe the woman who cut up Ronnie. She was the X factor in this whole situation. Why hadn't she gone to the police yet?

I paced Ronnie's den for a few minutes. I could worry about the woman later. Since I had no way of identifying her or finding her, there was no point worrying about her right now. *Set goals. Focus on what is knowable and doable.* First, I needed to clean Ronnie's car and then take a bus back over to Ukrainian Village to retrieve my truck.

Then I needed to figure out what to do about this detective, Owen Pall.

* * *

That night, I visited a dive bar on Milwaukee called Robert's. I arrived at ten o'clock, and the establishment was full. Although the place had a notorious reputation because supposedly the owner was related to someone in the mob, everyone I knew who drank there was a cop.

I found the particular cop I was looking for, Carl Whitney, slouched at the bar, smoking a cigarette and drinking Hamm's.

I sat down beside him.

"Carl Whitney, how are you?"

Whitney was thick-necked, with short gray hair and pink eyes. He glanced at me and nodded to himself, then turned back to his beer.

The bartender was an old guy in a Bears sweatshirt. I told him to get me a bottle of Hamm's. He pulled one out of the old glass door refrigerator behind him and popped the top. I paid him and had a sip.

I glanced around. Above the bar, the menu was spelled out in plastic letters on a mounted board that looked like it'd been stolen from a racetrack in the sixties. Taped to the bottom of it was a yellowed handwritten sign that read: NO SMOKING. Below *that* sign was another sign announcing cigarettes for sale. On the walls hung framed photos of mobsters and boxers. The Rat Pack. A *Goodfellas* banner. The jukebox was playing some crooner. Not Sinatra, I think, but somebody like that.

"Nice place," I said.

"On Friday nights, the fucking hipsters take over," Whitney complained. He didn't say it quietly, and he directed it over my shoulder toward two guys with porkpie hats and bowties drinking Old Style at the other end of the bar. They didn't seem to notice or care. "They come here to gawk at the wildlife in its natural habitat before they jump on their bicycles and peddle back to Wicker Park," Whitney grumbled. "Fucking idiots."

"Whole world's going down the toilet," I said.

"Fuckin A," Whitney answered.

"Can I buy you a drink?"

He glanced at me. "What do you want, Reid?"

"Just being friendly."

"Yeah, exactly. You ain't friendly, and you ain't my friend. So you come here why? To cash in your chip?"

About two years before, Whitney had slammed some gangbanger's head into a sidewalk so hard it left the kid's face permanently paralyzed on one side. Normally that wouldn't have been such a big deal, but it turned out that this particular gangbanger had a grandmother who worked in a state senator's office. She raised all kinds of hell about her grandson's rights being violated, and it eventually led to a use-of-force investigation. Since I'd been at the scene patching up some other gangbanger with four bullets in his leg, I was questioned as a witness about the incident. I'd gone on the record saying that Officer Whitney had only applied the reasonable amount of force needed to subdue the suspect. That was a lie—Whitney had drummed that guy's skull on the concrete like he was dribbling a basketball—but it helped get him cleared and reinstated for duty.

"Well," I said, "now that you mention it, I did need a favor."

Whitney raised his eyebrows and took a pull on his beer.

"You ever hear of a guy named Owen Pall?" I asked. "A private detective?"

"Sure."

"Really?"

"Sure. Everyone knows that piece of shit. He's the one who bugged Buzz Bazzano and got the poor bastard killed. You don't remember that?"

"The cop that got gunned down at the Heart O' Chicago?"

"Laying there with his dick in the carpet and his brains on the wall. Poor bastard. Why you asking about Owen Pall?"

"I think maybe he's sniffing around a friend of mine."

Whitney put down his beer and turned to really appraise me now. "Your friend named Vukov?"

"No, why?"

"Because just yesterday Owen Pall nearly fucked up a federal stakeout on a Croatian gangster named Josip Vukov. Heard about it from a couple of cops who had to pull this Vukov guy off Pall. I guess Pall was trying to put a tracker on his car and the guy caught him and just about killed him."

"Why was Pall trying to track him?"

"Oh, hell, it's probably a wife thing," Whitney said. "That's what the cops thought. This buddy of yours, he fucking around on his old lady?"

"Maybe."

"Yeah, that figures. It's about all Pall does anymore. Some of the guys think he blackmails people too. He hasn't been busted yet, but when it happens, he's going to go down hard."

"Does this Vukov guy know why Pall was trying to track him, or did he think Pall was with the cops?"

Whitney picked up his beer. "I got no idea. I just know Pall nearly fucked it up."

"Does 'nearly' mean that they busted Vukov?"

"No, they weren't looking to bust him. They were just following him to some meeting with another guy. Now they're following the other guy. I'm not privilege to the details of the case, but I don't think they're even on Vukov anymore." Whitney sipped his beer. "Still, it didn't earn Pall any points with anybody."

As soon as I stopped asking him questions, Carl Whitney sank back into whatever drunken funk he'd been in when I walked into the place. When I pushed my beer away and told him I had to go, he barely even nodded.

* * *

Driving home, I weighed the new intelligence I'd collected and came to some conclusions. Logical conclusions, it seemed to me.

First, I was in trouble, the biggest trouble I'd been in since I'd left the army. That meant I needed to make some big moves, decisive moves, and I needed to make them sooner rather than later.

According to Whitney, all Pall did was divorce work, which sounded about right. I'd bet anything that Heidi had put him on Ronnie's tail. If he was following Ronnie last night, then he must have seen something. He could've saved Ronnie from bleeding to death in the alley just to shake him down.

Ronnie was still fucked up, out of his mind on painkillers, so maybe Pall was just biding his time, waiting until he was recuperated. That's when he'd come to him with blackmail demands.

I was sure he had the knife and the body bag. He might have pictures or even video of the attack too.

That left Ronnie in a bad fix. He had no money of his own. The house belonged to Heidi. If he couldn't pay Pall, Pall could give him to the cops. And even if Pall didn't, there was no way Ronnie could go much longer without seeing a doctor. Either the doctor or Heidi was bound to report Ronnie's injuries. Every direction I thought about this thing, it seemed impossible that Ronnie would be able to get through another week without having to answer questions from the police.

And once you thought about it like that, my next move was so obvious as to be inevitable. On a practical level, Ronnie was of absolutely no use to me now. Quite the contrary, he was the biggest liability I had. He'd fucked up everything, and he'd turned himself into a walking piece of evidence. I didn't think for one second that he would keep his mouth shut if the cops pulled him in for questioning. He'd tell them it was all my idea, tell them I'd supplied him with the knife and the body bag, and he'd lead right them to my door, right down to my basement.

I would still have to figure out the best way to deal with Pall, but I knew I needed to deal with the Ronnie problem right away. The longer he was around to talk to Heidi, to Pall, to the cops, to anyone, the more danger he posed to me. I drove straight home, picked up what I needed, and then I went to go get him.

As I walked to the bus stop, I weighed whether or not I should kill Heidi and the kid as well. Heidi was the one who'd hired Pall, after all. Who knew what he'd told her? That meant the kid might know too.

I could text Heidi from Ronnie's phone, pretend to be him and have her bring the kid over to see him. Then I could kill them all and make it look like a murder-suicide.

But that was risky, far riskier than I liked. It meant an investigation, detectives, autopsies, crime scene technicians, all manner of things I'd have no control over. One fingerprint or fiber in the wrong place, and I'd be implicated.

So, looking at the situation and assessing it logically, I came to the conclusion that it made more sense for Ronnie to simply disappear.

CHAPTER

30

PAYING WITH CASH, I took the last bus of the night over to Portage Park, got off on Milwaukee and walked the rest of the way to his place, coming in the back through the alley. At midnight, the alley was empty, with an orange tint from the streetlamps. When I walked in the house, I found him lying on the couch in his living room watching *Man vs. Food*.

"We need to move you," I said.

He raised his hands to ask *Why*?

"I want to keep you away from Heidi and her detective. I went and did some checking on him. Son of a bitch does adultery work."

He just stared at me as dumb as a cow.

"She hired him to follow you, dipshit. He saw everything. He probably has pictures, video, God knows what."

His mouth opened. His hairy white belly showed between the Blackhawks T-shirt and blue shorts he was wearing. The more I looked at him, the more I hated him. I had to calm myself down because I was afraid I'd get too excited and murder him where he lay.

He grabbed his pen and paper. *That fucking bitch*, he wrote.

I shrugged. "What can you do? Let's get you up and get out of here. We need to put some distance between you and her for the time being."

He scribbled something on the pad. Just watching him write out his stupid little thoughts made me want to crack his skull open like an egg.

What will she think if I just leave? he wrote.

"Opinions are like orgasms," I said, "I don't care if a woman has one or not."

Ronnie smiled at that like an idiot.

I went and threw some of his clothes and toiletries in a bag. Just enough to make it plausible that he'd run away. "Here," I told him, handing him the bag. "Give me your cellphone. I'll carry it and your wallet. You just get some shoes on."

Once he was ready, I threw the bag over my shoulder and helped him to the door. He was moving well, still weak but able to walk on his own. I helped him to move the process along faster. We were out the door and across the yard with a minimum of fuss. Ronnie worked hard, so as not to disappoint me. He was always such a pleaser.

In no time at all I had him in the car.

"I'll lock up and be right back," I told him.

I ran back into his house. In the front den, I placed his wallet and cellphone on the coffee table. I didn't worry about prints, since my prints were all over the place anyway. But then I gently took a small plastic bag out of my jacket pocket and unzipped it. Inside was the note Ronnie had written to Heidi the day he tried to kill himself, the day I had saved his life. This I had never touched in a way to leave fingerprints, and now I carefully set it down on the coffee table next to his other things.

* * *

We got to my place about one in the morning. Mrs. Holding's light was off, which was a favorable bit of luck. I pulled into the garage and secured the door behind us.

Ronnie was already grimacing and making noises as I helped him out of the car. He gently touched the bandage on his throat.

"Hurts?" I said.

He nodded.

"I'll get you something."

I stuck my head out the door. Lights were off on either side of my place. Looked like the neighbors were in bed. Why not? People had to get up and go to work the next day.

I helped Ronnie across the backyard and up to my back door without much problem.

I unlocked the apartment and led him inside. He immediately went for the couch and laid down. He reached for the remote and turned on the television. Some family sitcom was on. A teenage girl smarting off to her befuddled father. I could hear the canned laughter as I walked into the bathroom and retrieved a couple of fentanyl from the stash I kept hidden under the sink behind the cleaning stuff.

After I got a glass of water from the kitchen, I went into the living room.

"Put out your hand," I said.

Ronnie lifted his hand, and I dropped the little blue pills in his palm. After he washed them down, I sat next to him and watched him watch television. As the shitty sitcom ground on Ronnie's eyes got a little droopy. Eventually, they shut completely. His mouth hung open. I waited about ten minutes, until he was in a deep sleep, and then I left.

I drove his car a couple of miles away and parked in a tow zone. I had a screwdriver with me and removed his license plate and scraped off the car's VIN number and the city sticker. Then I walked back home. Along the way, I ditched the license plate in a dumpster. When I got home, I moved my truck, which I'd parked out front, to the garage.

As soon as I walked in, I shook Ronnie awake. "You need more medicine," I told him.

He blinked drowsily at me and frowned, as if to ask *Already?*

"Yeah, you've been groaning and clawing at your throat. This will help you sleep through the night."

He didn't know the difference, so he washed down two more pills.

While I waited for the pills to take effect, I sat next to him and watched some other sitcom about a nerdy guy trying to work up the courage to talk to a blonde he had a crush on. At the end, the pathetic nerd got the girl.

I shut off the television and shook Ronnie awake again.

"We need to get you up," I said.

He was barely conscious, and he couldn't have spoken if he'd wanted to. His eyelids could barely open.

I knelt down, got his arm over my shoulder and lifted him up.

"C'mon," I said. "You need to help me. You're too big for me to move around like a ragdoll. You got to use your legs."

He didn't know where he was or what day it was anymore. Even if he had a voice box left to speak with, he probably wouldn't have been able to remember his own birthday, much less have the wherewithal to ask me questions. But he did whatever I told him. All he knew was that he should do whatever I told him. It's all he'd ever known, really.

I walked him over to the basement door, unlocked it, and walked him downstairs. That was an ordeal because he couldn't really judge distance anymore. But I finally got him downstairs and took him to the butcher shop. As I steadied him so I could unlock the door, he looked around, groggy eyed, at the basement's newly soundproofed walls.

"Yeah," I said. "Just finished this the other day. We could have had good times together down here, man."

He made some irritated, pained sounds.

"Almost done," I told him, unlocking the door and kicking it open wide enough to get him inside.

I turned on the light.

"Let's lean you over the sink here, man," I said. It was a sturdy, old cast-iron sink, heavy and solid, mounted to the wall in the back and standing on two legs in the front.

I leaned him over, with his head in the sink and his arms hanging over the sides. I had some rope underneath. I tied it around the legs of the sink and bound both his hands in slip knots.

Even then, he didn't fight me. As soon as his weight was resting against the sink, he just slipped into unconsciousness again. He didn't wake up until I grabbed his hair and pulled his head back. Then I took the skinning knife and slit his throat from one exterior jugular vein to the other.

Now he started bucking, his panic fighting against his drug-induced sluggishness. To hold him in place, I lay over him, my weight pressing him down into the sink, my mouth next to his ear.

"This is happening because you're stupid, Ronnie," I said, as he bucked harder and tried to scream. "Let that be your last, pathetic thought. You're dying because you were too stupid to go on living."

Finally, he bucked hard one last time, wiggled around limply for a few seconds, and stopped. His arms slumped and the ropes went slack. The last thing he saw was his blood pouring down the sink, and then he stopped seeing anything at all.

* * *

I returned to the garage and retrieved what I needed out of my truck. I had gotten four five-gallon plastic buckets with lids at Lowe's the day before. I carried them inside, used the hacksaw to decapitate Ronnie, and then dropped his head into one of the buckets. It landed at a tilt, and his face stared up at me as pale and pocked as a head of cauliflower. After I untied his hands, I used a pair of bolt cutters to snap through his wrist and elbow joints, and sawed through the rest. I dropped his hands into the bucket with his head.

* * *

It took me hours to cut up the rest of Ronnie. It was my first time out, and it was messy, but it was also instructive and I learned a lot.

I ruined the clothes I was wearing, which I really should have foreseen, but I wasn't too focused on what I wearing. I should have put down tarp, and I should have mounted a hook in the ceiling so I could have hung him up and dressed him properly. Instead, I put him on the table and slid the gore into the sink or into buckets. The saws and knives all worked fine, but my best investment turned out to be the big heavy-duty bolt cutters. They made the bone work go a lot faster. None of it was pretty, but it got the job done, and I was in a hurry anyway.

When I was finished, I had four full buckets. I'd brought in the big Rubbermaid garbage can from the garage, and I put the rest in there. The garbage can would have been large enough to transport Ronnie in his entirety, of course, but I figured it would be a lot easier to do it in pieces. I could make shorter, faster, quieter trips if I was only moving a few sections of him at a time. After I cleaned everything, I stripped down, threw my clothes in the trash can, tied down all the lids with bungee cords, and went upstairs to take a shower.

When I was good and clean, I got dressed and checked the time. A little after five AM. I drew back the curtains, no sun yet, but the sky was light blue.

I made some coffee and toast and sat down at the coffee table to eat. When I was done, I took my dishes to the sink. As I was washing them, Mrs. Holding's bell rang.

It startled me so bad I dropped the coffee cup. It hit the floor and broke into three big pieces.

Cursing her, I left the broken cup and ran upstairs to her flat. The door was open.

"What do you want this early?" I demanded.

She was out of bed, sitting in a chair by the window in her front room. She wore a beige caftan. She looked like depression itself.

"I thought I heard you up and about," she said.

"That doesn't mean you should be ringing that goddamn bell. It's five o'clock in the morning, for Christ's sake."

"Will you be able to help me today?" she asked.

"No, actually, I can't. I'm up early because I have a ton to do today. The basement is flooded, did you know that?"

"Oh, no," she exclaimed.

"Yeah, that's right. '*Oh, no.*' And I've been down there working on it. It's okay now. Don't you go down there or you'll break your goddamn neck."

"Oh, Eric, you know I couldn't get down there if I had to."

"Yeah, I know that." I turned back toward the door. "Is that all? I need to go. Like I said, I've got a lot to do. I need to take some of the stuff that was ruined in the basement to the dump."

"Oh, okay," she said. "Well, if you're back in time, you could have lunch with me, if you want."

"Yeah, I'll be sure and hurry back for that," I said and walked out.

Downstairs, I cleaned up the mess in the kitchen. Then I went to the basement, made sure all the lids were securely closed and tied down, and started hauling them upstairs. Crossing the backyard into the garage, I tried not to look around. I was just a guy hauling some shit out of his basement. No reason to look around. I had to make three trips. Two buckets the first time, two buckets the second time, and then the garbage can. After the third trip, as I was crossing the yard to go back and lock up my apartment, I looked up and saw Mrs. Holding sitting at her window. She'd been watching me the whole time.

I blew the old bitch a kiss.

CHAPTER

31

By the time I got back from Indiana, I was exhausted. The disposal process itself had gone smoothly enough, but it had all taken a lot longer than expected. I'd slipped out of Chicago and over the state line, and sunk Ronnie's earthly remains into the marshes outside of Gary. It was cold, wet, messy work. Once it was done, I changed clothes again—my third pair of clothes in the last eight hours—and drove back home, stinking of swamp water the whole way. The real pain in the ass, though, was the goddamn traffic I hit as soon as I got to Chicago. I-90 was absolutely choked in both directions, and the whole thing took two hours longer than I'd planned just because of the gridlock.

When I finally got back home, the old lady wasn't in her window. I crept into my apartment and took all my filthy clothes down to the laundry room. I had my own private basement, but Mrs. Holding and I shared the laundry room. Since she never came down here, though—because I did her washing—I could do whatever I wanted. I loaded up the washer and went back upstairs.

I took out my cellphone and texted Ronnie's phone. *Hey, man, you feeling better this AM? I'll be taking care of Mrs. Holding all day but let me know if you need anything important.* I figured I would send him another text that night, and maybe one the next day.

It didn't hurt to leave a trail of texts showing me expressing concern for my buddy.

I plugged in my phone and took a shower, scrubbing the murder and swamp off me. Then I went to bed. It was Saturday, and I hadn't had a full night's sleep since Wednesday. I threw off my towel, and I was asleep before it hit the floor.

When I woke up, it was dark already. I was hungry. I seasoned a steak in the fridge with some salt and pepper and let it sit at room temperature while I put some frozen tater tots in the oven. I waited until the tots were golden brown, and then I cooked the meat medium rare in a small stainless steel skillet. When everything was ready, I took an Old Style out of the fridge, and sat down at my coffee table and ate.

When I was done eating, I sat back, picking my teeth with the point of the steak knife, and stared at the plate, empty except for a few pink, blood-soaked crumbles of tater tots. I didn't turn on the television. Instead, I reflected on how things were going.

I'd learned a lot that day, about how to butcher a body, about how to dispose of the pieces. I could put all of those skills to use in the very near future. I could learn from my mistakes. No more long drives to Gary. I'd need to reassess my ideas about carcass disposal, maybe investigate sodium hydroxide or potassium hydroxide, and dissolve the bodies in the sink. As long as I didn't get busted by the cops anytime soon, I'd have plenty of opportunity to refine and improve my practices.

But, of course, all of that depended on staying free. I couldn't plan for this to go on forever, of course. Nothing lasts forever. Certainly, no man on his own, up against the whole damn world, can count on longevity. At some point, the cops were going to come pound on my door, and then we'd all go down in the history books together. I didn't dread that eventuality. I kind of looked forward to it. Nothing about old age appealed to me in the first place, and I sure as hell didn't plan on living out my days as an old man in a jumpsuit behind bars.

But I wanted to stay free long enough to fulfill my purpose, to do some real hunting on the streets of Chicago. And staying free meant taking care of my other problem: Owen Pall.

* * *

Sunday morning, the old lady kept ringing me, so I placated her by going up and having breakfast with her. I had to make the breakfast, of course, because as soon as I stepped into her flat, she became an instant invalid.

So I scrambled eggs and fried bacon and toasted bread while she sat at her kitchen table, yammering on about nonsense. She had nothing new to say, but she said it at length—recounting old personal resentments or horrible stuff she'd seen on television, then dismissing it all with some sentimental platitude of one kind or another. She was the kind of person who would tell you about a mother drowning her baby in a bathtub and then sum it all up by saying, "Well, at least he's at peace now, in heaven with the angels." All her stories started horrible and had a happy ending.

We sat down to eat and she droned on, talking while she chewed her food. I just thought about what I needed to do with the rest of my day. When we finished breakfast, she went to the bathroom and took out her teeth. When I was done with the dishes, I came in to tuck her into bed. As I was heading for the door, she begged me not to go.

"I have things to do," I said, pausing at the door.

"You always have things to do," she said. "What about me? I give you my home, all my money, and you're still always leaving."

I closed the door like we needed privacy. I walked back over to her bed and climbed up on the mattress, throwing my leg over her, straddling her, my knees on either side of her spilling girth, my face hovering just above her bug eyes and her stinking, toothless mouth.

"You'll get what I give you, Mrs. Holding. Look at yourself, old and infirm and forgotten by everybody who ever met you. Except me. I made your fucking breakfast, didn't I? I tucked you into your fucking bed, didn't I? Into sheets that *I* washed, in a bed that *I* made for you? If you look at it that way, I'd say you were getting a goddamn good deal. Wouldn't you?"

She nodded her big head, her big wet eyes in her paper-dry face. "Yes, please, Erik. I know all you do for me. That's why I need you, Erik. That's why I love you. You know that. I just want to show you that I love you."

I stared at her. "You want to show it?"

She swallowed. "Yes," she said.

"Then, if anyone asks, you tell them I've been here with you for the past couple of days. You understand? From Friday afternoon to this morning."

She frowned. "But why, Erik?"

I leaned down so close to her face our noses were touching. "Don't ask me why. If you want to show me that you need me, you'll do this for me. From Friday afternoon, about four, until this morning, I was with you. I didn't leave, and I didn't go anywhere."

"Yes," she said. "You were here with me." Her hand reached up to touch my side.

"Good," I said, climbing off of her.

* * *

I'd bought the fentanyl I had off of Stanislav Gotovac, a pharmacy tech at the CVS over by Saint John's Cantius Church. Stan had a system worked out where he faked inventory checks from different distributors and walked out the door with bottles of everything from generic alprazolam to hydrocodone. I'd gotten the fentanyl just in case I wanted to use some on prey. I could have swiped some of Mrs. Holding's Lunesta, of course, but I didn't want to use a drug that could be traced back to her and, by extension, me.

I found him having a smoke break by the back door of the CVS. When he looked up from his cellphone and saw me coming around the corner, he grunted and shook his head.

"The fuck you doing here, man? You want me, you need to call me. We meet somewhere else."

I waved that away. "I don't need anything like that. I'm just here to talk."

Stan had short, dark hair, but it was curly and wild and stuck out all over his head. He always looked like he'd just climbed out of bed. He glanced back at the door again. "I still don't like you being here, dude."

"I need to ask you something."

"Then ask it and get the fuck out of here."

"That Croatian gangster you used to sell to, you still sell to him?"

Stan stared at me. He lifted his cigarette and took a long, slow drag.

When he didn't say anything, I told him, "I need to speak to him."

He took another drag, staring me down like I was a narc. "How about you go fuck yourself, man? I don't sell anything to anyone." Then he dropped his cigarette and headed for the door. It slammed shut, and I was alone behind the CVS.

* * *

That night, I caught him walking down into the CTA station by his work. He had a backpack slung over one shoulder, with big noise-canceling Bose headphones covering his ears.

I tapped his shoulder. "Stan . . ."

He jumped, but when he saw me, he slipped the headphones down around his neck. "Jesus Christ, what the fuck, man? I told you to fuck off."

I followed him down into the subway, all the way to the platform. Stan stood away from the other people waiting for the next train.

"I need to speak to that guy you know," I said.

"You show up at my job talking about illegal shit. You know how suspicious that is? You wearing a wire or what?"

"Of course not. I just need to—"

"Why you need to talk to Ivo, man?"

"*Ivo*, right. Ivo. I need to see if he can get me in touch with someone."

"Who?"

"Does it matter? Do you really want to know? You told me this Ivo was in with some people. I want to know if he knows somebody specific."

"Who? C'mon, man. Don't give me that 'you don't need to know the details' shit. You want my help, I need to know what this is about."

"Josip Vukov. I want to know if your guy knows someone named Josip Vukov."

Stan shook his head and looked down the tracks into the tunnel. "And what do you want with Josip fucking Vukov?"

"You know him?"

"I asked what you want with him."

"I want to talk to him."

"Talk to him about what? Hurry up, man, my train's coming in a couple of minutes."

"I got some information about a private detective that might be following him."

"You planning on cutting me in?"

"In on what?"

"Well, you're planning to sell him this information, right? How much of that do I get?"

I stared at him. I'm always shocked by greed. I can't imagine trying so hard to hold on to the things of this world.

"I'm not going to sell him the information, Stan. I'm going to tell him about this guy just so he'll know. For me, it's more about fucking over the detective. But I'll tell you what I'll do, I'll be sure and let him know that you put me in contact with him. So he'll owe you a favor. Good enough?"

* * *

That night, about one AM, I met Josip Vukov in a parking lot behind a defunct electronics store over on W. Devon. I pulled into the lot and parked next to a silver Lexus SUV, the only vehicle around. Two men sat waiting for me. The big man in the passenger seat nodded at me to get out of my truck.

When I climbed out of my truck, he stepped out of the SUV and opened the back door.

"Let me see you leave your cellphone in your truck," he said. "Then you get in here with me."

I did as I was told and he slid into the SUV behind me and put his hands on me, patting me down. I said nothing, just lifted my arms and let him have his way around my body.

Once he was satisfied that I wasn't wearing a wire, he pulled my wallet out of my pocket. He handed my wallet to the driver of the SUV. "Take a picture of his driver's license and any other IDs you find," he told him. While the driver did just that, the big man stared at me.

I said, "Are you Vukov?"

He tapped his knuckles against his knee. "Why you want to talk to me?"

"I have some information."

He waited.

I told him, "The guy you found behind your car on Thursday, the guy you were beating the shit out of until the cops showed up? He's a private detective. Has a business called Security Solutions over on Irving Park. He was trying to put a GPS tracker on your car. He's working for your wife."

Vukov didn't react to any of this information, but he stared at my eyes while I spoke.

"How you know this?" he asked.

I didn't want to mention the cops. Instead, I said, "I've been following the detective. I've been chasing him while he's chasing you."

"Why?"

"That's my business."

He leaned closer to me. "The fuck you mean it's your business? I don't know you. What you want me to do with this information you give me? Why should I listen to you, some stranger who contacts me out of nowhere?"

I nodded at the driver in the front seat taking cellphone pictures of my identification. "Well, you know who I am now. You have all my information. But it doesn't matter. I'm just a guy who doesn't like this detective. And I thought you might like to know that he's been following you for your wife."

"You know my wife?"

"Nope."

"So what, you just want to fuck things up for this guy?"

"Yeah, that's right. That's why I'm talking to you, just to fuck things up for this guy. What you do with the information is up to you. But if I was you, I wouldn't want someone out there thinking he could plant surveillance bugs on me and follow me around and watch me and get away with it. Who knows what information he might have gotten on you already, just by accident? Who knows who he might give it to?"

The driver handed my wallet back to Vukov.

Vukov passed it to me. "So," he said, "what's this motherfucker's name?"

"Owen Pall," I said. "P-A-L-L."

CHAPTER

32

When I saw the two of them slipping out the back of Security Solutions the next day, Vukov was panting hard and his driver was carrying an aluminum baseball bat stained red with blood. Looking around, they hurried to the SUV, jumped in, and drove away.

And then everything was normal again. Traffic drifted by on Irving Park. I caught some motion in my review mirror, and I tilted it to see a woman and a little girl crossing the street about a block behind me.

I went back to staring at the detective agency's front door. I'd been sitting there, parked up the street, for a couple of hours now. I had almost been ready to leave when I'd seen Pall drive up and run inside. He'd been followed about ten minutes later by Vukov.

Now I was wondering if they'd killed him. That would be nice for me, of course, and if all the cops in Chicago really did hate Pall as much as Whitney had told me, there might not even be much of an investigation. But I couldn't take the chance. I needed to know what Pall had uncovered about Ronnie, and it seemed worth the risk to go inside and see what I could find out.

I got out of my truck. Cars stopped at the intersection when the traffic light turned red, and when the pedestrian crossing sign came on, I crossed the street, strolled up to Security Solutions, and stepped inside.

The lights were off, but the sunlight coming in from the windows illuminated the place just enough for me to see my way around. There was an office door in the back, light peeking out from underneath. I pulled some purple latex exam gloves out of my back pocket and slipped them on.

I opened the door.

Owen Pall was lying in the middle of the floor. His face was a bloody sinkhole, but his chest was still rising and his hands were twitching. Blood splattered the floor and ceiling and walls, and his respiration was ragged, but he was still alive.

The place was trashed. A computer lay on its side on the floor next to a smashed cellphone. I walked past Pall to the computer and picked it up. It had been kicked around and cracked, but it was a rugged laptop, the kind you could drop a cinder block on, and it was still working. I wondered why Vukov didn't take it, but I knew why. It was the same reason they'd left Pall alive. This beating was just a message to stay away—*far* away—from Josip Vukov and his business.

Then something caught my eye. My name on the computer screen. I sat down with the computer to do a little clicking around.

I didn't have a lot of time, of course. I needed to get out of there. But I saw enough. He had Ronnie cold, on video attacking a woman in an alley. He had the woman cold too, hiding from the police and running away.

Worst of all, though, he had me.

While I'd been sitting outside his store, he'd gone to my apartment. He'd been inside. He had video footage of my basement. The butcher shop.

It all chilled my blood to see. He'd been so close.

I tried to ignore that, to ignore the surge of adrenaline I felt. I needed to think quickly and clearly about what to do next. Take the laptop—and his cellphone too, just in case. I'd destroy them, but not before I had a good long look at all his files.

In particular, I wanted to study the one about her. Hardy, Alice; age, 40. The woman in the video. I could see what Ronnie had seen in her. One look at her, and I knew she was everything we both hated. Too bad I couldn't finish what he started . . .

Then, as if to remind me that I had other business to attend to first, Owen Pall started choking and spitting up blood.

Part IX: Monday

Owen Pall

CHAPTER 33

THE CLICKING OF the keyboard above me. The creak of my office chair.

I see nothing. When I try to move, I feel dipped in amber, sticky and hard. I cough and almost choke.

My left thumb can still move, so I use it to wipe blood out of my eyes. Only one eye works. I take a breath and my face feels like a loose jumble of disconnected pieces.

I hear footsteps, feel their vibration through the floorboards.

Erik Reid over me.

"Can you hear me, Owen?"

I try to answer, but all that comes up is another bloody wad.

"I've just been reading your notes. Very thorough stuff, man. I salute you. You've been working hard."

I shut my eyes. I feel the floor, hard and wide, expanding beneath me.

He's just above me now, his face inches away. "I wonder what you wanted out of this," he says. "Was it about money at first? Maybe you planned to sell that video to the news? You must have known that would be valuable. But then, what, something happened? You fall in love with her? Develop a conscience?" When I don't say anything, he sighs. "I guess we'll never know, will we?"

I open my one working eye.

He smiles down at me, that hateful joyous smile I've been told about. He pats my splintered chest.

"Thank you for bringing her to me," he says. "Alice Hardy. I never would have found her on my own."

He keeps talking, but I won't hear the rest of what he says. I won't hear another human word. When he's ready, he clamps his hand down on my smashed face, and I sink into the floor. What's left of my mangled assembly of broken bones and torn muscles jerks and fights for life, but he presses down harder and pushes me further into the expanding floor until I slip free of his grasp, until I'm down so far even he can't touch me. I slip away, away from him, away from the gangsters and the cops, away from the shadows and the whispers, away from this whole theater of suffering. I slip away for good and as I do I send one last message up, one final prayer, hoping she'll hear it somehow.

I'm sorry, Alice. I'm so sorry.

Part X: Monday

Alice Hardy

CHAPTER 34

When I woke up Monday morning, I was still pondering how to find my attacker and the two other men from the alley. It wasn't until I walked into the bathroom and sat down to pee that I noticed that my knee was better. The bruises had faded to a rusty yellow, and the pain was only an echo of what it had been.

After I showered and bundled my hair up in a towel, I put on my bathrobe and went downstairs and poured a cup of coffee. Greg and Tuck were both pulling on their coats and grabbing their bags.

"Hey, where's everybody going?" I said, trying to sound cheerful.

"Work beckons," Greg said.

"What about you?" I asked, nudging my son.

He nodded out the front window at the waiting car. "Julia beckons."

I patted his back. "Ah. Well, don't keep her waiting."

He nodded and slung his backpack over his shoulder.

I gave him a quick hug. "Have a good day."

He mumbled a hasty "You too" and hurried out the door to his girlfriend. I poked my head out after him as Tuck skipped down the steps. Julia sat in her car, tapping on her phone, and didn't look up.

I asked Greg, "Think they'll keep dating when they go off to different schools?"

He watched our son climb into the car and then watched it drive down the street before he answered, "Chances are, they'll date long distance for a while, get bored with it, and break up."

I turned to him. "You're such a romantic, Greg."

He shrugged and checked the contents of his bag to make sure he had everything before he left. "You didn't ask me for a love poem, you asked me what I thought. What do you think?"

I blew on my coffee, had a sip, and said, "I think they'll date long distance for a while, get bored with it, and break up."

"See?"

I smiled. "Okay, but can I have the love poem now?"

He grinned and checked the time on his phone. "Sadly, I gotta go. The poem will have to wait until later."

As he drove away, I took my phone out of my robe's pocket and scrolled through the local news. As usual, there was nothing. No man with his throat cut. If the other two men that Glen Samuels saw were friends of my attacker, then they must have been able to get him some kind of emergency medical care without it being reported to the police.

I ran upstairs and got ready for work, then I had a light breakfast—just some more coffee with toast and fruit, but at least I finally had my appetite back—and hurried out the door. On the way to school, I kept thinking about the night of the attack. I was certain that I cut his throat. It was so serious, he'd collapsed at my feet, his hands on his throat. I thought he was going to die right there in front of me.

Maybe he did? What if the other man in the alley, the one in the car, picked up his dead body and took it somewhere?

At work, I parked and walked to my Semiotics and Biblical Interpretation class. I felt steadier than I'd been on Friday, both physically and mentally. For the time being, I put the questions about my attack on a shelf in the back of my mind, and I focused on the job in front of me, which was teaching my class. With that mindset, I strolled into my classroom, said hello to my students, and proceeded discuss the Gospel of Mark with them for the next fifty minutes. By the time the class ended, all things considered, I was feeling more like myself than I had in days.

As students dispersed and I gathered my things, a girl named Brianna Kizmya walked up to my desk.

"Professor Hardy," she said, "could I talk to you?"

She was a tall girl with stooped shoulders, her poor posture compensating for her awkward height, who usually showed up late to class in a bulky winter coat thrown over a T-shirt and sweatpants. She'd failed most of the daily quizzes, struggled all semester to keep up with the readings, and had contributed absolutely nothing to our classroom discussions. I was certain I knew what she wanted to talk about.

"Sure, Brianna," I said, adjusting my bag.

"I came to see you during your office hours on Friday, but you weren't there."

The day I'd left early to go see Jason. Damn.

"I'm sorry about that," I said. "I had a family emergency. I meant to email everyone to tell them I wouldn't be there, but I must have forgotten."

"You have your office hours now, though, right? Could we talk now?"

"Sure," I said.

We walked over to my office in silence. I tried to make small talk, ask her how she was doing, but she only muttered half-formed replies. When we got to my office, I unlocked the door and gestured her to a chair.

We sat down and I asked her, "So, what can I do for you, Brianna?"

It was a wide opening, and I hoped she'd dive right through it. Since she had never evinced any interest in the subject matter of our class, I assumed this meeting was going to be about the only other thing students ever cared about: their grade. I hated waiting for the inevitable plea for mercy.

She took a deep breath. She didn't look at me.

"I don't know . . ." she began. "I don't know who to talk to."

I stared at her. Or, rather, I stared at her forehead as she stared at the office carpet.

"Is something wrong?" I said.

"Kind of. Yeah. Yeah, something is wrong."

As she lifted her head and tried, with great visible effort, to rally her strength, I looked at her smooth young face. She wore no makeup, and her bottom lip was chapped. She sucked it into her teeth and gnawed on it. Her brown eyes darted up and caught my gaze, and she released her lip.

"Brianna," I said, "dear, do you want to tell me what's wrong? I feel like this isn't about your grade in class."

"Yeah, I'm sorry about my grade in class," she said in a rush. "You must think I'm a real dumbass. Or just lazy."

I waved that away. "If there's something more important that you want to tell me, I don't care about the class," I said. I leaned forward, my elbows on the corner of my desk. "If you'd be more comfortable talking to someone else, a counselor maybe, we have good people on campus. I'm happy to—"

"No," she said, drawing another fortifying breath, "I wanted to tell someone I know. I can't talk to my friends from my high school, from my neighborhood, because everyone knows each other. And I don't really have any friends here yet. And my parents . . ." She shrugged. "I wanted to tell you that something happened over Christmas break. I was hanging out with this guy I knew from high school. We were drinking."

Suddenly, sensing what was coming, I felt something collapse inside me, some inner fortification of repression. I thought I'd burst out crying in front of this poor girl before she could finish unburdening her soul to me—to *me*, a virtual stranger to her, really.

"I was flirting with him," she said, "and I guess he got the wrong idea."

"You're not responsible for the ideas other people get," I said. "You're certainly not responsible for the actions of anyone else."

She pulled at a loose thread on her coat. "I know. But he got the ideas he got, and before I knew it he was on me. I said no, but I was trying to laugh it off, you know, like it was silly. Because at first it was like we were just messing around. But he didn't stop. And by then I just thought I should go along. So I did. But after I did . . . something was different. I don't know how to explain it."

I leaned closer. "I'm so sorry, Brianna."

Without looking at me, she waved away my sympathy as if she were turning down another helping of ice cream, something that wasn't good for her. "It's not a big deal. I'm being stupid. I've had sex before."

"That's not the point. The sex isn't the point. The fact that you didn't want to do it is the point."

She chewed her lip some more. "Since then, I've felt weird. You know? It's like I . . . it's like I got locked out of my house that night, and I can't get back inside."

I felt myself swallow. I wanted to tell her, this poor nineteen-year-old girl, what had happened to me. I wanted to both confess my sins and lay bare my trauma like she was a priest and a shrink rolled into one.

Instead, I drew my own deep breath, and then I told her that we should walk over to the counselor so that she could talk to someone who was trained to deal with a problem of this kind. I told her that she wasn't alone. I told her that there was help. I said all the stuff, I guess, that you're supposed to say.

Then I walked her over to the university's wellness center and got her an appointment to talk to a counselor. We got lucky. There was a slot open in fifteen minutes.

I sat down to wait with her. The silence was awkward. We didn't have much to say to each other. While Brianna looked at her phone, I noticed the girl at the front desk doing some paperwork, and something suddenly occurred to me.

I turned to Brianna. "I need to tell you something, Brianna."

She looked up at me. "Okay."

"Do you know what a 'mandated reporter' is?"

"I'm not sure."

"It means that if a student tells me they're in serious distress or that a crime may have been committed, I'm legally mandated to inform someone."

Her smooth brow furrowed. "Like the police?"

"No, like people at the school. I have to file a report with the Center for Student Assistance. It's called a personal concerns report." I leaned closer to her, stared right into her eyes. "You're not in trouble in any way. The report does not go on your transcript. It's not a negative thing at all. It's just a way to make sure you get the assistance you need."

She avoided my eyes and looked down at her hands. "Do you have to do that? I'd rather not get the whole school involved."

"Yes, I'm sorry, I do. But, really, I promise it will be fine. It's confidential. A case manager will reach out to you, probably within twenty-four hours of me filing the report. Just to make sure that you're doing what you're doing right now, talking to someone who can help you."

The counselor came out and called Brianna's name.

She stood up.

I told her, "Everything will be okay."

She turned to me. "I'm sorry I bothered you with this. Thank you for trying to help me, though."

"It was no bother at all. I'm glad you talked to me. If you'd like to talk again, at any point, just let me know. Okay?"

She nodded at that, barely, and turned to go.

I stood up. "Brianna?"

She turned around. "Yeah?"

"Can I ask you something? Why me? Why did you pick me to talk to?"

She shrugged. "I don't know," she said. "I guess because you're the only professor I have this semester who isn't a guy."

CHAPTER

35

St. Ignatius sits on the shore of Lake Michigan, and after I left Brianna, I wandered over to the shoreline. The sun was out, and I had to squint against the white sheen reflecting off the water. Since I'm from the sandhills of western Nebraska originally, I wasn't prepared for the size of the Great Lakes when I first saw them. Where I'm from, a lake is something you can see across. Lake Michigan, by contrast, looks like an ocean, with incessant waves lapping the shore and a horizon that stretches to the sky. Since it does such a good imitation of an ocean, most people treat it like one. It has sandy beaches, sunbathers, surfers. In a kind of mass delusion, everyone here sort of pretends it is the ocean. As mass delusions go, it's a nice one.

As I stood there on the walkway following the shoreline along the edge of campus, a couple of tattooed girls in tank tops and shorts strolled by holding hands. A shirtless guy on a bicycle coasted by in the opposite direction, bobbing his head to the beat of "Blinding Lights" wafting up from the cellphone sticking out of his pocket.

It was a beautiful day, the warmest day of spring so far, and it seemed to promise warmer days to come.

I thought I might cry.

Without knowing what she was doing, Brianna, the poor kid, had turned a mirror on me. I'd seen myself in full for the first time since the attack. For the first time, I could see what I'd done. I thought I might choke on my own hypocrisy.

I'd let him get away. Yes, maybe he was dead, but maybe he wasn't. For all I knew, he was somewhere recuperating, getting better, getting stronger every day. For all I knew, he and his friends were already out there, doing it again, preying on other women.

I'd been trying to protect my family by keeping the attack a secret. I was trying to protect myself. I didn't want my husband to divorce me. And I *desperately* didn't want my son to hate me. I didn't want my friends and colleagues to gossip about me, and I didn't want my life reduced to a story on the news. I thought I could simply bear it all myself.

What I saw now, with absolute clarity, was that I could not bear it all myself. It wasn't mine to bear alone, and it never was, not if there was any chance he could attack someone else.

Brianna, a teenage girl who barely knew me, had gathered her strength and come to me to reveal a secret that was drowning her in shame. And what was I doing? I was hiding in the library stacks, reviewing my notes. Hiding, while my attacker was still out there.

My hair was blowing in the cool winds coming off the water. I gathered it together, twisted it into a rope and pressed it to my chest.

I took a long, deep breath. If that man out there attacked another woman, raped her, hurt her, or worse, while I placated myself with fantasies of *maybe* finding him . . .

I let go of my hair.

I was about to blow up my life. How odd to realize so clearly. I'd had a similar moment of clarity the first time I'd ever gone over to Jason's apartment. I'd known right then what I was doing. *I'm about to fuck this guy*, I'd thought. *I'm about to cheat on Greg.* But I'd plunged ahead, turned on by that very lucidity.

This was worse, much worse. I didn't know what would happen with Greg and Tuck, much less with the police and the press and the people at work. But I had spent the last few days living as if I'd already died, as if I'd been killed in that alley. It was time to step out of the shadows, no matter what followed me into the light.

CHAPTER

36

When I saw Greg's car pull up, I walked upstairs. I wanted to talk to him alone before Tuck got home, and I didn't want Tuck to walk in and find us weeping in the family den, so I went and planted myself on our bed.

I heard him come in downstairs. As I listened to his footsteps climb the stairs and waited for him to come find me, I drew in long, slow breaths.

As soon as he walked into our bedroom, before I said a word, he knew something was wrong. I don't know if I looked guilty, angry, or something else. But I must have made quite the sight to see sitting there waiting for him.

"Please sit down," I said.

He raised his chin and took in his own long, slow breath. Beneath his rumpled black blazer his beige dress shirt was untucked, which was normal when he came home from teaching. He liked to untuck it as he headed to the car at the end of his day. He still had his bag of books and papers slung over his shoulder, and he lifted the strap over his head and dropped it at the foot of the bed. Pouring himself into the chair by the window, he slowly crossed one leg over the other and stared at me.

"I have some things to tell you," I said.

His eyebrows raised. I could almost hear him think *Well, I don't like the sound of that.* But he thought better of giving it breath. He lowered his head, hands in his lap, rotating his wedding ring around his finger. "Okay," he said.

I took a breath like I was about to jump off a cliff.

"First, you need to know . . . I've been seeing someone."

He stopped messing with his ring and stared at me.

"I've been seeing someone," I said again. "Not a friend of ours. Not a colleague. No one like that. But I've been seeing him for a few months."

His eyes were blank, waiting for more, knowing there was more.

"I went to see him the other night," I said. "And something happened. That's the other thing I have to tell you. Something terrible happened."

"The night you fell down."

"Yes."

He shook his head and looked down at his hands. "What happened?"

"I was leaving his place. I was walking to my car. And I was attacked. A man with a knife pulled me into an alley. I thought he was going to kill me, Greg. The way he looked at me. He ripped my blouse, he held the knife up to my throat."

When I'd thought about the moment I'd tell my husband about the attack, I'd imagined myself crying. But when Greg looked back up at me, his face was so blank I couldn't feel anything at all. He didn't look mad, and he certainly didn't look sympathetic. He wasn't going to let any emotion out until he knew everything. He never knew how to feel about something until he knew what to think about it, and he wouldn't know what to think about it until he had all the information. If my emotions were a wind at my back, pushing me along until I harnessed them and directed them toward some useful purpose, his emotions were a place he arrived at, the solution to a problem that he'd worked his way through.

"What happened next?" he asked.

"We fought and I managed to get the knife away from him and slash his throat."

He blinked at that. "You *slashed* his throat . . ."

"He didn't die," I said. "But I thought he might. I ran back . . . I ran back to the apartment I'd just been in. When we came out to check on my attacker, he was gone. We decided not to call the police."

"'*We* decided.'"

"Yes, me and . . . and the man I've been seeing."

"Who is he?"

"Greg . . . did you hear what I said? Someone tried to kill me."

"I just find it odd that you won't speak your lover's name. Seems like if you can fuck him, and if you can make life-altering decisions with him, you should be able to say his name."

Though his voice and face hadn't changed, at least now he was angry. At least now he *knew* he was angry.

"It's Jason Brennan," I said.

He blinked several times. "The guy who retiled our kitchen. You've been banging the guy who retiled our kitchen." He nodded. Smiled an ugly smile. Cocked his head ironically. "Jesus, you and the earthy man's man type, Alice. It must go back to your hard-scrabble Nebraska roots. You know what this reminds me of, right? That Marine you were infatuated with. What was his name?"

A year after we got married, right before I got pregnant with Tuck, I'd met a Marine at the gym where I used to work out. I hadn't slept with him, but things had gotten complicated.

"Greg . . ."

"No, that's my name. What was the Marine's name?"

"Greg, what does it matter? Are you listening to me?"

He shifted in his seat, uncrossed his legs and sat up straight, his hands on his knees. "His name must matter to me. I asked for it."

"You remember his name, Greg."

"No, Alice, actually I don't. I forgot it, on purpose, because I thought it didn't matter."

I took a deep breath. "Chuck."

He nodded. "*Chuck*, right. How could I forget? Chuck. And now Jason. *Real* men. I'm enough of a sports fan to understand the appeal. No, I mean it. The physical type who's comfortable with his body. You've always been attracted to that type. You know why, right? It's because you've always been a guilty intellectual. You spend your days with your nose buried in those old books, reading about the Gnostics and the Ebionites or whatever, but there's some part of you, deep down, that's afraid you're throwing your life away. Which, by the way, you are. We all are. One way or another, we all throw our lives away. That's the thing you can't face up to."

My face turned hot. I perched on the edge of the bed and leaned forward, trying to contain my rage. "I know you're hurt. And I am *truly* sorry I hurt you. But I was *attacked*. A man *dragged* me into an alley and tried to murder me."

"But when you and Jason the Tile Guy went back, your attacker had left."

"Yes."

"And so you left. And didn't call the police."

"No."

"And you didn't tell me, either."

"No. I was in shock. I was traumatized. And I was so confused by what had happened. He tried to kill me, and I thought I'd killed him. Then he just disappeared. By the time I got home, I just wanted it all to go away. Jason. The attack. All of it."

"So why tell me this now?"

"Because . . ." I ran my fingers through my hair. "Because today I realized I can't just let it go. I need to go to the police. At first, I thought maybe the man had crawled away and died. Maybe I was even hoping he had died, so I wouldn't have to deal with it. But I've been checking the news, and there's nothing. That means he's probably still out there. I went back to where it happened, and I talked to a man who saw a car parked there. He might be able to identify my attacker. I need to tell the police what happened, so they can try and catch him. I couldn't live with myself if he did this to someone else."

The infidelity, the attack, and now this. Greg just stared at me.

I wanted to stand up and go to him. Now wasn't the moment, though. I knew that, but I stayed on the edge of the bed to be ready.

Greg said, "So what now? You just call the police? You go to the station?"

"I've been thinking about that. I don't know what kind of trouble I might get in for not reporting the attack. I think it's best to take a lawyer with us. Maybe we should talk to Ben Powell tonight before we go to the police tomorrow."

"Powell handles wills and trusts."

"Right, but maybe he can recommend someone we can talk to."

"*We*. Now it's you and me making decisions."

"Yes." I sucked my lips in. "I know I hurt—"

He grimaced like some sudden shriek had hurt his ears. "*Stop* saying that you know you hurt me. It does me no good for you to keep acknowledging that you hurt me. It's actually a way of making this about you."

I shut my mouth. Greg looked at the floor.

After some time, he said, "What about Tuck?"

I put my face in my hands, cupping my eyes with my palms. "Once we bring the police into this, I don't see how we can keep it from him. If they catch the guy, I might have to testify. I might wind up on the news. So, I think we should tell him now." I lowered my hands and lifted my face to look at him. "And I think we should tell him together."

For a while, Greg didn't reply. He just stared at me in cold fury.

Finally he said, "You want me to walk in there with you and tell my son you've been fucking the tile guy. And that you stabbed somebody in an alley and ran away without reporting it to the police. And that everyone is going to know about it now because we're all probably going to wind up on the evening news."

There was nothing to say in reply because that was exactly what I wanted him to do. I knew he'd hate me for it, and that Tuck would probably hate me for it too, but I also knew it would be better for both of them, for all of us, if we did it as a family. I was in no position to press the point, but there really was no other way. As upset as I was, I understood this one thing with perfect clarity. We would either come together as a family to get through this, or this would tear our family apart. And I wasn't going to let it tear us apart.

"I'm afraid so," I said.

"Why don't you call the tile guy, ask him to come over and hold your hand while you explain the situation to our son?"

"Greg . . ."

"Where is he? Where's *Jason*?"

"We're done. He and I are through. I promise you that."

"Nice. He fucks you and leaves, and I get to deal with the trauma and the public scandal."

I waited on him. When he'd not spoken in a while, I said, "I just want you to know, I felt so guilty the whole—"

Without a word, Greg stood up and walked out of our room. I heard him go downstairs, and then the front door opened. I got up and ran to the bedroom window in time to see his car back out of the driveway and head down the street.

Shaking my head, cursing myself, I wandered out to the hall and discovered my son trying to slip silently back into his room.

He turned and his eyes told me the story. He'd come home early. He'd heard it all.

I stepped toward him. "Tuck . . ."

Looking suddenly so very young, he was red-faced with shame, as if he'd wandered innocently into my bedroom and found me standing there naked. As he rushed back into his own room, he shook his head and waved me away, not in anger or rejection, but with a kind of terrible mortification.

"I'm sorry," he muttered, shutting his door before I could reach him.

And for a moment, I was left there in the hallway alone, dazed between the rooms of my home and swaying on my feet, not knowing where to go or what to do with myself.

CHAPTER 37

I STOOD AT HIS door.

"Tuck, we need to talk. Please, son."

His door opened. He must have been standing on the other side of it unsure of what to do with himself. Unable to look at he, he stared at the floor like he was about to be yelled at.

I suddenly felt claustrophobic in the hallway. At the same time, his room seemed suffocatingly small too. I needed to get out of the house altogether.

"Can we go outside?" I asked.

"Outside, why?"

I closed my eyes and put my hand on my throat. "Please," I said. "I need some air."

"Okay," he said.

He followed me downstairs and out to our back patio. I pulled two patio chairs side by side and sat down in one. He sat down in the other.

I tried to think of how to start, but before I could, he said, "You were attacked?"

"Yes," I said.

His Adam's apple jerked in his throat. "Are you okay?"

I shut my eyes. I reached out and took his hand, felt it in mine, and tried not to break down.

"Yes," I said.

"Where did it happen?" he asked.

"Over by Humbold Park. Walking down the sidewalk, the night you and Dad went to the game. A man pulled me into an alley."

He looked at my knee. I was wearing a long skirt so it was covered, but I put my hand on it to answer the question he hadn't asked.

"Yeah, that's how I hurt my knee. He knocked me down."

Tuck's face flushed.

"Some fucker *attacked* you . . ." he said, his voice cracking.

I gripped his hand tight.

"I'm okay, Tuck. I'm okay."

His eyes marbled with tears. "I hope he's dead. He better be dead. If he's not, Mom, I swear to God I'll fucking find him, and I'll fucking kill him."

I held on to his hand with both of mine.

The profanity, the vows of violent retribution on my behalf—I knew they were his way of handling the shock of what he was feeling, the abrupt realization that his mother could die, and not just someday, but any day, at any time, for no reason at all. My poor son.

"It's going to be okay," I told him.

"You stabbed him?"

"Yeah. I grabbed the knife he had."

He squeezed my hand when I said the word *knife*.

"But he got away?"

I nodded. "I don't know how. I guess he crawled away. Like I told your dad, that's why I need to go to the police. I should have done it last week when this happened. I'm ashamed that I didn't."

"You were scared. You were in shock. Anyone would be in shock."

I hung my head. "Yeah," I said. "But that's not why I didn't go to the police."

He drew his hand back. Not quickly, not pointedly. But he drew it back and sat with his hands in his lap.

"You didn't go to the police because you didn't want anyone to know about the other thing."

I took a deep breath. "You heard what I told your dad. About where I was, who I was with?"

"Mr. Brennan. The guy who retiled the kitchen."

I hated hearing him say Jason's name, but my heart really sank at the mention of our kitchen. All families have rooms where they naturally, habitually congregate. We'd always been a kitchen family. While I cooked—and I did most of the cooking—my boys revolved around me like satellites. Tuck digging through the fridge, picking at leftovers while he told us about the new movie he'd discovered in his film history class. Greg sitting at the kitchen table, reading something to us out of a sports column, usually something he disagreed with. And after we ate and they did the cleanup—and they did all of the cleanup—I'd lean back with a glass of wine with my feet up on a chair and watch them, father and son, rinsing dishes and loading the dishwasher. Me with my boys, my men, with their wild enthusiasms, with their fragile egos cloaked in midwestern stoicism, and I would feel truly at home.

Now that kitchen would always be the room where Jason Brennan had been. They'd remember him there in his jeans and toolbelt and his sweaty T-shirt, and they'd wonder at what I'd done there when they weren't around.

"Yes," I said. "Jason Brennan."

"Are you in love with him?"

"No."

He blinked at that. "So like . . ." he prompted me.

I wasn't sure what he wanted me to say. Like good progressive parents, Greg and I had been matter-of-fact about matters of sex, love, and procreation when Tuck was little. When he and Julia had started dating, we'd revisited the topic to encourage safe sex, much to his obvious discomfort. But my son and I had never discussed *my* sex life before. I didn't want to discuss it now, but *not* discussing it was no longer an option.

"I don't know what to say, Tuck. I want to be honest with you, but I'm not sure what to say. There's nothing much to know, really, outside of understanding that Jason—that Mr. Brennan and I had a brief relationship."

"Are you going to leave Dad?"

"No."

"Is he going to leave you?"

I swallowed. "I hope not. But it's up to him. I've hurt him, so it's really his call to make."

As if the mention of his name had summoned him, we heard the garage door, and Greg walked through the kitchen. He opened the door to the patio and stood in the doorway.

He looked at us both sitting there, our knees almost touching, and his mouth tightened. With Greg, the purest evidence of his emotions was the visible effort used to restrain them. As he moved toward me, his mouth looked tight enough to splinter his teeth.

He put a hand on my shoulder. I took it. I stood up, and he pulled me into his arms. He reached for our son and pulled him to his feet to join us. The last time the three of us had shared a hug together, I could still carry Tuck on my hip. Now Greg held us both.

"We almost lost her," he told our son, kissing my forehead. His voice broke. "We almost lost her."

CHAPTER

38

OUTSIDE OF GETTING speeding tickets, I'd never met a police officer before. Dana Schweickart was not what I expected. I'm ashamed to say that when our lawyer Ben Powell said he could bring his "cop friend" by our house to talk to us that night, for a kind of preliminary meeting before I filed an official report with the police the next day, I was expecting a man, some tall strapping pillar of law and order. Instead, Dana Schweickart was a woman, shorter and stockier than me, with blonde hair pulled back in a ponytail. She dressed like an insurance claims adjuster, in slacks and a blouse, with scuffed, sensible black shoes.

When we'd contacted Ben and explained the situation, he suggested we speak to his friend in the CPD before anyone else. Better to start with someone friendly than a complete stranger with a badge, he said. When Detective Schweickart fixed her humorless blue eyes on me, though, she didn't seem particularly friendly. She had a broad, flat face with a lipless mouth that stayed clamped shut when she wasn't speaking. Sitting at one end of the couch in my living room, a fat spiral notebook resting on her thick knee, she jotted down notes while I sat at the other end and told her everything that had happened. As I spoke, she stared at me like a builder estimating the cost of a repair.

I detailed everything that had happened in the alley, what the man had looked like, what he had said, and how our struggle had ensued. I told Detective Schweickart about hiding from the cruiser, running back into the apartment, and my decision with Jason to go check on the man in the alley. Once we discovered him missing, I told her, we decided not to notify the authorities. I ended by telling her that I went back on Sunday and talked to the neighbor, Glen Samuels, who had seen three different men and a car parked in front of his garage.

Greg, Tuck, and Ben sat around us. Ben sat in a chair that we'd brought in from the kitchen, leaning forward with his elbows on his knees, his eyes locked on me in lawyerly concentration. Greg sat in an armchair and stared at me, his brow furrowed, gently shaking his head in quiet horror as I described the attack. There had been some talk of sending our son upstairs, but Tuck insisted on staying. As I detailed what had happened to me in the alley, he sat in another kitchen chair, staring down at his hands, unable to look at the rest of us.

When I was done, Ben asked the detective, "Dana, what we need to know, first off, is whether Alice broke any laws here in not reporting the attack until now."

"I doubt it," she said in a flat voice. "Under certain circumstances you're obligated to report a crime, especially if in not reporting it you're essentially aiding and abetting the perp in the commission of the crime, but on a deal like this? There's no chance the DA's office would press failure-to-report charges against the victim in a situation like this."

"Thank God," I said.

"That's assuming your attacker didn't die from his wounds, of course. That might complicate matters."

"Right," I said. "Of course."

Detective Schweickart read over her notes and lifted her eyebrows. "I am wondering . . . You describe a pretty violent attack. Were your clothes ripped?"

Knowing where this was going, I took a breath. "Yes."

"Blouse, stockings, that sort of thing?"

"Yes. My blouse, stockings, and the skirt I was wearing."

"Any blood get on them?"

"Yes."

"May I see the clothes?"

I took another breath. "I threw them away."

I felt everyone looking at me.

The detective seemed to speak for all of them when she asked, "And why did you do that?"

"Like I said, I was . . . afraid. I know it was a stupid thing to do, but in the moment, I panicked. I just wanted to pretend that the attack had never happened. I wanted to get it as far way from me as possible."

"You threw away your clothes, with your blood and the attacker's blood?"

I nodded.

"In your garage can outside or . . ."

"Outside. The garbage was collected the next day."

She stopped looking at me so she could jot down some notes. As she did, she shook her head.

I told her, "I was just so panicked. In a state of shock. I didn't know what to do."

She looked up from her notes with the same empty stare as before, devoid of anything like pity. "What you should have done was notify Chicago Police immediately," she replied. "You should have flagged down that cruiser when you had the chance. Then we'd have the guy in custody. You wouldn't have to go through this. Police wouldn't have to go out looking for him. And since you tossed your clothes, even if they do find him, the chances of there being physical evidence left to tie him to the attack is pretty slim. You did pretty much everything you could have done to make it difficult for us to find your attacker."

Ben cleared his throat. "But just to reiterate, Dana, you don't think Alice is in any legal jeopardy regarding the, ah, the destruction of clothes?"

"Destroying evidence of a crime is more serious than a simple failure to report. That's obstruction. We're talking one to three years in prison, a $100,000 fine." Detective Schweickart registered the shock on our faces and shrugged. "But look," she continued "let's be blunt about this. The DA is not going to file charges against the victim of a violent crime, especially not a white woman from the suburbs."

I saw my son flinch at that, his face a mix of relief and disgust.

"So what do we do now?" I asked the detective, wanting to get her out of the house as soon as possible.

"Well, this happened in Central's jurisdiction. You should go down to the Detective Bureau on Wentworth and talk to Detective Andrew Kantzavelos in Violent Crimes. He's the one you'll want to speak to, if you can. I'll call him and let him know you're coming." She spelled out his last name quickly, as if she had it memorized.

I held up my empty hands, already overwhelmed with details. "I should . . . I should write all this down."

"I've got it, Alice," Greg said. He had his phone in his hand, taking notes on his Notes app.

Detective Schweickart read over her notes and tapped the page with her pen.

"Well, Doctor Hardy, I think that's about it. I'll pass this information on to Detective Kantzavelos. Is there anything else you can think of before I go?"

"No, I think that's all."

Detective Schweickart stared at me a moment. Then she glanced at Tuck, who was grimacing down at his hands again. She turned back to me.

"May I have a glass of water?" she asked me.

"A glass of . . . Sure. Tuck, buddy, would you go get the detective a glass of water?"

He rubbed the back of his neck. "Sure," he said.

The detective watched him leave, and when he was out of the room, she leaned closer to me and said, "This friend you were seeing over by Humboldt Park, we'll probably want to talk to him too."

"Oh. Uh, sure. His name is Brennan, Jason Brennan." I cleared my throat and gave her his phone number. I glanced at Greg, who was looking at the floor.

The detective jotted down the name and number and clicked her pen closed. "Okay," she said, "that should do it."

Tuck came back in and handed her the water. She set it down on the coffee table without drinking any and stood up.

"I think I have all I need, Doctor Hardy. I'll give Kantzavelos a call and let him know that you're coming his way. I'd suggest you call him first thing in the morning to arrange a time to come in and sit down for an interview. He'll probably want you to look at pictures. If the sketch artist is there, Kantzavelos may ask you to talk to him as well. We're down to one sketch guy in the whole department, though, and he floats between stations, so you may have to make a separate appointment to see him."

I felt a bit overwhelmed at the thought of talking to one or two or possibly more police officers, but I stood up and extended my hand. "Thank you for coming by, Detective Schweickart. I appreciate you taking the time to come talk to us. You've been very helpful."

Her handshake was one quick, hard jerk. "Good luck, Doctor Hardy." She stepped over and gave the same terse handshake to both Greg and Tuck. Then she turned to Ben. "Now, mister, you owe me a steak dinner."

"Indeed I do, my dear," he said with a smile.

Greg and I walked them to the door. The detective headed for Ben's car, but Ben paused before he stepped outside. "Dana will reach out to Kantzavelos tonight. Let me know how it goes when you talk to him in the morning."

After they'd driven away, I felt a little dizzy. I couldn't really remember anything the police detective had told me. I just remembered her tight, judgmental mouth as she listened to my story and scratched down her notes. I slumped down on the couch with my hands steepled against my lips.

Tuck and Greg sat down on either side of me.

"You okay?" Greg asked.

I raised my eyebrows.

"She was rather rude," he said.

I shrugged. "That's what I'm in for, I guess."

Tuck looked away from both of us. "Only bougie white people expect the police to be nice."

Greg said, "Well, son, I don't know how to break this to you, but we are bougie white people."

Tuck stood up. "I'm going to bed."

I reached for his hand. "You okay, buddy?"

"No," he said, pulling away. "Not really. This is all so fucked up."

"Son . . ." Greg began, but Tuck was already headed upstairs.

"Let him go," I said. "He's just upset, lashing out. Give him space. He needs to process this."

Greg rubbed his face. "Don't we all." He dropped his hands and looked at me.

I just stared back at him.

He shook his head.

"How about you?" I asked. "How are you doing?"

He had to think about that, like he always did, as if his emotions were a bank account that he needed to check.

"I'm mad at you," he decided.

I nodded.

"You hurt me."

"I know. I'm sorry, Greg. I really am so sorry."

He nodded. "Yeah. I know." Sighing, he said, "Right now, tonight, frankly I'm more relieved that you're okay." He stood up. "Jesus, I am exhausted. I'm sure you must be too. Let's go to bed?"

"I'll be up in a bit? I need to just sit here and be quiet for a few minutes."

He nodded. He didn't kiss me goodnight, but he patted my shoulder. I touched his hand, and he walked away.

* * *

As my men settled in upstairs, I sat on the couch and felt the room spin. Part of it was relief. So much weight had been taken off of me, I was thrown off balance. But I still dreaded what was coming. Tomorrow, I would call that police detective, whatever his name was. I'd have to go in, look at photographs of violent men—rapists, thieves, killers. I'd have to talk to more police officers, detail the attack, explain that I didn't stop the police cruiser when I had the chance because I wanted to hide the fact I was cheating on my husband. I'd have to be up front about destroying evidence. I'd be condescended to. Maybe I'd get more lectures about what I should have done.

I stood up and carried Detective Schweickart's glass of water into the kitchen. I poured out the water and loaded the glass into the dishwasher.

I checked the locks on the windows and the doors, and I reset the alarm. Greg had already set it, but since the night of the attack, I'd needed to reset the alarm myself two or three times before I could go to bed.

I climbed the stairs to go up to my bed and listened for sounds behind Tuck's bedroom door, particularly the telltale signs of whispering that meant that he was on WhatsApp with Julia. Instead, I heard a gentle movie score and the sound of Japanese dialog.

I smiled. He'd gone through most of Kurosawa and Suzuki already. His current passion was Ozu. I could picture my son on his bed, iPad propped up on his chest, watching a movie on the Criterion app, his face aglow in the darkness. I touched his door with my hand as gently as I'd caress a burn, and then I left him to his movie.

Greg was already asleep in our bed. He wasn't pretending either. He'd simply undressed, slipped beneath the sheets and passed out, exhausted from the emotional labor of the last six or seven hours.

I got ready for bed as quietly as possible and then slid in beside him.

The house was quiet, my son with his movies, my husband with his dreams. I closed my eyes and tried not to think too long on what tomorrow might bring.

And I didn't. Before I realized what was happening, I'd slipped off, silently and peacefully, into sleep.

That night, for the first time in a long while, I had no nightmares.

Part XI: Monday–Tuesday

Erik Reid

CHAPTER

39

I DON'T THINK ANYONE noticed me leaving Security Solutions, but given what I had found on Pall's laptop, I wasn't sure of anything anymore. You never knew who was watching. I got out of there in a hurry, carrying his laptop, with his cellphone, thumb drives, and an external hard drive shoved into my pockets. When I got home, I checked all my locks and seals. I could see where someone—Pall, of course—had come in while I was gone. I went down into the basement and set up his computer.

I spent the rest of Monday night looking over all the material he'd gathered. When I was done, I walked upstairs, changed for bed, and got some sleep.

The next morning, I was getting dressed when the front door buzzed. I picked up the Mossberg and went into the front room to peer through the window curtains.

There were two plainclothes cops outside. I knew they were cops even before I spotted the badges and guns clipped to their belts. I knew the type.

I stuck the Mossberg under the cushion on the armchair where I could grab it if the situation escalated. Then I walked out to the foyer and opened the front door.

The police detectives were both middle-aged guys in crisp blue shirts and dark slacks. One guy was taller and more fit. His partner was darker, shorter and softer.

Once they had my name, the taller guy introduced himself. "Detective Heller." He nodded at his partner. "This is Detective Alvarez. You work with Ronnie Dunlap?"

"Oh, Jesus," I said. "What did he do?"

"Is he here?"

"Here? No."

"Can we come in for a moment to talk?" Heller asked.

"Yeah, sure," I said. I showed them inside to my apartment. They walked in slowly, casual but still silently checking their corners. Then we all stood awkwardly in my den, a few feet from the door.

While Heller asked, "When was the last time you saw Mr. Dunlap?" his partner tilted his head to glance into my bedroom.

"Last time I saw him?" I said. "I don't know. Friday afternoon, about three? He was fucked up. Someone cut his throat Thursday night. Is that what this is about?" I looked back and forth between them. "C'mon, guys. Tell me. Did something happen?"

"His wife found a handwritten message from him at their house early this morning. Sure looks like a suicide note. He also left his cellphone and his wallet behind with it. No sign of him or his car."

"Oh, Jesus, no," I said. I shook my head. "He finally did it . . ."

"His wife said he has a history of suicidal attempts. Said you were present for one."

"Yeah. A few months ago. He took some pills."

"He leave a note that time?"

"Not that I know of. Seemed spur of the moment to me. Like he just spiraled one night and tried to . . . you know. Tried to end it."

Heller looked at his notes. "This wound to his throat, that was Thursday night?"

"That's right. Insane. I asked him about it, you know, but he wouldn't tell me shit. Just said it was an accident and he didn't want to discuss it."

"Did the wound appear to be self-inflicted?"

"Well, that's what it looked like to me. Besides, what the hell does 'I had an accident' mean? So, yeah, I figured he'd done it himself." I shook my head. "I think some guy found him in an alley and brought him home that night. You'd have to ask Heidi about that. I didn't catch the guy's name. And I'm not sure why she didn't take Ronnie to the hospital."

"You didn't think to take him yourself?"

"Well, I mean, I *told* them both that he should go to the hospital to get it looked at, but Ronnie's a grown man. Heidi's his wife. Who am I? It's up to them to make those kinds of decisions. I can't make Ronnie do anything he doesn't want to do. The wound had already been cleaned and dressed, so I didn't think he was in any immediate danger."

"You haven't gone back to check in on him since then? Since Friday?"

"Oh, I texted him a couple of times over the weekend, checking in. Didn't hear back from him, but that's just Ronnie. Like I said, he was kinda cryptic. I was thinking I'd pop over there today."

"You know his wife had left him?" Alvarez asked. It was the first time he'd spoken, and his voice was so loud it almost startled me.

"Yeah. I saw her leave."

"You know why she left?" Heller asked.

"Not really."

"You didn't ask Ronnie?"

"Sure, but he didn't want to talk about that either."

"You ever know Ronnie to be violent? Toward her or toward anyone else?"

"No."

"He ever tell you what kind of stuff he liked to look at on the internet?"

"The internet? No, why?"

"She said he liked to look at some pretty disturbing stuff."

I shrugged. "We never discussed that kind of thing. We mostly talked about work."

"Why didn't you stay with him?" Alvarez asked. His voice was just as loud and blunt as before. "He's hurt, his wife leaves, why didn't you stay with him?"

"Well, look, he's my buddy, but I'm not his mother. We don't even work together anymore. I have responsibilities other than babysitting Ronnie. I'm the caretaker for Mrs. Holding, the old lady upstairs. I have to stick around here most of the time. So, you know, I made sure Ronnie was okay, that he had soup and stuff to drink, and I told him to text me if he needed anything. I was worried about him, but I got other things on my plate."

"So, you were here with the old lady upstairs all weekend?" Heller asked.

"Yeah, pretty much. You know I ran out to the store or whatever, but, yeah, I was mostly here taking care of her. Why is that important?"

Heller shrugged like it was no big deal. "Just trying to establish who last saw Mr. Dunlap and when they last saw him." I couldn't tell if the *it's no big deal* attitude was sincere or a technique for putting the interviewee at ease. He added, "Is she home now, the lady upstairs?"

"Sure. She never leaves."

Heller turned to Alvarez. "You want to go talk to her?"

The other cop just nodded and headed for the door. Watching him leave, I asked Heller, "Why do you guys need to talk to Mrs. Holding? She doesn't know anything about Ronnie."

Heller gave me another no big deal shrug. "Just dotting the i's and crossing the t's."

I tried to appear unperturbed by that. I switched to being the worried friend. "Poor Ronnie," I said sadly. "Poor dumb bastard."

We listened to Alvarez climb the foyer stairs and knock at Mrs. Holding's apartment. Through the ceiling, we could hear her plodding across her floor to answer the door, followed by the muffled sound of her discussion with the cop slowly going back and forth. He wasn't as loud with her as he was with me.

Heller asked me, "So you and Mr. Dunlap were partners on which ambulance?"

"Ambulance 43. Engine company 83. Over on Wilson."

Heller glanced at his notes. "But you're not there anymore, is that right? Mrs. Dunlap said you quit recently?"

"That's right."

"Any reason you quit before you got to retirement age?"

"It just got to be too much, man. Too much shit."

"Hey, I hear you," he said.

"That's the thing. Me and Ronnie, we were both burned out on the job. I quit and went to work for Mrs. Holding. Sort of her full-time caretaker. It's a pretty sweet deal. Nice and quiet most of the time. I know Ronnie wanted to quit the ambulance too, but he doesn't have a situation like mine to fall back on. Plus, he's got the wife and kid. He's kind of stuck where he is."

Heller nodded and consulted his notes. "This throat wound," he said. "Someone patched up, according to his wife."

"Yeah. It was a real professional job too. The sutures were tight but not too tight. The wound had been cleaned and irrigated. So he must have seen a doctor *somewhere*." I watched the cop write that down. "You might want to talk to the guy that found him."

Heller raised his eyebrows. "Yeah, we're checking on that. Owen Pall. You know him?"

"Just met him for a couple of minutes on Friday when I saw him with Heidi."

"Well, between you and me, he's kind of a known lowlife. Real sleazy. Did 'detective' work, if you want to call it that. Specialized in cheating spouses. Mrs. Dunlap hired him to follow her husband. Looks to me like Pall followed your partner, saw him either get hurt or saw him hurt himself, got him fixed up, and brought him home. Now, exactly how he planned to make a dollar off of that, we don't know. But he and Ronnie were trying to keep something secret."

"Well, if you don't mind me asking, what does Pall say about all of this?"

"Nothing. He's dead."

I stared at him.

"What do you mean?" I said, finally.

"Found dead at his shop last night. He had a little 'museum of detection' at his place. Some couple came in on a lark to see it and found him."

I did my best to look shocked. "Jesus Christ, how did he die?"

"Bludgeoned to death. You think Ronnie could have had something to do with it? You said he could get up and move around."

"Ronnie? No, I don't think so. He could get up and move around, but he was too weak to get into a fight, much less to win a fight."

As he recorded my impression of Ronnie's physical state, I asked, "You really think Ronnie had something to do with it?"

Heller raised his eyebrows. "For him to leave a suicide note and disappear on the same weekend that this guy Pall gets killed—the same guy who found him with his throat cut in an alley—that's one hell of a weird coincidence. Too big of a coincidence not to look into."

"Sure, I understand."

"But look," he added, "I know Ronnie is your boy and you're worried about him, so I'll just say that given the nature of the crime scene over there, and the nature of Pall's work, there are other persons of interest worth talking to."

"Yeah?"

Heller leaned in closer to me, as if to confide a secret. "Alvarez and I aren't at liberty to really talk about it. Pall is someone else's case. *But* let's just say, your partner isn't the only one Owen Pall's been following around."

"No kidding?"

Heller raised his eyebrows again.

Alvarez came back downstairs. Heller stepped out to confer with him in the foyer for a moment. Then they came back.

"Well, thank you for talking with us," Heller said, handing me a card. It had his name, desk and mobile numbers, and his email. "We're sorry to show up here with news like this. I really hope your partner is okay. Obviously, if you hear from him, or if you think of anything that might help us, let us know."

I assured them that I would, and then I shook hands with them both and showed them to the door.

CHAPTER

40

As soon as the cops were gone, I went downstairs and disassembled Pall's laptop. I needed to get everything of his as far away from me as possible, as soon as possible. I'd already reviewed what he had, and the son of a bitch had it all. He had video, good video, of Ronnie's attack on the woman in the alley. And he had information on all of us. Ronnie. The woman. And me.

His notes on me were even more detailed than the notes on Ronnie. He'd seen my discharge papers or talked to someone who had. He'd talked to Rusnok. He'd talked to my fucking stepmother. It was quite the psychological profile.

And, of course, he'd been in my apartment. I would have felt violated if I hadn't already killed him.

I filled up the sink and submerged all his devices. After they were good and ruined, I pulled them out and pried them apart with a hammer and screwdriver. The rugged laptop was a bitch, but I got it disassembled eventually. When everything was broken, I hauled the pieces to a dumpster behind a taco place a mile away and ditched them.

I knew, of course, that Pall could have everything backed up on some cloud somewhere, but there was nothing I could do about that. I also knew from his notes that he'd scooped up the knife and body bag from the car, and since I'd seen a safe in his office, I suspected that that's where he'd stashed them, along with the woman's torn blouse, the one she'd tried to throw away. Wasn't much I could do about any of that either. I'd eliminated both Ronnie and Pall, and I'd disposed of all the evidence and background research that I could get my hands on that could tie either one of them to me or to what had happened in the alley. What happened when the cops popped Pall's safe was out of my hands.

After I disposed of Pall's devices, I checked the tow zone where I'd left Ronnie's car. As I expected, it was gone, hauled away and sucked into the scrap yards where all such anonymous cars went to die. Good old Chicago. The buses might not run on time and the politicians might all be liars, but the goddamn tow trucks always do their job.

As I drove back home, I thought back over my conversation with the cops. So far, the story was holding. Ronnie was a suicide. He'd left a note and disappeared. The throat wound only helped feed that story, as did the previous suicide attempt.

I couldn't be sure if the story about Pall would hold as quite as well. Everything pointed to Vukov, and while Vukov would deny any involvement, if the cops got him into a tight enough corner, he could point them right at me, tell them that I was the one who led him to Pall. If that happened, I basically had only one card left to play: I could point the finger right back at the cops—tell them that yes, I had wanted to get Pall the sleazy divorce detective off my buddy's back, sure, but where had I gotten Vukov's name from in the first place? I'd gotten it from my good buddy, Chicago Police officer Carl Whitney. I was betting the cops wouldn't really pursue the murder of a deadbeat like Owen Pall, someone they already didn't like, if the case was going to point back at them.

Of course, if that gambit didn't work, and if they came to get me anyway, then I'd pull out the Mossberg and we could all figure it out together. Some part of me was excited at that prospect, of dying in a shootout with the cops, but we'd have to wait and see how the investigation panned out.

When I got home, I opened a beer and carried it to the couch. I realized that I'd never felt better in my life.

I should celebrate . . .

I thought about that woman in the alley.

Alice Hardy, a professor at St. Ignatius. Pall had collected a lot of information on her. Married with a husband, a son, and a house in Evanston. He'd saved some screenshots of her. A picture from the university website showed a middle-aged woman with long, straight hair, dressed in a pantsuit with her arms crossed, trying to look smart and professional. Apparently, she'd been sleeping with some guy named Jason Brennan when Ronnie jumped her. I gathered that's why she'd try to cover up what had happened in the alley. Doing anything to try and keep up appearances, a feminine trait if ever there was one.

What happened if she decided she didn't want to keep her secret anymore? The disappearance and suicide of a firefighter who'd been called a "Chicago hero" by the mayor not long ago was definitely going to rate some news coverage. What happened if she saw Ronnie's picture on the six o'clock news tonight, recognized him, and decided to come clean? You can't trust a woman to stay consistent. There was also that bloodstained blouse in Pall's safe. Maybe it could be traced to her.

I laughed at myself. I was just trying to justify my urge. I wasn't really scared of her. Hell, if she found out Ronnie was dead, maybe she'd be happy. Maybe she'd continue to keep her mouth shut. And if she didn't? So what? Even if she talked, or even if the stuff in Pall's safe tied her to Ronnie, none of it implicated me. I looked at it from every angle I could think of, and when I did, I didn't think any of it could lead back to me.

So why did I still have an irresistible urge to go kill Alice Hardy? Was it that I had come so close to having her the night Ronnie grabbed her in the alley? Was it that there might still be some miniscule chance she could tell the cops *something* that would cause them think he had a partner? Maybe. Or maybe I just didn't like her face. Maybe she was just the kind of smug woman that I hate the most.

Who knows? Maybe the answer was what they'd always said about me in school and in the army. Maybe I just lack proper impulse control. Maybe all my urges are irresistible.

All I knew was that my basement hadn't been put to its proper use yet. Ronnie had just been a trial run.

I'd built it for someone exactly like Alice Hardy.

CHAPTER 41

When I had everything ready in the basement, I headed upstairs and grabbed the keys to the truck. I was about to walk out the back door when the old woman buzzed me. I'd been so busy with everything else, I'd forgotten about her. She was easy to forget. As much as I wanted to just ignore her, though, I needed to talk to her and see what she'd said to the cops. Besides, I reasoned, I would need to knock her out if I was going bring Alice Hardy into my flat without being seen. I'd need to talk the old woman into taking a nap, slip her a couple of Lunesta, and be on my way.

I ran upstairs.

When I came in, I started to tell her, "Hey, I'm going to be busy later, but—"

"I need to talk to you," she said. She stood in her doorway, looking more worried than I'd ever seen her. "About what's been going on around here."

I sighed. As soon as she said it, I realized that I'd probably have to kill her too. It hadn't really been part of the plan—at least it wasn't part of the short-term plan—but now it seemed unavoidable. The question was *when*. I'd have to ponder that.

"Okay," I said. I came inside and shut the apartment door behind me. "Why not? Let's talk."

She nodded at that and walked into the kitchen. I followed her.

"What are you doing?" I asked.

"I was about to have some coffee," she said. "I'll make you some, and we'll talk. God, you know, we haven't sat and had coffee in so long. We used to do it all the time, when you first moved in."

"I told you I've been busy," I said.

"I know, Erik," she said, pouring herself a cup. "But if you want me to keep lying to the police for you, then maybe we should sit down and talk."

She turned around and held her chin up, and I just stared at her big watery eyes for a moment. I couldn't bring myself to feel sorry for her, of course, but there was *almost* something sad about watching someone so helpless try to be brave, try to take charge. *Maybe*, I thought, *I should just go ahead and kill her now*.

But I stopped myself. Now wasn't the time. I had too much to do first. Besides, I still needed to know what she told the police.

I walked in and sat down at her kitchen table.

With my most understanding smile, I said, "Okay, let's sit calmly and talk, Mrs. Holding."

She poured me a cup of coffee and set it in front of me like we were an old married couple.

"Just the way you like it," she said, smiling nervously. Two seconds ago, she was trying to be tough, now she was trying to be sweet.

I sipped some of the shitty coffee and told her it was good.

"It's been so long since we sat and had coffee together," she said.

"You said that already," I told her.

"I guess I did," she said.

"So, what happened with the cop?"

"He asked me about your friend."

"Ronnie."

"Yes," she said. "He asked me if I'd seen him. Did something happen to him?"

I drank my coffee. It really was awful, even by her standards. "I don't know," I said. "I haven't seen him in a few days."

"Oh."

"What did you tell the cop?"

"Just what you told me to tell him. That you were with me all weekend."

"Good. Because I was."

She said nothing to that. I nodded. Good.

"Anything else?" I said.

"Oh, Erik," she said, "you're not leaving already, are you? Can't you stay with me a while and talk?"

"No. I have a lot I need to do."

"You really have to go out again?"

"Don't worry about what I need to do."

She shook her head. "Please, Erik," she pleaded. "Can't we finish our coffee first? I don't ask much. Can't we just have one cup together like we used to?"

I couldn't take much more. I picked up the coffee she'd given me and downed it in one gulp. Then I set the cup back down and said again, meaner this time, "Anything else you want, Mrs. Holding? I haven't got all day."

She looked sad, even sadder than usual. "I'm just worried."

"About what?"

"So many things . . ."

Jesus Christ. I rubbed my eyes. I was exhausted. First Ronnie, then Owen Pall, then the cops, now this. How was I still going? "Well, I've had a long weekend, so can we get to the main thing that's worrying you?"

She looked out the kitchen window and sipped her coffee.

"Did I ever tell you about my first husband, Erik?"

I sighed and sat back and kind of zoned out for a while. The old lady had been stewing in her regrets so long it never occurred to her that someone else might not care about them. As she talked about her husband, I yawned and pondered how I was going wrap up Alice Hardy in a way to keep her quiet long enough to get her into my apartment. A gag with tape over her mouth?

"He died here, you know, in this apartment," Mrs. Holding was saying.

"Huh?"

"In this room, in fact."

When I turned to look at her, I realized she'd grown fuzzy. Everything around her seemed soft. I seemed soft.

"Are you okay, Erik?"

What the hell?

I stood up and my head was swimming. I heard my chair fall over, but when I tried to say something about it my tongue felt thick.

"Please, sit back down," she said. "You'll fall over."

I grabbed the table and shut my eyes. My head felt like it might roll off my shoulders.

"Erik . . ."

I opened my eyes and she was standing there, staring at me. Staring right at me.

"What the fuck?" I said. "What did you . . ."

I went for the door, but it was like I was walking in mud, in that deep thick muck where I'd sunk buckets of Ronnie.

"Gaaamm *bitch* . . . I'll *kill* you. Whtdyooo . . . *do*?" I bit my tongue, but I couldn't feel it at all.

"I'm just trying to protect you, Erik."

I got to the door and opened it and my fingers were numb and I stumbled out to the top of the stairs.

"Erik," she said again.

I swung around to punch her in the face, but when I did she was already there and she put both hands against my chest and pushed.

Part XII: Then and Now

Mary Margaret Holding

CHAPTER

42

I'VE ALWAYS HAD bad luck with men. Like most things in my life, it started with my father. When I was very young, he worked at a brokerage firm down in the Loop until suddenly, one day, he didn't. I was never told what happened. I'd never understood how we'd gotten rich in the first place, and I never understood what happened to make us poor. All I knew was one day we had to move out of our ivy-covered house in Hyde Park and go to Bridgeport to live in a crowded tenement. After that, I stopped getting new dresses whenever I wanted them. My father went to work keeping books for the Carey brickyard, and my mother was always sad. When I was a girl, I thought being sad was just a natural part of getting old. I still think that, to tell the truth.

I was quite pretty in those days. Hard to imagine now, I guess, but it's true. I was. I had auburn hair and a good figure. That's what we used to say back then. A good figure. Despite not being very smart, I had a good personality too, and I was well liked. I was married by the time I was nineteen.

When Roy and I got married, I thought he was shy, but I came to realize that he wasn't actually shy, he just didn't have anything good to say. He was a clerk at a bank, and every day he put on a suit and a smile and went to work. When he came home, he took them both off. His own father had been very strict and had beaten Roy and his brothers too much when they were children, which had turned Roy dark and moody. It seemed like he was always mad at somebody—his bosses, his clients, the people on television—but he didn't take it out on any of them. He took it out on me. That man blamed me for every problem in the whole world.

Of course, it didn't help that we couldn't have children. We tried for the first few years of our marriage, but nothing happened. My mother had only managed to have one baby, so the doctors just scratched their heads and told me that maybe there was something wrong with the women in our family.

All I know is, once it became clear that we weren't going to have a baby and that his position at the bank was never going to improve much, Roy started drinking. And when he drank, he went from being mean to being cruel. It didn't happen gradually either. For Roy, alcohol was like a virus. Once it got in him, it destroyed the man I'd married. He'd smack me around and burn my arms with cigarettes and then yell at me for crying about it.

Those were the toughest years for me, the years of living in the cold shadow of Roy's resentment and cruelty. That's when the eating started. After years of being thin, it was like I discovered food about 1965. I couldn't help myself. Roy had stopped touching me except to beat me or burn me with his cigarettes. So I'd eat all day long. Of course, once my figure went and I started really putting on weight, he only hated me more. He was one to talk. By that point, he had pink skin and a big potbelly. That was okay for a man, but women weren't supposed to get fat, especially back then. It was like you'd broken some contract you'd signed with your husband.

Then about 1971 we bought the two-flat in Lakeview. Back then this area wasn't so nice, but Roy was good at saving money and he said the place was a smart long-term investment. We took the unit upstairs so no one would be over us, and we rented the downstairs unit to another couple with a little boy. The Sullivans.

They were paying us rent, but Roy used to compare us to them. Never favorably, of course. Kathy Sullivan was no looker. She was pale and had freckles and orange hair. But she was skinny and she'd had a baby, so Roy would always ask me how he'd managed to get stuck with the fat wife who couldn't even give him a kid.

I finally got a job. Roy had never wanted me to work because he thought it made him look bad, like he wasn't a provider. His own mother had never worked. But he told me that if I wasn't going to give him a child I might as well do something useful. So I got a job and started working five days a week. Of course, he still expected me to come home every night and make his dinner.

But I was happy to go to work. I got a job in the museum gift shop at the Art Institute. On my breaks, I liked to go downstairs to the gallery where dozens of tiny model rooms were displayed in glass cases. They were like different dollhouses from different eras and different countries, from French palaces to American farmhouses. I'd stare at those perfect little rooms and imagine the lives of the people who lived in them.

Then one night, it was snowing hard and the buses were running slow, and I was almost an hour late getting home from work. When I came in, Roy was sitting at the kitchen table, sipping bourbon. He still wore his shirt and tie. He'd been sitting there since he'd gotten home, which I knew was bad news for me. Whenever he started drinking before dinner, I was in for it. I told him I couldn't control the weather or the buses, but he bawled me out for being late anyway. I didn't say much. I just hurried up and cooked him a steak and boiled him some potatoes and set the table. The whole time I was cooking he sat there silently sipping bourbon, watching me.

It was still snowing, and there was already a foot of snow on the ground. Our windows were caked in ice and frost. We always had the television going, and Tony Orlando was on in the den. When I brought the food to the table, Roy put down his glass and started eating like he was starving to death.

I was nibbling at some potatoes. I always served myself an extra-small portion when we ate together because otherwise he'd make a comment about it. I was trying to keep my head down and stay quiet, but when I looked up, Roy was staring at me like I'd just insulted him.

"Bring me my cigarettes," he said.

"Your cigarettes?" I said.

He stuffed some potatoes in his mouth and nodded. "Yeah, they're in my coat."

I got up and went to the coatrack and dug through his coat and found a half empty pack of Chesterfields. I brought them to him. I was wearing a floral-print dress with three-quarter sleeves, and as I sat back down I tried to pull the polyester cuffs all the way down to my wrists.

He shook a cigarette out of the pack. "What am I supposed to light this with, a spark of inspiration?"

"I'm sorry," I said. I jumped up and got him the box of kitchen matches from the drawer.

He lit the cigarette and stuck it in one side of his mouth. Then he sawed off a big piece of steak and shoveled it into his mouth on the other side. As he chewed and swallowed, he said, "Let me tell you something."

Then he coughed, hard, and the cigarette fell out of his mouth. The falling cigarette dropped sparks and ashes on his white dress shirt, but he ignored it.

He thumped his chest with his fist and tried to cough again.

"Roy?" I said, starting to get up.

He waved me away, so I sat back down. He coughed again, or he tried to, but he couldn't quite do it. Then he tried to retch, which made him look like a cat. When that didn't work, he slapped his chest with the palm of his hand, trying to dislodge the meat. But that didn't work either. That's when he started waving at me to help him.

I stayed in my seat. I wonder how my face must have looked. He grabbed my arm, but I pulled it away. He punched the table.

He took a swing at me, maybe to knock some sense into me. I'm sure he wanted to beat the hell out of me, but he was starting to panic. His eyes went from being angry to being terrified. He waved his hands like he was trying to flag down help. When he fell out of his chair, he fell so hard it shook the house, and I knew that the Sullivans must have heard it.

I stood up and backed away from him. He kicked the kitchen table. I backed up all the way to the wall and slid down until I was on my knees. I don't know how long I watched him choking, maybe only a few seconds, but it was more than enough time to come to my senses. It was more than enough time to realize that Roy was about to choke to death right there on the kitchen floor. I knew that no matter how much noise he made the Sullivans would not come up to check on him. They'd been listening to Roy beat me for years, and they'd never once said a word about it. I was all alone with him, and I had more than enough time to realize that if I did nothing, maybe my life would change.

But then he started to get up. He was in a blind panic now. He must have realized I was just going to sit there and watch it happen, so he lurched for the door, maybe to run downstairs and get some help from the Sullivans.

That's how fast life happens to you. One moment, you think you can just sit there and do nothing and things will change on their own. Then suddenly you have to commit yourself. As Roy threw himself at the door, I grabbed his ankle and jerked him back as hard as I could.

When he turned around, he looked surprised. He hadn't been surprised by anything I'd done since I married him. But he was sure surprised that night on the kitchen floor.

I straddled his back to keep him from getting up. His panic gave him even more strength, and he bucked and kicked, but I sat all my weight on the small of his back and pinned his shoulders to the hardwood floor. I could hear the clogged wet suction in his throat getting tighter and tighter, until finally there was no sound at all coming from down there because it was sealed completely shut. The veins on his neck stood out like power cords, and his skin turned purple. Fury kept him going once the air ran out, but then even the fury ran out. The bucking stopped. He stopped trying to get up at all, and his hands crept back to his throat.

He twitched hard a few times, terrible shudders running through his whole body. His eyes had bulged out as big as eggs. He died like that, with his hands at his throat, still trying to dislodge the meat.

I rolled Roy over and listened to his lifeless chest for a few minutes. Finally, I got up. I picked up what was left of his cigarette and placed it on his plate next to the rest of his steak. Then I walked to the door of our unit, took a deep breath, opened the door, and screamed for help.

CHAPTER 43

ROY HAD A very good life insurance policy, and his father helped me to invest it well. That, along with the rent from the downstairs unit, kept me comfortable. Even the neighborhood eventually turned around. Gentrification, they call it. I kept working just to have something to do, and that provided me with even more income. But I didn't know what to do with my money, which is another way of saying that I didn't know what to do with myself. I mostly just saved it, but I didn't have some grand dream of what I would do with it one day. I'm a romantic by nature, I think, but Roy had beaten all the dreams out of me by the time I had any money to spend.

So I got addicted to comfort instead. I locked my front door against the world, and I became very selective about who came through. As a revenge for their years of silence, I immediately got rid of the Sullivans by raising their rent far beyond their budget and then lowering it again once they were gone. After that, I only rented out the downstairs to people who interested me. That usually meant single boys in their twenties or thirties who needed someone to look after them. Most stayed a few years and moved on. One boy got so mad at my intrusions on his privacy he left after three months. Another stayed eleven years. We grew close, but then he got married and moved his new bride in with him. I immediately stopped speaking to him and raised the rent until they had to move out.

Then one day Erik showed up. I was old by then, too old to pretend I was anything else. You get to an age where there are no more illusions available to you. The first time we spoke I knew he was trouble. He had the same dead-eyed friendliness that had been Roy's stock in trade when we were courting. He even told me he liked that I'd had the whole place painted in baby blue and powder pink, which was such a transparent lie that I laughed when he said it. He thought I was giggling because he'd charmed me. Pride was always Erik's main flaw.

He was different from all the others. As soon as he moved in, he immediately began wooing me. I let him do it. I hadn't had so much attention from a man in decades. He'd come upstairs every day, and we'd sit and have coffee together. He did little odd jobs for me around the place. For months, he was flattering, helpful, attentive. But his meanness was always just below the surface. I could feel it the same way you can feel someone's pulse just below their skin.

I let him in, further and further into my world than I'd ever let anyone. I let him think what he wanted to think about me—that I was a foolish old woman, alone and abandoned, easily coddled. He didn't know that I'd rejected the world. He thought it had rejected me, and he held me in contempt for that. Soon he started showing up late with the rent. At first, it was just a few days late. Then a week or two, a month or more. With his salary, that boy could well afford to pay me, but he just didn't want to. It was a game he was playing, seeing how far he could string along the old landlady upstairs. He even started staying with me at night sometimes, sharing the same bed with me, almost daring me to ask for rent after he would stoop so low.

Of course, I knew his pride blinded him to what was really going on. Without him even noticing, Erik was becoming more and more dependent on me, not the other way around. He thought that the more he used me the more control he had over me, but the truth was he was becoming addicted to his own comfort. I saw an

Oprah show once about "How to Spot the Narcissist in Your Life" and, boy, did Erik fit all the criteria. The selfishness, the anger. Oprah said that a narcissist thinks the world should belong to him and he lives his life in a rage because it doesn't. Well, that was Erik.

Then there was the question of girls. The boys downstairs had always had their girls, of course. The ones they brought home drunk late at night. The ones they brought home sober at more reasonable hours. The ones they eventually married. I always ended up jealous, always ended up annoying them in the end. In the mid-eighties, I tried moving a boy in downstairs who clearly had no interest in girls. He was a quiet young librarian with soft, delicate manners. But I figured out pretty quickly that I was just as jealous of the handsome male friends he brought home. A gay man, I learned, will break your heart as quickly as any other man.

Again, here Erik was different. When I first met him, I assumed the contempt I sensed from him was specifically aimed at me. But he hadn't lived downstairs more than a few months before I realized that it extended to every woman on earth. There was not even any regular lust in him. He didn't go out looking for girls, and he never brought any around.

The only person he ever brought around was his partner on the ambulance, that Ronnie. Erik introduced me to him one day as they were coming inside. I could tell Erik wanted to show Ronnie to me. Seeing them together, I understood why. Ronnie was in love with him, and Erik liked that. He wasn't in love with Ronnie, of course. I don't know much, but I am sure that Erik could never love anyone. It's just not in him. Ronnie followed after him like a dog, though, and Erik loved showing off his dog in front of me. He'd bring Ronnie around because he wanted me to know that he had a life outside of me. It was his way of pointing out that I didn't have a life outside of him. It was one of his petty little games.

But then things got serious the night he switched my pills. He gave me a couple of my Lunesta to knock me out so he could go through my apartment while I was unconscious. He was too prideful, and too contemptuous, to wonder why I had let him handle my pills in the first place. He always assumed I was needy and stupid, and it made him careless. I knew he was giving me the wrong pills, but I said nothing about it and stuck the pills under my pillow just to see what he would do. Sure enough, he waited until I was supposed to be asleep, and then he went through my things. He could have been looking for money, but I actually think he did it just to do it. Finding nothing, he came and sat down next to my bed and stared at me. He said my name a few times, louder and louder, like pulling on a door handle to make sure it's locked.

When he was satisfied that I was out like a light, he laughed and started talking. He started by cussing me out, telling me how much he hated me, telling me how disgusting I was. But then he kept talking, talking for a long time, and the more he talked, the more he told me. It was the first time he was ever truthful with me. What poured out of him that night was a vile sewer of abuse. He hated me—he hated all women, but *especially* me. He said he'd cut me up and eat me one day. Said he wanted to eat me and crap me out and flush me down the toilet. Then he kissed me on the nose and left.

I didn't move, but my heart was pounding so hard I thought I might have a heart attack.

It was exhilarating.

I hadn't felt such white-hot hate from a man since Roy. The others had come and gone. Some had pretended to care for me, others had barely tolerated me. A few had told me that *I* was the narcissist, that I was possessive, that I was no better than a stalker. One threatened to go to the police if I didn't stop pestering him and his girlfriend. But that was all a long time ago. You get to be my age and everything divides in two, between right now and a long time ago, separated by a big empty space. And I was thrilled to be living in the right now. My relationship with Erik was the most intense relationship I'd ever been in. Who lucks into that kind of situation in their old age?

Still, I suppose people will say that I should have kicked him out, should have kicked him out the moment he switched my pills. But we don't always do what we're supposed to do. A lot of time we only do what we're supposed to do because we think we'll be judged for it later. I gave up on caring about that a long time ago. If I'd done everything I was supposed to do, I'd still be married to Roy.

Not that I doubted Erik was really capable of murder. That's what made it exciting. I'd found out the hard way that anyone is capable of murder. And Erik, I had no doubt, was more capable than others.

It's not that I wanted him to actually hurt me, of course. I just didn't want him to be taken away from me. That's the hardest part of this whole deal for me to admit. As much as I was using Erik and lying to him, I wasn't lying when I said I loved him. Everything I'd done, I'd done to keep him close to me. He really was my whole world. If he ever did something truly bad and the police came and took him away, I'd be all alone, maybe more alone than I'd ever been before.

I didn't think I could live that way.

CHAPTER

44

THEN LAST FRIDAY he came home very late. He was driving Ronnie's car. He tried being quiet, but I'd been watching out the window for hours, waiting for him to get home. Ronnie was with him, but something was wrong. I had my light off, and I watched them crossing the yard. Ronnie had a big white bandage around his throat, and he could barely walk. Erik almost had to carry him. They climbed the steps into the house and shut the door.

I wondered what it was all about. I heard them moving around downstairs, and then maybe fifteen minutes later, Erik went back out to the garage, got in Ronnie's car by himself and left. He was gone maybe forty-five minutes. I watched for the car to return, but instead he came back on foot. That's when he moved his truck. It had been parked out front all night. Now he came up through the alley and pulled into the garage. He crept back into his flat. There was more movement, heavier movement, like he was moving Ronnie. Then I heard the basement door. Erik didn't know that I could always hear when he went downstairs into the basement.

Then everything was silent. Silent for hours. It got so quiet that I almost fell asleep. Then I finally heard his basement door again. After spending all night in the basement, he was coming back up.

I heard his shower running, and then I heard him in his kitchen. I wanted to have a closer look at him, to see what he'd been up to, so I buzzed him. A few minutes later he stomped into my apartment.

"What do you want this early?"

I was in my chair in the front room. I liked the way it filled with sunlight in the morning. He stood there bathed in all that white light, looking bright and guilty.

"I heard you were up."

"So what? Doesn't mean you should be ringing that goddamn bell at five o'clock in the morning."

I had to stop myself from smiling at that. He had installed the bell to make me more dependent on him, but it had always been a shackle around his ankle.

"Will you be able to do some things for me today?" I asked.

He told me the basement had flooded and that he'd spent the night cleaning it out. I knew that was a lie, of course. I have a basement specialist over at All Seasons Plumbing who comes in every autumn to check the pipes. Besides, although the basement hasn't flooded in over a decade, it's flooded enough times over the years that I would have recognized the smell immediately. It stinks up the whole house. And the idea that poor Erik, so arrogant and overconfident, could fix it himself was ridiculous. I didn't say any of that, though. I just let him stand there and lie to me while I tried to figure out why he was lying. Why wouldn't he just say he was with Ronnie? Why make up a story about the basement?

After he went back downstairs, I moved to my bedroom. I thought I might get a little sleep, but then Erik went back down to the basement and started carrying buckets outside to the garage.

He carried out two buckets, went back and carried out two more, and then he dragged out a big Rubbermaid garbage can.

He saw me watching him and blew me a kiss with the same spirit people use when they give you the finger.

Then he left. Alone.

For a long time, I sat there by the window staring at the empty yard.

Finally, I got up and took my keys and went downstairs. I don't go downstairs much because I'm a physical wreck. My doctors all yell at me for not taking better care of myself. But I'm not the invalid Erik thinks I am. He doesn't understand that my whole life has been a lesson in withstanding pain.

So I got myself downstairs, breath wheezing and bones creaking, and I knocked on his door. I knocked loud, for a couple of minutes. Then I unlocked the door.

"Hello?" I called.

When no one answered, I went inside. I hadn't been inside Erik's flat in years. He hadn't done much with it. That boy never had much style. I went in all the rooms. There was no Ronnie. I went to the basement door. I unlocked it.

It looked like a cave. It was all black. I went down the stairs holding on to the wall. It was all puffy, thick, and black. In the basement, everything was normal. There certainly hadn't been any flooding.

The door to the back room was open. It had locks on it, but I guess he wasn't done doing what he was doing down here and hadn't locked it up. There were knives and saws hanging on the wall of the little room. Everything was clean.

I felt a shudder run through me. I didn't touch anything. I turned around and climbed back upstairs. I locked the basement door. I locked up Erik's flat. I went back to my flat and laid down on my bed. Everything hurt, and I was gasping for breath from climbing all those stairs.

I lay there for a long time thinking about everything I'd seen and heard. He brought Ronnie here, spent the night in the basement with those knives and saws, then he carried out buckets, loaded them into his truck and drove away. He got rid of Ronnie's car, and he lied about flooding in the basement to explain why he'd stayed down there all night. And now Ronnie was nowhere to be seen. You didn't have to be Miss Marple to figure out what had happened down there, though figuring it out didn't make it any easier to accept.

The real question was what I was going to do about it. Of course, I didn't care about Ronnie. I didn't even really know him. Maybe he'd done something wrong to Erik. And besides, with him out of the way, Erik was more mine than he'd ever been before.

But I worried about how long it would take someone to catch Erik. He was so helpless and arrogant, so sure of himself, that it made him blind. Should I try to protect him somehow? Could I? Could I find a way to keep him with me? How do you protect someone from himself?

* * *

The next morning he came up and joined me for breakfast. He seemed agitated, even more than usual, but he was doing his best to keep it under control. When he was done eating, he did the dishes and tucked me into bed. That's when I knew he must really be desperate. He hadn't been this nice to me in months. When he tried to leave, I started to act petulant. I knew it would make him angry.

"I give you my home," I said, "all my money, and you're still always leaving."

He stopped at the door. He closed it. Then he turned around and came back to the bed and climbed on top of me.

His weight on me was terrifying and exciting. His hips pressed into mine. Hate was the only passion he had, and he hated me more than he hated anyone, I think.

"You'll get what I give you, Mrs. Holding," he said. His pocked face was just a few inches from mine. "Look at yourself, old and forgotten by everybody who ever met you. Except me. If you look at it that way, I'd say you were getting a goddamn good deal. Wouldn't you?"

I batted my eyes at him. "Please, Erik. I know all that you do for me. That's why I need you. That's why I love you.

Then I set the trap. I added, "I just want to show you that I love you."

He was *so* satisfied—poor, arrogant, stupid boy.

"You want to show it?" he said.

"Yes," I said.

"Then, if anyone asks, you tell them I've been here with you for the past couple of days. You understand? From Friday afternoon to this morning."

"But why, Erik?" I asked, as innocent as a lamb.

He leaned down close enough to kiss me. "Don't ask me why. If you want to show me that you need me, you'll do this for me. From Friday afternoon, about four, until this morning, I was with you. You didn't see me leave and go anywhere."

"Yes," I said. "You were here with me."

"Good," he said.

I lifted my hand and touched his side. He rolled away like a snake had bitten him.

When he was gone, I lay there in my bed, basking in the warmth of my triumph.

He needed me now, needed me more than he'd ever needed anyone.

CHAPTER 45

THEY CAME FOR him a few days later.

I saw them park in front of the house, get out of their car, and walk to our front door. Two men in shirts and ties with guns on their belts. They looked like police detectives you'd see on television except they were older and flabbier. Erik met them at the door and invited them inside. I couldn't move. I was more scared than I'd ever been in my life. More scared than I was the night Roy died or when Erik told me for the first time what he wanted to do to me.

I was terrified they'd take him away right then and there. He was so dumb, and he'd made so many mistakes. Maybe they'd already figured out what he'd done to Ronnie, and they were here to arrest him. I was scared I'd never see him again.

Then I heard footsteps on the stairs, and one of the police officers knocked at my door.

I went to the door and opened it and invited him in. We sat down in my front room, in the light, and he asked me questions. He was Mexican, I think. Very polite and professional. He had a pen, and he took notes on a little pad that he rested on his knee.

He asked me if I knew Ronnie Dunlap. I said I'd met him. He asked when I'd last seen him. I told him I couldn't quite remember.

A few weeks ago, perhaps? Maybe more? He asked if Erik took care of me. I said he did. He asked me about Erik's temperament. I said I'd always found him to be a levelheaded boy. He asked if Erik had been with me all weekend. I said he had. He asked if I paid much attention to what happened downstairs, if I ever noticed anything that might indicate a problem between Erik and Ronnie. I said as near as I could tell they were good friends.

He thanked me and gave me his card and left.

I wanted to cry.

I had no idea if that policeman believed me or not, but I was certain that he didn't believe Erik. The way he asked about him, as if he was subtly inviting me to tell him that Erik was a liar and maybe something much, much worse.

When I heard the police leave, I watched them walk back to their car. They climbed in and sat there a while, talking. Finally, they drove off.

It wouldn't be long now. They'd be back, I was sure, and when they came back, they'd take Erik away.

Maybe he could sense it too. I heard him go down into the basement for a while, and when he came back up, he hurried out to his truck carrying another bucket. Then he drove away, fast.

As I watched him turn at the corner and disappear, I sat there in the sunlight in my front room, thinking about my life. I'd buried both of my parents and my husband a long time ago. I'd seen the city rise up and fall down and rise up again. I'd been in this same upstairs flat for almost fifty years, watching the snow pile up and melt away and pile up again. The boys downstairs had come and gone, but I'd never been into anything as deeply I was into this situation with Erik, and now that was coming to an end too. They'd take him away soon. I was sure of that now.

I couldn't even think about what it would be like the day after they took him away. I'd be alone, with the police and reporters coming around, with people going through my house. Once it was over, I'd have to hire movers to come in and take out Erik's things.

I'd have to go through the whole rigmarole of finding another tenant for the flat. It didn't just exhaust me to think about all that, it filled me with a sick dread. I was too old, too spent, too alone, to deal with all that mess.

I just couldn't do it.

So I went to my bathroom and washed myself. I did my hair, and then I dressed myself in the best thing I had that still fit me. I crushed up pills on the chopping board using a rolling pin, then I swept the powder into an empty coffee cup and put the cup back on the shelf. Then I washed the chopping board and rolling pin, dried them, and put them away. About the time I had everything the way I wanted it, I heard Erik come in downstairs.

CHAPTER 46

I BUZZED HIM. IT took him a while to come up. When he did, he only opened the door and poked his head through to tell me he couldn't stay.

"I'm busy," he said.

"I need to talk to you," I said, standing in the doorway of my bedroom. "About what's been going on around here lately."

He stared at me, then he sighed and hung his head. "Okay," he said. He came inside, shutting the door behind him. "Why not?" he muttered, as much to himself as to me.

I walked into the kitchen.

"What are you doing?" he asked.

"About to have some coffee," I said. "Will you sit down? I'll make you some. God, you know, we haven't sat and had coffee in so long. We used to do it all the time, when you first moved in."

He didn't move except to cross his arms and scowl at me. "I told you I was busy," he said.

"I know, Erik," I said, pouring myself a cup, "but if you want me to keep lying to the police for you, then maybe we should sit down calmly and talk."

That got his attention. He came in and sat down at the kitchen table.

Glaring at me with hate in his eyes, he forced his mouth into a smile. "Okay," he said. "Let's sit calmly and talk."

I took down the cup I'd prepared for him and poured coffee in. I put in plenty of cream and sugar, and I set it in front of him. He never liked it too hot or too strong. "Just the way you like it," I said.

He sipped some. He nodded, as it to say *It's fine.*

I sat down across from him and sipped mine. I take it black.

"It's been a while since we sat and had coffee together," I told him, trying to be pleasant.

"You said that already."

"I guess I did."

He crossed his arms again. He asked me about my visit from the police detective. I told him what happened. None of it seemed to worry him, or at least he didn't want to appear worried. But I could tell he was agitated. He said he needed to go.

I held my cup with both hands and grimaced. "Please, Erik. Can't it just be normal, just for a minute? Like it used to be. I don't ask much. Can't it just be normal long enough for us to have one cup of coffee together?"

His mouth twisted into a mean smile. He picked up his cup and gulped down the coffee like a petulant child trying to prove something. Then he tossed the cup back down on the table.

"So what *else* do you want, Mrs. Holding?"

I sighed again. "I'm worried."

"About what?"

"So many things . . ."

He rubbed his eyes. "Well, I've had a long weekend, so can we get to the main thing that's worrying you?"

I looked out the kitchen window. I sipped my coffee.

"Did I ever tell you about my first husband, Erik?"

"What does that have to do with anything?"

"Please, humor me."

He rubbed his eyes again. "You've mentioned him. Ray."

I smiled. "Roy."

He shook his head. "Right. Roy. What about him?"

"You remind me of him."

"That right?"

"Yes."

I tried to tell him about Roy. I tried to explain. I'm not sure why. I'm not sure what difference it made, or what difference it could have made. Maybe I just wanted him to know that I had lived a life, that my life had led me here just like his life had led him here.

He wasn't really listening, of course. Who knows what he thinking about, but it wasn't me.

I said, "He died here, you know."

"Yeah?"

"In this apartment."

"Huh."

"In this room, in fact."

Erik heard that, but he was shaking his head again, faster now. He squeezed his eyes shut and reopened them, like he was trying to blink away dizziness. When he looked up at me, he must have seen the same thing Roy had seen.

"Are you okay, Erik?" I asked.

He stood up, shooting up so quickly he knocked over his chair, but he was unsteady on his feet.

"Please, sit back down," I said. "You'll fall over."

He blinked at me, squeezing his eyes shut and popping them open again and again.

"Erik . . ."

"What the fuck?" he said. "What did you . . ."

He staggered toward the door, shaking his head like he was trying to shake something loose.

He tried to curse me, tried to threaten me. It mostly came out in a garble, though.

"I'm trying to protect you, Erik."

He flung open my apartment door and stumbled to the stairs. I was right behind him, limping along on my cane.

"Erik," I said. I was close enough to touch him.

He turned around at the top of the stairs. Maybe to curse me again, maybe to beat me to death. I'm not sure. But when he turned around, I put both hands against his chest and pushed.

His fall made a terrible racket. He tried to grab at the wall, but all he did was knock a framed picture off its nail. The picture shattered on the hardwood floor while Erik was tumbling down the stairs like a boulder. When he landed on the bottom floor, he just laid there.

I cussed myself for shoving him. I hadn't been thinking. I wanted him upstairs with me, not down there on the floor.

I hobbled down after him as quickly as I could, which wasn't too quickly. I didn't want to slip and wind up on the floor myself. When I finally got down there, I was relieved to find that he was still breathing.

"Erik," I told him. "Honey, you've got to get up."

His face was bleeding. I guess he must have smacked one of the steps hard on the way down. The blood spilled out of his nose and his lips.

His eyes rolled around like he couldn't control them, like he couldn't focus on anything.

I bent over him and pulled at his arm. "You need to get up and come upstairs with me before you pass out," I said. "If you don't, the police will find you. You hear me, Erik? They'll get you, sweetie. They're coming for you."

"Wha—" His mouth tried to form words, but he'd lost control of his tongue.

"You've got to come now," I told him. "We've got to hide you from the police."

I pulled at him and kept telling him the police were coming. It took some coaxing, because he was swinging in and out of consciousness, but he tried to get on his feet. That was too much for him, but he did manage to roll over and get up on his hands and knees. I pushed him toward the stairs, told him we needed to climb.

No one could see us, but we must have looked like quite a pair—Erik slowly crawling up the stairs on his hands and knees, his face dropping big splotches of blood on every step, me behind him with my cane, encouraging him and warning him that he needed to keep going.

The poor boy didn't know where he was or what he was doing. I kept telling him I was going to hide him from the police. Maybe in his delirium he believed that. Or maybe he just figured he'd go along with whatever I told him until he could recuperate and get even with me. It didn't matter, at any rate. He wasn't in his right mind, or he wouldn't have listened to me at all. Even after what I'd done, he didn't have it in himself to be afraid of me. He just crawled up the steps and back into my apartment, pushing himself until the moment he could collapse.

I got him all the way into my bedroom, but when I tried to get him up on the bed that's when he gave out. The drugs finally took hold of him completely. He just lay there on the floor as flat as the rug.

I had to get him onto the bed by myself. I sat on the mattress, leaned over, and tried to lift him. I managed to get him up in a sitting position, but that was it. I couldn't get him off the floor.

I thought about it for a while. Then I went to the bathroom and got the belt from my bathrobe. I tied it around his right hand and walked around the bed and ran it under the bedframe. I walked back around, got my arms under his armpits, and used my weight to pull against the belt and hoist him up by the arm at the same time I was lifting him.

It was like those stories you hear about a mother lifting a car off a baby. I screamed like someone was stabbing me, but I held on, hoisting and pulling, and I finally got him up there with me.

When it was done, I wiped away my tears and straightened him out and laid down next to him. I had to rest for a long time, had to let my breathing return to normal. I tried to match my breathing to his, slow and steady, but it was difficult to concentrate with the pain

I was in. I knew I'd done permanent damage to my hips and back, but at least I knew that *permanent* wasn't going to last much longer.

I opened my bedside table drawer and took out my pills. I already had a glass of water waiting. You get to be my age, you need to plan ahead for everything. I unscrewed the bottle of pills and washed them down a few at a time. It took me a while to get the whole bottle down, but I managed it.

Then I took out the box cutter. It was old and the blade wasn't so sharp anymore, but when I cut Erik's wrist, it sliced through his skin like it was packing tape. As his blood poured out, he groaned and twitched and tried to pull his arm away, but he didn't come out of his sleep, and I held on to him, held him close.

I put my leg over his and drew the covers over us. Soon, my pills took effect and I felt the first wave of relaxation ripple through my body. The next wave loosened the muscles in my back. With the third wave I emptied my bladder and smiled and held Erik closer to me in the warmth.

Eventually, he turned cold, but by then it didn't matter. I just held him closer as my whole body grew numb. I'd left the curtains open on purpose, and sunshine came in through the windows just the way I'd hoped and filled the bedroom with light. I heard a bug going zzzt zzzt zzzt against the windowpane. Somewhere down the street, a car passed. I didn't wonder who it was or where they were going. I didn't care anymore. I let go of myself, my body, the whole world. Everything but Erik. My boy. Mine forever. I just held him closer and closer and closer.

Part XIII: Now

Alice Hardy

C H A P T E R

47

Bette Davis is dancing on the beach, twirling in black and white. The crowd gathers around her in a drifting circle. Two cops at the edge of the crowd suddenly spot Joan Crawford's body in the sand and rush over to her. Music and waves crash and the silver screen goes dark.

As the curtain comes down, the lights go up. There's a smattering of applause throughout the theater, and Tuck and I grin at each other and get up to leave.

Outside, we pause beneath the Music Box marquee to let our eyes adjust to the light, and Tuck says, "Jesus Christ."

"The sun or the movie?" I say.

"Both," he says.

I nod. "Sushi?"

"Yes," Tuck says. "I'm starving."

We walk up Southport to the sushi place across from the grocery store, discussing the insanity of *Baby Jane*. I feel my phone buzz in the back pocket of my jeans. I ignore it until we get to the restaurant, and then I go to the bathroom.

I lock the stall behind me and pull out my phone.

It's a text from Detective Kantzavelos. It's been a couple of weeks since I went to see him and spent the day looking at mugshots and talking to the sketch artist. Since then, we've been exchanging text messages every few days. These primarily consist of me asking how the investigation is going. Most of his replies are the equivalent of a shrug.

This one is different.

This is a long shot, he writes. *But did you see the story on the news about the two paramedics?*

I heard about it, I write back.

Everyone's heard about it. One guy went missing, and the other guy was murdered by his landlord in some kind of suicide pact. The police are still sorting it all out. I haven't really followed the story, but it's been impossible to miss completely.

The guy who's missing was named Ronnie Dunlap, the detective tells me.

OK, I text back. The name is vaguely familiar from the news reports I've skimmed.

He texts me a photograph of the man who attacked me in the alley.

I put my hand to my mouth. I almost drop my phone as I'm calling Kantzavelos.

"*That's him*," I say when he picks up. "That's the man who attacked me."

"I fucking knew it," he says. I can almost hear him smile. "If you'll excuse the language. But I fucking knew it."

"How?"

"I ran into Danny Heller, the detective who's working the Reid-Dunlap case. He told me Dunlap's wife said he showed up one night with his throat cut. That part hasn't been in the news yet. Obviously, it got my attention. As we were talking, I realized it happened the same night you were attacked."

"Jesus Christ."

"So here's the deal: a couple of days after he attacked you, Dunlap goes missing. His wife calls the police, and they question Reid to see if he knows where his buddy is. The next day, Reid and his landlord kill themselves. Police go in and find out that Reid's basement is a torture chamber. Knives, a surgical bone saw, rope. Forensics found some of Dunlap's blood and skin in the fibers of the rope, and more traces of blood around the sink's backsplash. So, the theory, at this point, is that Reid killed Dunlap, hacked him up, dropped the pieces somewhere. Then the landlord and Reid killed themselves. Or maybe she killed him. We're not sure yet."

"Jesus," I say again.

"Oh, one more thing. We think a private detective named Owen Pall—who was hired by Dunlap's wife—might have witnessed the attack on you and tried to blackmail Reid and Dunlap. That got *him* killed. Might also be the reason Reid decided to kill Dunlap."

I pull the phone away from my ear and look at the photo of Ronnie Dunlap again.

"It's him," I say. "I'm sure that's the man who attacked me."

"Listen, when the press finds out about you—and they will—they'll be camped out on your lawn. For a while anyway. They already love this Dunlap story, and it was about to die down. Now they'll have more to run with. You should come in tomorrow so we can talk with Heller."

After I agree to meet with the detectives the next day, we hang up. I think of calling Greg to tell him, but I decide against it. He's at home, chasing his equations. I'll leave him to it for a few hours more.

I walk back out to my son.

I'm about to tell him about the phone call, but before I can, he looks up from his phone, where he's been reading IMDb, and asks, "Was Joan Crawford dead at the end of the movie?"

"What?"

"On the beach. Did she die? I can't tell if it was a happy ending or not."

Before I can answer, the waitress comes around, drops off a couple of glasses of water, and we order the sampler platter of maki to split.

When the waitress leaves, I take out my phone, turn it off, and lay it face down on the table.

"So it's a happy ending if she lives and sad if she dies?" I ask.

"Well, not exactly," my son says. "Pretty dark either way. But if she survives, isn't it less dark?"

I catch myself before I say the first thing that pops into my head—that none of us survive, not really, not in the end. Instead, I smile. I raise my water like it's a glass of wine.

"Well," I tell my son, "let's hear it for the lesser of two dark endings."

ACKNOWLEDGEMENTS

First and foremost, my profound thanks to my remarkable agent, Nat Sobel. Without him, this book would not be in print. And thanks to Judith Weber and everyone else at Sobel-Weber who read early drafts, provided invaluable feedback, and helped shepherd this book into publication.

A huge thank you to my editor Tom Wickersham at Crooked Lane.

Thanks to Thai Fantauzzi Pérez, Lunaea Weatherstone, and the whole team at Crooked Lane for all of their hard work.

Merci beaucoup to Oliver Gallmesiter for giving my books a home in France.

And a special thanks to Sophie, Edie, Mitch, Dwayne the Rat Johnson, Bernie, Duke, and Sid.